ENCHANTMENT

PIETRO GROSSI

ENCHANTMENT

Translated from the Italian by
Howard Curtis

PUSHKIN PRESS
LONDON

Pushkin Press
71–75 Shelton Street, London WC2H 9JQ

Enchantment first published in Italian as
Incanto in 2011

This edition first published by Pushkin Press in 2013

ISBN 978 1 908968 16 6

Set in 10.75 on 14 Monotype Baskerville
by Tetragon, London
and printed and bound by CPI Group (UK) Ltd, Croydon, CR0 4YY

www.pushkinpress.com

This project has been funded with support from the European Commission.
This publication reflects the views only of the authors, and the Commission cannot be
held responsible for any use which may be made of the information contained herewith.

ENCHANTMENT

S o HERE I WAS AT LAST, standing in a daze with the receiver of my parents' old grey telephone in my hand, those damned words echoing in my head like the first rumblings of an earthquake, and the most lucid part of me immediately sensed that the tremor would leave behind it nothing but debris.

If anyone had asked me, even a short while earlier, I would have declared with a touch of naïve pride that the walls of what I persisted in calling "my life", which had taken me so much effort to build, were quite solid. And yet now, it was as if overnight I had detected some alarming cracks, and was gradually starting to suspect that someone had mixed the mortar in the wrong proportions. Now, as everything started to shake and I was forced to admit that pieces of plaster were coming loose from the walls, I felt an overwhelming need to discover the exact moment when it all started.

A few hours later, lying staring at the ceiling, I managed to pin down the moment of time when the tectonic plates that were now shifting had given the first signs of drift. When it had happened, nobody had realized that the ground was moving, and even if we had noticed that the landscape was tilting slightly, the view in front of our eyes had been anything but unpleasant.

And yet the exact moment when that cosmic roar invaded my universe was the imperceptible fraction of a second during which a small area of skin struck the shiny surface of my window. That had been my Big Bang: the muted rapping of knuckles on a window pane in the dead of night.

ONE

Rocky Road

1

M Y HEART AND LUNGS trapped in a vortex of terror, I instinctively pulled the blankets over my head. My breath warmed the sheets, draining the oxygen from my body. More sinister knocking. My heart thumped in my chest. After a few seconds I turned down the blankets slightly and took a look.

A dark figure was curled up outside the window. I huddled under the blankets again, trying to convince myself I was still asleep and this was only a nightmare. In a moment I would calm down and wake up properly: the figure would be gone and I would laugh and fall asleep again and have something to tell my friends the next day.

But the figure was still there, still tapping at the window pane and waving at me, motioning for me to approach. With the blankets still up to my nose, I squinted, trying to see better, then dropped my head back on the pillow and cursed. I immediately lifted my head again and took another look. For a moment, I concentrated on catching my breath and listening to my heartbeat slowly getting back to normal. I threw off the sheets and blankets, sat up on the edge of the bed, glanced at the window another couple of times, then got up and walked to it. I quietly opened one shutter, closing the other and trying not to make a noise.

Outside, squatting on the roof of the back porch beneath the window, was Biagio. He was chewing a long piece of wood and looking at me as if everything was perfectly normal.

"Are you mad?"

"Get dressed. There's something you have to see."

"What time is it?"

"I don't know. Get dressed."

I again looked down and around. The moonlight glinted on the lawn in front of the house.

"How did you get up here?"

Biagio gestured with his head, behind him and to his left. Beyond the roof on which he was squatting, down the corner of the main wall of the house, ran an old copper pipe, blackened with age, which I seemed to be seeing for the first time.

"All right, I'll put something on. In the meantime, go to the shed behind the house and find Enzo's ladder. I'm not going down that pipe."

"You big cissy," Biagio said with a smile as he turned away.

Once I had climbed down the ladder and crossed the garden as silently as possible, we headed left and out of the village.

It was one of those nights at the end of May when the air, although still crisp, starts to smell of summer. I tried to ask Biagio where we were going, but he simply told me to wait and not to worry. When we got to the end of the street, we turned right, and when we came level with the old school buildings Biagio started down the stone steps that led to the washhouses. I had never seen anybody there, but my dad always said he could remember the women washing the clothes, singing and beating the linen on the edges of the

14

tubs. As children we had sometimes bathed there, and in summer, when they were overrun with tadpoles, we would fish out frogs using the heads of daisies.

For some reason Biagio was always going out for walks by himself at night. The first time his mother had discovered it, he was nine. She had woken up in the middle of the night and, on her way to the kitchen to get herself a glass of water, she had half opened the door of the boys' room and glanced in. Biagio's brother, Graziano, was sleeping like a stunned animal. Of Biagio, though, there was no trace: his bed, which was opposite Graziano's, was unmade and empty. Betta took the length of the tiny corridor in a single step and looked in the bathroom, and again in the kitchen. Then she went back into her sons' bedroom and shook Graziano. He snored and turned over.

"Graziano!" she cried, shaking him more violently.

A grunt rose at last from that mass of limp flesh.

"Biagio. Where is he?"

Graziano raised his big square head and looked at the empty bed opposite. "How should I know?" he muttered.

"Haven't you seen him?"

"No."

"Are you sure?"

Graziano turned, gave his mother an angry look, grunted again, and went back to sleep.

Betta got the keys from the kitchen and went outside. She first checked the yard, then walked up and down the road for a few hundred metres, and finally went behind the house, over towards the farms, softly calling her son's name. The only response was a flutter of wings in the hen house and a dog barking in the distance. Before going back inside, Betta knocked at her sister's window—her sister lived in the house opposite—and asked her if by any chance she had seen Biagio. She hadn't.

"He'll be back soon," her sister said, already closing the window again and disappearing inside.

So Betta went back home and sat down in the kitchen with a cup of hot milk. At the first light of dawn, by which time she had already decided to go and see the Marshal with her husband, she saw Biagio pop up at the kitchen window, which was fixed from the outside with a piece of cardboard. Biagio had jumped up and and laid his stomach on the window still, but once he saw his mum he froze. For a moment or two, they were both quite still, staring at each other, Biagio wondering what was the best thing to do, whether to keep going in or retreat, his mother trying with all her might to hold back her tears. But the next moment, Betta leapt to her feet and Biagio, his eyes wide, hesitated for an instant, then tried to jump back out. But big as she was, Betta was too quick for him. Darting forward, she grabbed Biagio by the sweater and pulled him in. Then, when he was on the kitchen floor, Betta began raining slaps down on his head. Shielding himself with his hands as best he could, Biagio tried to crawl to his bedroom. Betta's big hands, as hard as pieces of wood, still managed to land sharp blows on his head, which in the silence of the dawn must have rung out like thwacks of a stick. I remember those hands well: they were as tough as leather and it didn't take much for Betta to raise them. One day she had caught us throwing firecrackers in the hen house behind the house. I can still feel those sharp shovel blows on our heads as she screamed at us that the hens would stop laying eggs if we did that.

In the end, Biagio managed to get to his bed and Betta stopped in the doorway.

"We'll talk about it over breakfast," she said, closing the door.

A couple of hours later, as Betta was heating the milk and coffee on the stove, Biagio sat down at the little pink formica table in the kitchen.

"Where were you?" Betta asked without even turning round.

"Walking around."

"Around where?"

"Just around."

Betta turned with the saucepan of hot milk in her hand and slammed it down in front of Biagio on a small wooden plate covered with burn marks. "If you do it again I'll lock you indoors until you're twenty."

In the following five or six months, Biagio was caught a few more times and there were more slaps and more threats. And whenever his mum or dad asked him where he went, he would simply say, "Just for a walk." They even tried barring the doors and windows, but the only result was to find Biagio in a dejected mood in the morning, as white as a sheet and with two deep black pits under his eyes. He even had a fever. In the end, his parents reconciled themselves to the fact that every morning Biagio calmly came back to his bed, and that wherever he went on those walks of his, it couldn't be doing him any harm. So they decided to postpone their anxiety for two or three hours, until dawn, and then start worrying if they had to. They never had to.

At the time, I myself often wondered where exactly Biagio

went, and I liked to see that place, wherever it was, in a heroic, adventurous light. Now, though, I can't help imagining him simply walking around, looking at the mounds of snow in winter, listening to the crickets in the fields in summer. And I wonder if, when you come down to it, that was all he ever asked.

Biagio led me through the Sardinian's rapeseed field and beyond the old river bed and up again through Ninno's dad's olive grove. And every time I asked him where the hell we were going he would tell me to keep quiet and follow him. Then all at once we found ourselves on the edge of that big field under the cliff, where we'd stolen sunflower seeds the previous summer.

"Close your eyes," Biagio said.

"And then?"

"And then follow me."

"Are you mad?"

"Don't start crying. I'll lead you. Close your eyes."

I stared at him for a moment and sighed. "What a drag."

Biagio got into position behind me, grabbed my belt and started guiding me like a puppet. If I close my eyes I can still smell the scent of the night and hear the cry of an owl in the distance and feel the ears of corn caressing my trousers.

"Wait," Biagio said after a while, stopping.

"What is it?"

"The cliff."

"Can I open my eyes?"

"No."

"Come on, Biagio, what do I do?"

"I'll jump and pull you up."

I'd have liked to complain, to say that it was night and I was sleepy and had no desire to be there in the middle of the countryside with my eyes closed. It was quite cold. Biagio's feet slipped on the loose earth. Then I thought I heard him steady himself.

"Give me your hand," Biagio said, from somewhere a bit higher up.

"Where?"

"Here."

I reached up my right hand like a blind man, and Biagio grabbed me. As I climbed I felt him also going up a few steps, pieces of wood and branches cracking under his feet.

"There, relax now," Biagio said as I touched the ground with my other hand to steady myself and pulled my right foot out from under a root.

Suddenly I couldn't find any ground to touch and my right foot landed on what felt like grass. There was a strange, bitter odour of tar, which jarred with the fresh smell of the countryside, an odour I didn't want to recognize at the time, but which, when I think about it now, was unmistakable.

"Are you there?" Biagio asked.

I braced myself, as if expecting a sudden gust of wind. "Yes. I think so."

"Go on then, open your eyes."

All this drama made me smile suddenly, and I slowly opened my eyes. I stood there motionless, turning my head first to the left, then a long way to the right.

"Jesus."

Biagio was also looking right and left and nodding with a smile.

We were standing on the weed-strewn verge of the Rocky Road. The Rocky Road, as we had dubbed it several years earlier, was a stretch of more than three kilometres, part of the old road that joined San Filippo and Posta, twisting and turning between fields and hollows and low hills. The road had been in use for more than two hundred years, until the mayor and the leader of the local council had suddenly turned ambitious and decided to improve the provincial highway and build approach roads, roundabouts and fast lanes. Of the old winding road that had joined the two villages—the scene, so it was said, of bloody battles that were probably more like tavern brawls—all that survived were three sections, bordered on one side by the modified version of the provincial highway and on the other by a big new road which was always deserted, and which bypassed Posta and then led downhill.

The part of the old road that led to San Filippo had become the semi-private access road to a new complex of detached houses, where even Mauro, the butcher's son, had ended up. Mauro hadn't much liked the new arrangement and had suddenly disappeared, one day at the end of March. The boys said he was somewhere in South America, or travelling the oceans on a merchant ship, but the old men said only that he was a rotten fruit and the spring had replaced him. What he had been replaced with, the old men were always vague about.

Towards Posta, the old road had simply become an ordinary stretch leading from the roundabout to the cinema and the centre of the village. The leader of the council had been very pleased with that roundabout and, in his euphoria, had used words in his inaugural speech which at the time, as I listened, holding my dad's hand, seemed filled with wonders: Europe, progress, the new millennium. Apparently the idea had indeed been his, and it had come to him after a holiday in France with his wife, just before discovering that she was carrying on with a detergent salesman from Rome. The roundabout had been the poor councillor's attempt at redemption, which was why it would for ever after be called the Horn.

In the middle stretch there were still those three kilometres and more of bare, now useless road, at the mercy of brambles and brushwood and blocked on both sides by the barriers of the new roads. When we were smaller, we had often gone there on our bikes, or to try out an older brother's moped, but gradually the branches had taken away half the fun, and the blackthorn scratches and potholes were no longer worth those few metres of free road. It was at that time that we started to call it the Rocky Road. First, for just a few weeks, carried away by our innocent desire for a more glittering world, we had tried calling it the Runway, but the title didn't fit it well, and as well as creating new potholes, a few showers soon did away with that name.

And now there it was in front of me like a cobra, all black and clean, all covered and coated and polished: who had done it, and why, would long remain a mystery, and would also secretly eat away at our studied cynicism.

I shook my head and squatted on the ground. The asphalt glittered with millions of diamonds beneath the almost full moon. I moved my hand over it, and it was as if I could hear the roar of the engines, and the tyres clinging like claws at the rough surface. I picked up a handful of black powder from the edge: it seemed to have fallen straight from the sky, and to be made of the same material as the night.

Biagio was still standing there, looking at me and smiling.
"When did this happen?"

"I don't know. I was here last week and everything was exactly the same as before."

"Jesus," I said again, looking at that black snake disappearing into the countryside.

Later, as we walked home in silence, with our hands in our pockets, we felt like two mountaineers returning to base camp. Maybe, when you come down to it, all that separates men capable of amazing feats from everyone else is a single moment: the moment when—consciously or not—you smell the universe and realize that everything is possible. A man may ride the waves, understand the laws of electromagnetism or build a skyscraper, but sooner or later he is overwhelmed by the insidious, shattering intuition that the limits of his body and of the world are not as solid as he had always imagined. I wonder if that wasn't my moment: the moment when the palm of my hand brushed against the mystery of the fresh asphalt on the Rocky Road.

2

THE RUMOUR bounced around the walls of the school like a clandestine murmur. It spread so quickly that in the space of barely three quarters of an hour, after break, it came back to me from the side opposite to where I had myself launched it.

After almost two hours of lessons, as Signor Torello was trying in vain in his Calabrian accent to draw our attention to the wonders of the Renaissance, I couldn't resist any more: I leant slightly to my right and, while still pretending to listen, simply whispered, "They've tarred the Rocky Road."

Antonio, known as Tonino, the always neat and tidy son of a lawyer who had once resolved a spot of bother my dad had got into because of an accident, looked up from the exercise book in which he was making notes and frowned.

"What?" he whispered.

Again I shifted towards him, with my back resting on the chair and my legs stretched in front of me.

"They've tarred the Rocky Road," I said, with a complacent half-smile, like a film actor.

Tonino continued taking notes. "Oh."

I looked at him and shook my head, with the same contempt

I would have felt if I'd told him that Giulia Morelli would show her private parts to everyone that afternoon. Giulia Morelli was the blonde, green-eyed daughter of a watchmaker, who had joined the school just a year earlier and would leave again the following year to go to school abroad. A tall, generous girl, she had, in that short time, entertained various young men: her memory and the stories about her would haunt our masturbatory fantasies for years.

During the break, Biagio, Greg and I mostly kept to ourselves, thinking hard about what to do. We had the feeling that everyone was looking at us strangely and, although we didn't say it, we were convinced that those looks were the prelude to a great and imminent future.

We had told Greg at the main entrance as soon as we arrived. Even after several years, having to go to school in Posta every day had the frustrating taste of defeat. The bitterest moment had been almost six years earlier, on the morning of the first day of the fifth year of primary school. The previous year, the local council had decided that it wasn't worth refurbishing the old school buildings in San Filippo and had decided to amalgamate them with the schools in Posta. That first morning, as we looked out at the lime trees lining the road to Posta, we realized, reluctantly and unconsciously, what nasty tricks were concealed by the word *modernity*. And however many years had passed since then, and however many things had changed, having to go down to Posta every day, thus paying tribute to its subtle but unchallenged supremacy, always annoyed us. It was basically unacceptable that we, the historic inhabitants of San Filippo, had to lower ourselves to travelling every day to what until a couple of generations earlier had simply

24

been a place where wayfarers and mail coaches stopped for rest and refreshment, without the inconvenience of having to go up the hill to the village. The full name of Posta was actually Posta di San Filippo—as indicated on the half-rusted sign at the entrance to the village and underlined, in parenthesis, by a superfluous and wonderful "hamlet of San Filippo". It was our guest room, and that was something that occasionally got us into slanging matches or scraps. The hamlet, however, had rapidly grown in size. Encouraged by its easy access to the plain and its lenient housing policy, Posta had expanded over the course of time, and apart from attracting entrepreneurs from all over had taken away our businesses and our shops and our schools and most of our inhabitants.

A few days after the great disappointment of the fifth year, Biagio and I had decided to mount our little campaign for dignity and austerity by refusing to take the bus the school provided for us. "Thanks—we prefer to walk," we told the bus driver every morning for more than two months, with heads held high, until we stopped to ask ourselves why the rest of the boys pointed at us and made fun of us. It was now years later, and we were in secondary school, but arriving alone on foot every day still seemed in some absurd way to be a reassertion of our freedom. Greg, on the other hand, more to his embarrassment than ours, continued to arrive in a shiny dark chauffeur-driven car.

"Well?" he said, coming up to us, looking almost peeved.

"It's happened."

"What's happened, Jacopo?"

I looked at him some more. "They've tarred the Rocky Road."

It was a great moment, the kind where you delude yourself that life could be like a beautiful woman, full of surprises.

"What are you talking about?" Greg asked, coming closer and lowering his voice.

"I swear to you, they've tarred the Rocky Road."

"Who has?"

"How should I know who? All I know is that it's all nice and clean and tarred. Biagio discovered it last night."

"I was over that way and I saw it," Biagio said.

"You were on the Rocky Road?"

"Yes."

"Doing what?"

"Nothing, just walking around."

"I see." Greg looked at us for another moment and gave a little smile.

Later, back in the classroom after break, after barely ten minutes or so, Mario the Redhead leant towards me from the side opposite Tonino, and continuing to look straight ahead whispered, "They've tarred the Rocky Road."

I stared at him for a moment, then burst out laughing, bent forward and banged my head on the desk.

We didn't go back to the Rocky Road until the afternoon of the next day. From a distance, as we came past the old riverbed and moved on to the road that ran alongside the last field, we could hear the *vroom-vroom* of mopeds. Marco was there, going backwards and forwards on one wheel of his souped-up Garelli, in front of Giorgia and her friends. On either side of the road, under the trees and on the grass, were various people. After a while, Tino's brother came round a bend on his Lambretta: he turned for a second, clung to the brakes and, halfway round the bend, a bit shaky but with his body nicely tilted to one side, gunned the engine. As soon as he saw us, he did everything he could to pass as close as possible to us and started laughing. Even Giorgia and her friends laughed and clapped. After a few seconds Giorgia waved to us, then said something to her friends and they burst out laughing.

Marco passed us on one wheel, turned back and approached us. "What are you doing here, wankers?"

Greg and I stood there motionless, not quite sure what to say.

"Nothing," I ventured.

Marco looked at me, then turned to Greg. "Won't your mummy buy you a moped?"

"Marco, come on," Biagio said. Biagio's brother Graziano had been a schoolmate of Marco, and prided himself on actually having belted him one day, which—surely wrongly—had always made us feel partially protected.

After a few moments, even Tino's brother Luca came up to us, sitting astride his Lambretta.

"What's up?" he asked Marco, raising his head slightly. His eyes were a strange opaque yellow colour, and his voice was so harsh it gave you a sore throat just to hear it. His long, unkempt ponytail and the scar on his cheek had always struck me as quite alarming, and ever since I was small I had tried my best to stay away from him, especially as years earlier he had amused himself beating us up. It was at least two years since I had last seen Luca, and during that time people had been telling all kinds of stories about him: they said he had been in prison, that he had done a robbery, that he was on heroin, that he was a drug dealer. They said a whole lot of things about Luca, things that might not have been true at all but that contributed to making him a sinister and legendary character.

"Nothing," Marco said. "I was asking these cissies what they're doing here."

Marco was the good-looking bully of the village, the one who, among other things, was always the first to use his fists in feuds with Posta. Next to Luca, he was like a puppy wagging its tail.

"Come on, boys, leave them alone," Giorgia shouted from the distance with a smile on her lips.

"You don't own this place," Greg whispered. I turned and looked at him with a mixture of admiration and disquiet: half of me wondered where he had suddenly acquired all that initiative, the other half wanted to hide my head in my hands.

Marco pulled the Garelli back a couple of paces and leant towards us, scowling. "What did you say?"

Greg stared straight in front of him and I could sense an inexorable slide towards one of those situations that was bound to end in some kind of pain.

But thank heaven, at that moment the sound of an engine echoed through the countryside. Marco stopped and looked towards the village. Luca also turned and, as we listened to the sound and after a while saw that red and silver animal approaching, the sense of gratitude to a god I didn't know, plus a wave of excitement, swept through my stomach like melted chocolate. The shiny red animal was carrying on its back a large figure in tight black leathers and an old white helmet with two green stripes. Arriving at the entrance to the Rocky Road, the animal roared again a few times and went up a couple of gears, then slipped between the verge and the guardrail and came towards us.

Marco and Luca stood there motionless, watching that thing come closer. Luckily, they seemed to have lost interest in us and what we had to say.

"What's this?" Luca asked in bewilderment, shouting over the scream of the engine, when the animal and its rider came to a halt right next to him.

The rider took off the two snap-fasteners of the half-scratched visor and from under it appeared the squinting face of Paolino. The sides of the old helmet had creased the skin around his eyes and squeezed his cheeks.

"This is Sandra," Biagio said with a smile.

It had started on a day like any other, a few months earlier, an ordinary cold morning at the beginning of February. Greg had come up to us during the break and after saying hello told us to come to his house after lunch, because he had something to show us. Biagio said he had to give his dad a hand with something, and it wasn't an ideal day for me either: I had promised to go and study at Francesca's. Francesca was the quiet, well-brought-up daughter of the owner of the general store, and I had been going out with her for more than a year. Greg looked at us seriously for a second and said it was important, and it wouldn't take long. We weren't used to Greg being that intense, and we thought it might be best to go.

By five to three, we were already at the gates. When we got to the end of the long avenue of cedars, the butler was there as usual waiting for us at the front door, at the

top of the stone steps. He greeted us with an imperceptible nod and led us into the small room filled with rugs
and leather-bound books, which they called "the small
drawing-room".

"The young master will be here in a minute," the butler
said. "Can I get you anything?"

Biagio collapsed into a huge blue velvet armchair, which
greeted him with a big snort.

"I don't know. You fancy anything?" I asked him, feeling
a bit awkward. He played with a fold of the armchair and
shrugged.

The butler stared at us for a moment or two, unable entirely
to conceal his annoyance.

Greg appeared at the door. "Come on, let's go," he said,
motioning to us slightly irritably.

"Remember the appointment with your mother," the
butler said as Biagio and I slid past him and followed Greg
towards the front door.

"Yes, Franco, yes," Greg sighed. "I'll be back in a minute.
I promise I won't run away."

Once through the door, we went down the steps and walked
around the outside of the villa.

"Do you wind that guy up in the morning," I asked, "or
is he always like that?"

"I don't know," Greg said. "He belongs to my mum. I
found him already assembled."

For a while now, a few weeks at the most, Greg's impeccable
politeness had started to turn into something more obscure
and elusive. He was brisker, more distracted, and sometimes
his sense of humour took on a slightly bitter tone. Thinking
about it now, I can't help seeing in those little signs the

real beginning of everything, but at the time it was simply something strange I happened to notice, nothing but a slight deviation from a person who even at the age of seven had greeted my mother with a kiss of the hand and always let us through a door first.

We walked along one side of the villa, then down a little stone drive, and entered the grounds. We went around the pond, which was half covered with the flat leaves of water lilies. On the edges, a slight crust of ice had formed. Three years earlier, during the great frost, we had even run on it and had some spectacular falls.

We descended some steps covered in lichen and came to the big, white-painted glass and metal greenhouses. Next to them was a long wooden shed full of mowers and agricultural machines that we had often sneaked into and played in as children. There was also a dark old car covered in dust, which for some reason had always scared us.

We entered the shed and, taking care where we put our feet in the gloom, went all the way to the back, where we couldn't remember ever having been before.

"The other day," Greg said, clambering with some difficulty over a plough and two rusty carts, "I came here to take a look and... shit, I just caught my trousers on a nail... and as I was looking around I discovered this."

Abruptly, he pulled away a thick greyish tarpaulin, raising a cloud of dust as he did so to reveal what, to all appearances, was a motorcycle.

Biagio and I finished climbing over the plough and, taking care not to catch ourselves on any spikes, got past the first cart. We stopped before the second, but close enough to get a better look at what Greg was showing us. It was indeed an old motorcycle, covered in dust, its short handlebars, red fuel tank and thin leather saddle forming a single line. Under the fuel tank and the thin plates of the cylinder was what looked like a kind of metal egg and on the front mudguard an iron tag that resembled a flipper. The engine seemed oxidized, and the chrome plating was spotted with rust. And yet, despite everything, it was still a beautiful sight.

"Well?" Biagio said.

"What do you mean, 'well'?" Greg replied, visibly disappointed. "Can't you see how beautiful she is?"

"Greg, it's a heap of rust."

"Who cares? We can fix her."

"But whose is it?"

"How should I know? Nobody's. I asked, but they didn't even know it was here."

"Incredible," I said. "I don't even know what to ask for this Christmas, and he finds a motorbike in his garden."

Biagio let out a laugh. Greg gave us both a surprising look, as if from a long way away, both enthusiastic and desperate. "But don't you understand? This is our bike."

He seemed really terrified, and his tone was imploring. Our bike. All at once, driven by Greg's sudden urgency, those simple words sounded like the last footholds we had before we sank into a crevasse. It was as if a cloud of diamonds had fallen from on high and that heap of old iron had suddenly coughed and come back to life. As if that bike had been ours for ever, hidden somewhere in our memories by some trivial trick of the mind.

We stood there a while longer looking at it. Then Greg carefully covered it up again and we left the shed. Once outside, in a ray of sunlight, the frozen grass crunching beneath our feet, we formed a kind of circle, facing each other. Greg took from the breast pocket of his shirt one of those cigarettes he had always loved smoking, home-made and tied up with sewing thread. He always rolled the leaves in a kind of fern which he found in the garden, tied them with the thread, and left them to dry for a few days on a slice of apple or an orange peel.

"Well, what do we do?"

"Good question," Biagio said. "Give me a drag."

Greg took a puff of the cigarette and passed it to Biagio. Biagio took it between his thumb and index finger and, keeping an eye on it, took a big drag.

"I don't know anything about engines," I said.

Biagio let out the smoke slowly, then continued looking at the cigarette. "These are good, Greg," he said, his voice half furred by smoke. "Really good."

"They are, aren't they?" Greg said, really pleased, taking back his cigarette.

"Yes, really good."

They both nodded.

"Hey," I said.

They looked at me. "Huh?"

"Well?"

"Well what?" Greg said, letting the smoke out of his mouth and screwing up his eyes a bit.

"The bike."

"Oh, right, the bike."

Biagio turned to Greg. "Give me another drag."

Greg handed him the cigarette again and looked at me thoughtfully. "The bike, right. It's quite a problem." He nodded again, and stroked his chin. Biagio looked at him and burst out laughing. Greg, who had turned serious, now glanced at the hand he was massaging his chin with and also burst out laughing. I stood there listening to them laugh and watching him stroke his chin theatrically for at least two minutes until, fortunately, they pulled themselves together.

"Everything all right?" I asked.

"Yes," Greg said, laughing again with Biagio and passing his hands over his eyes, "everything's fine."

"Well?"

"Well, the only thing to do is talk to Paolino," Biagio said.

Paolino had been our classmate for one year in secondary school, before he took the wise decision that school was not for him and left to work in his father's workshop. Every day there were fists flying. He was like a caged animal. Outside school, he was fairly quiet: touchy perhaps, and you certainly wouldn't have wanted to tease him, but all things considered, he minded his own business. In class, though, stuck between those desks, you could almost see his nerves throbbing beneath his skin, and after a while he would blow up like a pressure cooker with whatever he had within reach.

"I can't go, boys," Greg said. "You heard the tailor's dummy: I have to see Mum."

Biagio looked at him gravely for a moment, then dismissed that hint of scorn with a slight shake of the head.

When we got to Paolino's, he was bent over the handlebars of a Lambretta. He still occupied the old workshop in the corner of the square: it was narrow and greasy and stank of petrol and stale oil, with motorbikes and mopeds stacked one on top of the other any old how. The glass panes in the front door were held in somehow by rickety frames with their blue paint peeling, and on days when the north wind blew a draught came in that could blow out a match at a distance of a metre. The inside of the workshop was so narrow and smelly that Paolino always preferred working outside, even on really cold days, as long as it didn't rain. I had seen him there on the pavement even when it was snowing. As we came close, Biagio gave me a glance and a nod, motioning me to go forward. I looked up, wondering when all these roles had been assigned.

"Hi," I said.

Paolino raised his eyes from the brake lever on which he was working, glanced at us, and without saying a word resumed his work.

Biagio and I looked at each other for a moment, not sure what to do.

"Listen," I said, "we need to talk to you about something."

Paolino continued working on the lever of the Lambretta. I turned towards Biagio, who simply shrugged, then I looked again at Paolino.

"We have a motorbike," I said after another little while, for a moment feeling taller by at least half a head.

Paolino picked up a spanner from the saddle of the Lambretta and started tightening a nut on the lever, still without saying anything.

I was rather embarrassed, but after a few moments I summoned up a crumb of courage. "Paolo?" I ventured timidly.

Paolino stopped and sighed, then raised his eyes and stared at us. "Listen, you wankers, I don't have time to waste on your bullshit. I don't know what you want. You talk to me about a motorbike that isn't here and—"

"You could come and see it. It's at Gregorio's."

Paolino stood up straight and pointed the spanner he'd just been tightening the nut with at us. "I wouldn't even go with you lot to see your mothers' tits. If you have something to show me, bring it here, and if you're not out of here in three seconds I'll kick you so hard that when you get home you won't be able to get through the door, your arses'll be that swollen."

"All right." I raised my hands. "Forget I said it."

"Okay," Biagio said.

The day afterwards, at school, Greg asked us how it had gone.

"He wasn't very keen on the idea."

It took us more than two hours to drag the motorbike with its deflated tyres from Greg's shed to Paolino's workshop. It was even colder than the day before. There were still patches of ice at various points in the grounds of Greg's house and in the village, and both Biagio and I slipped several times. On a couple of occasions—though to be honest without much enthusiasm—Greg offered to help, but we tacitly agreed that Greg was practically giving us a share in a motorbike, and the least we could do was sweat in his place.

We felt big and tough, and pride prevented us from asking for help: despite the cold we were sweaty, dirty with dust, and in one of the falls I hit my knee against the ignition lever, tearing my trousers and cutting my skin. Muscles I didn't even know I had were hurting.

I'm convinced that when Paolino saw us appear in the square, dishevelled and bloody, sliding on the frozen slabs of the pavement and steaming in the cold like hot linen, he felt a touch of respect for us for the first time. He leant on the wooden doorpost at the entrance to his workshop and waited for us.

"Here it is," I said once we were close, as soon as I had recovered my breath.

"What do you want me to do with this?" Paolino asked after a few seconds.

We looked at each other, not sure what to say.

"Make it go, I suppose."

Paolino looked at the bike for a while and then at us. "And who's paying?"

A wave of cold went through me, freezing every drop of sweat on my skin and making the cut on my knee throb with pain. How could we not have thought of it? Did we really think that Paolino would go to all the trouble of fixing up a heap of old iron like that, just for fun?

"I'll pay."

I turned. Greg was looking Paolino right in the eyes. For the first time, he had a hardness on his face that I'd learn to recognize only much later. Paolino looked at Greg, then again at the bike. He took a few steps forward to get a closer look at it. He crouched on the ground, passed a hand over the chain guard, removing a little dust, and for a few moments went over the bike from top to bottom. Between his teeth he had a small piece of rolled-up paper, which he kept shifting from one side of his mouth to the other. Then he stood up again and went back to the entrance.

"It'll need a lot of work."

Greg continued looking at him, as serious and motionless as a statue. "No problem."

They were like two gunfighters in an American western. Paolino looked at all of us again, trying to work out if he was being swindled or not.

"All right," he said finally. "In the meantime I'll take the hose and give it a wash down."

3

THE ROLES WERE SOON DEFINED. Greg, as the financial backer, asked for accounts and forked out the money as it was needed. Biagio gave Paolino a hand to find replacement parts in the area. Whenever he could, he took his father's Ape truck and went to Posta or down in the valley to a few car breakers to pick up couplings, levers, bands or gudgeon pins. Occasionally I went with him. I would sit down in the bed of the Ape and look at the countryside speeding past. It would have been good to have music, a saxophone solo, maybe one of those Frank Sinatra records my dad loved listening to. Greg had decided that I was the one with the best taste, so I had been automatically elected the panel beater.

That meant I would take care of repainting and scraping the various parts of the bike. The first part I took to Marino was the fuel tank. It was in a decent condition, but the red paint had turned opaque and in a couple of places was swollen with bubbles of rust.

Marino was perfectly round. When I was smaller, at the annual feast day of the village's patron saint, he'd amused himself having me with him for the tombola. I remember him standing on the steps of the church, already tipsy and

red-faced from the wine: for every number we had, he got me
to make a hole in the ticket with a toothpick and laugh. He
would say it brought luck. Once we even won the tombola,
the prize being a whole ham. So we decided to dine on that
instead of the suckling pig, and Marino surreptitiously made
me take a couple of swigs from a bottle of red wine.

When I put my head in through the entrance to his shed,
Marino was hard at work on a Fiat 128 half covered in
light brown patches. He was all dusty and was wearing
a mask.

"Hey, Jacopino, what are you doing with that?" he greeted
me, barely taking his eyes off his work.

"I have to repaint it."

Marino glanced at me, then went back to working on the
128. After a moment he straightened up, lowered his mask
and approached. In his blue overalls, he seemed even rounder
than usual: a blue ball with a head stuck on it.

"Whose is it?"

"Ours."

"No, I mean, from what bike?"

"An old Gilera."

"Yes, I see that, but where did you get it?"

"We found it at Gregorio's, next to the greenhouse. But
please, Marino, don't tell anyone. It's a secret."

Marino raised his eyes for a moment and stared at me, then
looked again at the fuel tank. "I think it was the old estate
manager's," he said in a warm tone and with a look in his
eyes I couldn't recall ever seeing before.

"What estate manager?"

"You weren't even born," he smiled, taking the fuel tank
from my hand.

"Are you saying he wants it back?"

"I doubt it."

"Are you sure?"

"Fairly sure: he's dead." Marino turned the fuel tank and studied the bottom. "It'll need sandblasting. Then we have to see if it's in good condition, and maybe repaint it. If not, it'll have to be replaced."

"What about the emblem?"

"It'd be better to find a new one. Then we'll give it a bit of a polish. How's the rest?"

"The rest of what?"

"My grandmother. The bike, arsehole."

"Oh. Well, it's quite rusty but I'd say it's okay."

"The rest will need sandblasting too."

I had no idea what sandblasting was, but all this renewed intimacy with Marino filled me with joy and I had no desire to ruin it.

"Do you want to do it?" he said at last.

"Do what?"

"The work. Sandblasting and all that."

"I don't know."

"You might enjoy it."

So I found myself a couple of days after that, late in the afternoon, at the back of Marino's shed, with a tube in my hand spreading sand at pressure on the fuel tank of our bike. The ease with which the paint came away was staggering. It was like rubbing out pencil marks with an eraser. I could have carried on for hours. I'd have liked to sandblast the whole village, and when I was already finished after barely half an hour I was visibly disappointed.

"It's come up well," Marino said, picking the fuel tank up

from the floor and turning it this way and that. "Luckily the rust was only on the surface."

"Do you want me to sandblast anything else for you?"

"No, thanks, it doesn't matter."

"I could have a go at the Renault."

"No, son, thanks."

"How about those old scraps over there?"

"Jacopo, go home. Tomorrow we'll choose a shade of red for the paint."

Everything took an unexpected turn one Saturday afternoon. We got to Paolino's workshop and found him on the ground, his back propped against the entrance, staring at the bike. So as not to show the bike to anyone, we had decided to always work indoors, and on the couple of occasions when Paolino—afflicted by splitting headaches caused by the gas and petrol fumes—had been forced to go outside, we had concealed it carefully under an old sheet.

We approached without saying anything and also started looking at the bike in silence. Nothing remained now but the frame, with dozens of nuts and bolts around it and the wheels laid on their sides. The shiny egg of the engine was lying on its side by itself, on three folded sheets of newspaper. It looked like an aluminium heart. Unsure what to do, we also stood there in silence for a few minutes.

Greg looked round at everyone, then shrugged. "Well?"

For a moment, Paolino continued to look at the bike, then wiped his mouth with the back of his hand. "What are we going to do?" he asked.

Biagio and Greg and I looked at each other without quite understanding.

"What do you mean 'what are we going to do'?"

Paolino raised his head, a distant look in his eyes. "With this. What are we going to do with this?"

I stared at Greg and Biagio and all three of us shrugged again. "I'm not sure what you mean, Paolino," I said.

"Right now we're fixing the bike," he began. "If we're lucky and find all the parts we may even manage to get it up and running. And then?"

"I don't know, Paolino. Then we go for a ride."

"But where do you want to go? It doesn't even have a licence plate. Take it out of San Filippo and the first carabiniere who sees you will make you put it back in the garage at the very least, and could even confiscate it."

"So what do we do?"

"We really get it to run."

I looked again at the other two without understanding. Paolino seemed different, all his hardness transformed into something unusually soft and dreamy.

"We fix it, we change it, we improve it. We turn this heap of iron into a racer. If we're going to do something illegal anyway, let's go for it."

We all looked at that eviscerated frame and those rusty parts. From the first, we had neglected to think about what we would do with the bike. The thought hadn't even crossed our minds. It was our bike, and that was enough for us. The fact that it was a bike was secondary: it was simply something of ours, something that was only ours, a first thrilling step into the magical world of emancipation, and it really didn't matter all that much if it was a vehicle on two wheels or a sleigh or some other object. But now we saw it all at once for what it actually was: a motorcycle, a complex mechanism with a very specific purpose.

Maybe, in a hidden place in our consciousness, we'd been thinking that once we'd fixed it we would ride it along the gravel paths in the grounds of Greg's house. But that bike wasn't made for gravel: in the now distant times when its lines had been drawn, its designers hadn't been thinking of stones and earth, but rough asphalt. In the meantime, though, years had passed, years in which the bike had remained in that shed gathering dust, while the world and technology had advanced and progressed. That was why Paolino's vision suddenly rose in front of our eyes in all its grandeur: to make that old bike even better than it was, to obliterate the years that separated it from us or, if not all of them, at the very least, a fair number. We immediately thought it was an excellent idea.

Greg, Biagio and I suddenly smiled, and although we didn't say it, the three of us understood for the first time that behind Paolino's tough exterior, his bulk and his silences, was a person capable of looking at the world.

"So what do we do?"

"We need to start again from square one."

"Meaning what?"

"We have to enlarge the tyres, the engine, the brakes, the carburettor. We have to make it lighter, throw out the useless parts, open the exhaust… we have to do a lot of things."

Paolino was speaking for the first time with a drive we had never seen in him before, and for a few seconds I thought I could hear particles vibrating at higher frequencies all around me.

"And you'll have to spend a lot more money on it," he concluded, though without his usual bullying tone, in fact dropping his voice slightly.

So we all turned to Greg, with the terrible sense that the whole vision might abruptly disintegrate in front of our eyes.

"No problem," Greg said.

Paolino was unable to hold back a smile and for the first time, although without getting up off the ground, he shook our hands one by one.

Paolino and Biagio started scouring all the wrecking yards on the plain, in search of parts they could use. The bike was completely dismantled.

The wheels and the lights and the brakes and the whole exhaust ended up in a cardboard box, gathering dust, while the engine was opened and disembowelled. For a while, Paolino wondered if it might not be a good idea to find a new engine that could be adapted. But he was unable to find one, and in any case he'd fallen in love with the dry clutch, which he said was a rarity. So he rebored and polished the cylinder thoroughly and from a mysterious character in Viterbo got a brand new piston with a double ring. He managed to recover and adapt a Dell'Orto 36 carburettor and he had a friend of his remodel and lighten the piston rod. Once the frame was sandblasted, we had it strengthened by Sergio, the locksmith, with four steel plates, and we had two new arms soldered on for the rear swingarm, on which, instead of the Gilera's narrow rings, Paolino managed to adapt those of a Ducati Mark 3.

Finally opening that package with the Swedish postage stamps was like turning the key in the lock of a safe. Through yet another of his contacts, Paolino had managed to get sent from Öhlins—and this time the money involved had made even Greg hesitate for a moment—two rear shock absorbers and an entire front swingarm composed of plates. They were all gilded, the springs canary yellow, and in the dim light of evening we really felt as if we were looking at a treasure. Paolino's eyes were shining like a junkie's over a load of heroin, and as we listened to him telling us that it was with shock absorbers like these that Eddie Lawson had won the 500cc world championship road race four years earlier, we felt as if were already surrounded by laurel wreaths and people in leathers.

Now Biagio put his hands on the bike as if it were his, and I started to feel useless and jealous. The new version of the bike had fewer parts than before on the bodywork, and it was quite a while now since Marino and I had finished sandblasting and painting what remained. Even though the painting had taken longer than anticipated—drops still formed, which I worked hard to get rid of, and Marino had stubbornly refused to help me—the whole matter had been resolved rather quickly. Moreover, the enthusiasm with which I brought back those shiny, refurbished parts had been greeted with a certain indifference.

I would drop by Paolino's workshop and find both him and Biagio dirty and bent over the bike, talking—as if they had always done so—about things I didn't know and that would have been too difficult to explain to me. Or else—and this was even more frustrating—in total silence, each at work by himself and yet perfectly coordinated: Paolino's hand appearing, Biagio lowering a spanner, then at the right moment a nut and a pair of pliers, then maybe a simple "go on" and Biagio holding a hose steady and Paolino tightening a bolt.

I tried at first to ask what this or that part was and if they needed a hand, but each time they told me they didn't, and the explanations between one job and the next were always vague. So I'd end up just sitting on a Vespa or some old wreck watching them work. It was during this time that the whole Sandra thing started. When Greg put his head in through the front door of the workshop one day, Biagio and Paolino were fiddling with a few parts at the work bench, under the light, and I was on my own, playing with a piece of inner tube.

"So, how's Sandra?" Greg asked.

I looked at him, bored, not understanding. "Who?"

"That, the bike."

"Oh, they're just fixing something on the engine. Paolino has found a new part."

Greg watched the others working for a minute. "All right," he said without even coming in. "See you."

The others did not even turn round, and the thing seemed to have passed without notice. But then we all gradually started calling the bike Sandra, and for some reason it always made us smile.

One afternoon I happened to glance at the photograph of Randy Mamola hanging on the back wall of the shop. He was coming round a bend, his knee almost on the ground and his head tilted the other way, astride his red and white Yamaha covered in inscriptions, with the yellow patch and the number 3 on the front. I saw that photo every day, and always went on to something else, as if indifferent to it. This time, though, I looked at it in another way: harbouring absurd ambitions in my boredom, it struck me that our bike could be like that, almost horizontal, defying the laws of physics.

And I suddenly realized that there was something I stupidly hadn't thought of before.

So I went to Marino's shed. He was inside a Fiat Uno that had been in an accident, dismantling something under the steering column, with a light attached to the wheel. After a few seconds he turned his head slightly and glanced at me.

"Hi, kid, how's it going?" he said, resuming his work.

"We have to cover the bike."

Marino stopped and put his head out, with a frown. "We have to do what?"

"Cover the bike."

"Cover it?"

"Yes, cover it."

Marino went back under the wheel. "Son, I don't know what you're talking about."

"You know racing bikes?"

"Yes…"

"All that stuff that covers it."

"The fairing?" Marino asked, continuing his work.

"If that's what it's called."

"What about it?"

"How do we make it?"

Marino laughed. "Good Lord, lad, that's not easy. They're made of plastic. We'd need the moulds." He put his arm out. "Pass me the pliers on the seat there."

On the back seat of the Uno there was a pair of long, thin pliers with blue handles. I grabbed them and put them in Marino's plump hand. I watched and listened for a moment or two as he moved about under the steering column. He came out holding a big metal ring and sat down on the edge of the car.

"You could try fibreglass."

"Fibreglass?"

"Yes. I can get you some if you like next time I go to the paint shop. They should have some."

"And what do I do with fibreglass?"

"Do whatever you like, but it won't be easy. It's a bicomponent resin that you soak sheets of glass wool in. Then you let it dry and it becomes very tough and resistant. A couple of years ago, I used it to cover the cracked sink behind the shed."

Marino got up with a sigh from the edge of the Uno, waddled over to the anvil on the workbench and, after putting the big ring down on it, picked up a hammer and gave it two good blows. Then he stopped.

"But you have to know how to make a fairing."

A few days later, having taken all the necessary measurements of the bike, Marino and I found ourselves in front of those big cans of resin and hardener and those white sheets of glass wool and started to try figuring out how to mould a resistant base on which to place and dry the soaked parts.

"Chicken wire," Marino ventured after a while.

"Chicken wire?"

"That's right, chicken wire."

"And what do you do with chicken wire?"

"You shape it and put it over the fibreglass. It should work."

For a moment I looked at Marino, trying to figure out if he was a madman or a genius. I had him lend me his moped and rode over to Testucci's to get two metres of chicken wire. Within quite a short time, looking at the photographs of a couple of racing bikes and trying to follow the measurements I had taken of ours, I managed to give the wire a vague shape. Marino lent me a pair of overalls and a table and a mask, and the three or four times I managed to find time to go to his shed I covered the wire with the pieces of glass wool soaked in resin. At first we were convinced we could cover the whole bike, just like a real one, but then it seemed a shame to cover the shiny egg of the engine so we decided to limit ourselves to a nice round windscreen, which would give the idea of a racing bike but not conceal it too much. I managed to make a decent base, and once we had the rough parts we found ourselves looking at the result again and wondering how to go forward.

"The only thing to do is fill and smooth everything."

"What do you mean?"

Marino went to get a big metal can and opened it. Then with a spatula he put part of the contents on a piece of wood, added a little red paste to it from a tube and mixed them together, turning the paste round and round until the red had completely disappeared, merging with the brown of the filler. He then took the windscreen and smeared a fair amount of paste on it, spreading it as much as he could. The irregularities of the fibreglass made the spatula jump, but quite a lot got filled.

"It's going to be a tough job," Marino said. "You'll have to fill everything, get rid of the excess, fill it again, discard the excess again, until it's completely even."

It was indeed a tough job. I spent hours rubbing the sand-paper over that damned fairing without ever seeing an end to it. I seemed constantly to be getting there, until I washed down the surface and saw that there were still dozens of frustrating irregularities. From time to time, partly to repay him for the time I was stealing from him and the tools he was lending me—not to mention the quantity of putty I was using and for which he would never ask a lira—I gave Marino a hand with a few little bodywork jobs. There, too, I found myself doing a lot of filling: by now I had acquired such a knack and the fairing was so difficult that the smooth surfaces of the cars were a breath of fresh air. It wasn't exactly what my parents or I had imagined for my future, but if the worst came to the worst I could always become a bodyworker. All things considered, it didn't seem a bad way to end up.

To perfect the job, Marino gave me some thick pieces of curved wood on which to lay the sandpaper and apply it uniformly. When at last I found myself faced with those smooth, polished contours, with the muscles of my arm still throbbing under the skin, I felt an unmistakable elation: they seemed the most elegant curves I had ever set eyes on, and it would be a very long time before I felt the same overwhelming satisfaction.

With all the work and the putty and the chicken wire we had used, though, the fairing was far too thick and heavy. So I used it as a mould. I smeared it in grease and covered it with another thick layer of fibreglass. Once dried, I separated the two surfaces and used the new shell as a mould to make the actual fairing.

The work held me spellbound for days. I spent all the hours I could at the bench that Marino had put at my disposal in a corner of the shed, with a mask on my face and wearing his blue overalls, which were too big for me. The resins and the flying particles of glass wool and the solvents made my eyes bloodshot. When I looked at them in the mirror in the evening, they were swollen and bulging, with red veins spreading from the pupils. My head throbbed, I couldn't breathe well, and at night I would often wake up with my throat dry and painful and couldn't get back to sleep even with two cups of milk and honey. And yet, every evening, Marino would push me away and force me to go home: I was feverish, feverish and compulsive, but happy in my way, as if every remedy for the world was in the viscous substance of the resins and in the ability of the glass wool to envelop the contours of things and harden and withstand shocks. If only some god had given me the opportunity, I would have covered the earth in fibreglass.

Even Francesca had started looking at me strangely. If I have to think of a word that best describes my relationship with Francesca, that word is *predictable*. It was predictable that she was my girlfriend, predictable that during the trip to Florence a year earlier, walking by the Arno, I had asked her if we could go out together, predictable that through a friend of hers she had later simply said "all right", predictable that the whole village thought we would get married one day and start a family and live happily ever after. It was predictable that on Saturday afternoons we'd visit one another's houses whereas during the week we had to study, and that our parents respected each other and saw our relationship in a very good light. The fact that suddenly my eyes would be bloodshot and that I would prefer the company of epoxy resins to hers was perhaps rather less predictable.

When I finally saw the fairing, right there in front of me, even I didn't think it was real. For a moment, the hours I had spent on it and my bloodshot eyes and aching arms all vanished: it was as if a courier had just delivered it from a spare parts company. Marino patted me on the back and told me I was stealing his work. In the end we decided to paint it red, with a silver circle in the middle and a piece of transparent plastic to make a tiny windscreen.

When I took it to Paolino's workshop, to place it over the bike and find the best points to fix it on, the others couldn't believe it. They particularly couldn't believe that I was the one who'd made it. Paolino suddenly looked at me with what actually seemed a fair amount of respect, and years later Greg would tell me it was the first time he'd had a clear inkling that I might one day do something in life that would surprise him.

In the meantime they had reassembled a lot of the bike, and Sergio had forged a trumpet exhaust, which Paolino swore would make a great din and above all would help Sandra go like a rocket.

We started Sandra for the first time outside Paolino's workshop as the sun went down, covered by the canvas so that nobody should see it. Paolino had to hit the pedal about thirty times to get it started. He continued adjusting the air and the tick-over, and for a few moments we were silently overcome with the terror that it could all vanish in a soap bubble. Then Paolino hit the pedal for the umpteenth time, Sandra gave a cough, screamed and started. Without taking one hand off the engine, Paolino yelled and raised his arm to the sky. It was like hearing the baying of the beasts in the forest, the first roars of an animal, and as we stood there, surrounded by these cries and in a big cloud of white smoke, we couldn't stop laughing and hugging each other.

4

T HE BEST RACES, to be honest, were those between the Vespas and the few Lambrettas in the area. In a hastily called conference, featuring the four of us and another handful of regulars of the Rocky Road, it was decided—for reasons of security: that was the formula we liked to use if anyone asked us—that we would limit the races to three vehicles at a time and everybody had to wear a helmet. For some mysterious reason that didn't really thrill me, the others decided unanimously that the only person they could trust if there were ever any doubt about a result was yours truly, so on one of the first days I was taken to the end of the course on the saddle of one of the mopeds, and, after drawing a line across the asphalt with a piece of brick, was left there to be the judge. I found a little seat of rock for myself a couple of metres higher up along the embankment, and ended up spending quite a bit of time alone and in silence. Sometimes Francesca came with me but, although she would never have admitted it, I think she found the whole thing rather stupid, and was secretly disconcerted by her sudden low opinion of me, so she often ended up finding some excuse and staying in the village.

One day Greg, thinking to make things easier for me, turned up with those huge radios his father had bought dozens of years earlier for an expedition in Africa. There had been a period when, just to have an opportunity to use them, we had made up games and battles in his garden, but after a while we'd started to get bored and feel stupid. For years Greg had been looking for a good reason to use them and when we saw him with them that day we doubled over with laughter. In the event, I found I liked having one with me when I was on my own at the end of the Rocky Road, and hearing my friend's voice crackle every now and again from the loudspeaker.

Seeing the Vespas and mopeds coming round the last bend was always a sight. The riders would be well forward, going flat out, the frames twisted, their faces drawn, as if the more they pushed the faster they went. When they were well matched, they even seemed to sway and bump into each other as they made their way through. Then, when the race was over, they always went back to the starting point quite fast, laughing and miming a few turns with their hands. Luca was among the fastest, and bit by bit, with all the victories I had witnessed, he ended up taking a liking to me. One evening he even gave me a lift back to the start of the course. It was like being behind a fierce and unpredictable animal, but getting off his Lambretta while everyone watched and giving each other a high five filled me with great satisfaction.

Gradually most of the bends had been given names. The S-bend just after the starting line had become the Romoli, because the first time Romoli's son came round it, shouting

"I'll show you!"—having already skidded at the first bend—he had skidded again and ended up in the ditch, to general laughter. The amazing bend that turned sharp left under the embankment became the Dwarf, because you went so close to the overhanging rocks that you had to lower your head, and Paolino had admitted that a dwarf would have gained at least half a metre of trajectory. The downhill exit from the S bend that directly faced the German's field, in which you could go as fast as you wanted as long as you held on tight, was the Satellite Dish. The next bend had become the Plane, because if you didn't take it correctly you could well end up wide and go flying straight into the field below. It happened one day to Nicolino, and even after I'd made sure he was fine and hadn't hurt himself my legs were shaking.

Nicolino was the Marshal's rather slow-witted son, who had shown up one day as we were adjusting something on Sandra, and told us that he had heard about the races and was a good rider.

When I managed to catch up with Nicolino, he was lying in the middle of the field holding his arm and laughing.

"Did you see how I flew?"

"Yes, I saw. Are you all right?"

"Great, wasn't it?"

Nicolino seemed excited and happy, as if he had finally done something worthy of respect and admiration. To be honest, I was more worried about the Marshal's Vespa lying five metres from him, with its handlebars bent and full of bumps. This didn't bode well, and for the first time I realized that in our great plan we had been unforgivably thoughtless. When Greg had told Paolino that he would pay for Sandra, I'd learnt something fundamental that sooner or later everyone would agree with: you can't do anything in this life without arms, but nor can you do without sponsors. I would only realize the full wisdom of that intuition much later, and yet already that evening I went home feeling more confident. There was, though, a third element we couldn't do without, and which in our innocent dreams of independence we had fooled ourselves we could ignore: the law.

I heard the other Vespas and mopeds coming up behind me, then people running down the cliff and into the field.

"Shit," Greg said when he came level with me. "What now?"

I was still looking at the Marshal's Vespa, lying broken in the middle of the stubble.

"Now we're in for it."

The Marshal came striding across the square just twenty minutes after we got back to Paolino's workshop. We were all sitting on the pavement, the Vespa propped against the wall next to the entrance. Apart from a few scratches on the front shield and the engine guard, one tyre had been torn off and the rim twisted, which had made pushing it all the way to the village rather laborious. It was a hot afternoon in June, and school had been over for at least a week.

When Nicolino saw his dad enter the square he leapt to his feet and ran to meet him.

"Don't worry, Dad, I'm fine."

"Not for long," the Marshal said, walking straight past him without even looking at him and carrying on towards us. Paolino and Biagio and I got to our feet. Greg, as usual, had already found an excuse to go, leaving us to push the Vespa.

The Marshal was now less than half a metre away and had started staring at his Vespa behind us. For more than two minutes, he stood stock still and looked at it gravely.

We even had time to exchange glances and gestures, asking each other what on earth he was doing. The Marshal then lowered his head and looked all three of us in the eyes, one after the other. His gaze came to rest on Paolino.

"Let's say my Vespa was making a strange noise, and let's even say that for some incomprehensible reason I decided to take it to an idiot like you to get it repaired. Let's say also that I have the bad luck to have broken a part that's hard to find. I'll be back here in five days, and if my Vespa isn't the way I saw it this morning when I left home I'll arrest you all for theft, damage to property and circumvention of an incapable. Is that all right with you?"

"Of course, Marshal, perfectly all right."

"Excellent, goodbye then," the Marshal concluded. He turned, took a few steps, then stopped and looked at us again.

"Oh, and if I see any vehicle on wheels, even a wheelbarrow, going at more than ten kilometres an hour along the old road, I'll take that damned bike you put back together and any others and send them to a friend of mine to make them into a container. Is that clear?"

"Of course, Marshal," Paolino replied, although with much less enthusiasm, perhaps with even a touch of ill-concealed resentment.

When the Marshal turned his back on us, Nicolino got into step behind him, following him at a distance of a metre.

"It's better for you if you go to Giorgio and have him make you up a bed in the barracks, because if you come home tonight I'll give you all the bruises you didn't get with the Vespa."

Paolino worked every evening until late fixing the Marshal's Vespa and in order to finish it in time I promised Marino

I'd help him out in the body shop until September. When the Marshal came back, his Vespa was already there on the pavement waiting for him, like a prize. He walked around it and looked it over from top to bottom, then got on it and gave a sharp tug to the lever. It came on immediately and the engine seemed to throb like an athlete's heart. Paolino had dismantled it and cleaned and polished it well. While he was about it, he had also sorted out the carburettor. The Marshal insisted on revving for at least a minute to make sure that everything was in working order, then pulled it out of the kick-stand and put it in first.

"Thanks," he said gravely but unconvincingly.

"You're welcome," Paolino said, shaking his head and spitting on the ground as he watched him leave.

Our relations with the authorities were compromised in any case. In one go we had played all the cards in our hands, and the thought of our bikes and mopeds being confiscated scared everyone. Overnight, the summer seemed to revert to the same lazy rhythm of previous years. Those who had cars waited for Saturday to go to the sea, and we wandered through the village, kicking stones, each of us wondering without saying it how we were going to fill the weeks to come. Francesca was pleased to have me to herself again, and demonstrated it with a new and unexpected pride. We'd be out for a walk and all at once she'd be clinging to me like a true fiancée. Even in bed, when her parents weren't there and we started on that mechanical exercise we had the effrontery to call love, for the first time she actually gave a few barely perceptible moans.

*

Up until that afternoon.

About three weeks earlier I had been alone at the end of the Rocky Road waiting for the arrival of two Vespas, and had started to wonder if there might not be a place from which to see a larger section of the course. At the starting point, Luca had had a few problems with his Lambretta and Greg told me to wait a minute. To kill time, I'd clambered up the rocks and discovered a spur from which you could see the Satellite Dish and a stretch immediately before the Dwarf. The spur was quite difficult to reach and I'd only gone back there once or twice, and hadn't given it much thought. But when the problem of the Marshal arose, I remembered it, got Biagio to give me a lift, and climbed it again. Once I was at the top, out of breath, Greg's father's radio suddenly took on an even brighter colour than anticipated.

"I knew it," I said, smiling and looking further down, beyond the Rocky Road.

Biagio stared at me as he caught his breath, then shook his head and also looked into the distance. Sure that the only reason I'd asked him to follow me was to have a bit of company, he did not seem very happy. "You knew what?"

"There and there," I said indicating two points in the landscape.

Biagio squinted at the horizon, then gave me a puzzled look. I went closer and put my finger as close to his line of sight as possible.

"There. And there." I pointed first to the left, then to the right.

"What?"

"What do you mean, 'what'? That's the exit from the road that leads to Posta and the end of the Rocky Road. The one down there, on the other hand, is the stretch of the provincial highway that goes all the way to San Filippo."

Squinting again, Biagio stared at both spots. "Are you sure?"

"Yes. Do you see that grey thing?"

"Yeah."

"That's the milestone that Mirco's brother hit. You can see the broken tree stump next to it."

Biagio looked for another moment or two. "I think you're right."

I stood there, gazing out at the view with a smile on my face and my hands on my hips. "I am. Anyone trying to get to the Rocky Road, we'll be able to see from here."

So the races began again more or less as before, but with more care taken. In the end, I was the one who lost out more than anybody else, having to climb up to the spur every time, but I was gradually rewarded with two well-toned legs and a strong spine. On the rare occasions someone decided to go with me, the satisfaction of waiting at the top, as fresh as a daisy, for them to arrive, red-faced and sweaty, was absolutely priceless.

"I'm not going up there," Francesca said to me one day, visibly irritated and disappointed by this new turn of events, as I was already climbing the spur.

The first time the Marshal's car decided to turn in the direction of the Rocky Road was a great moment. I had already seen it on a couple of occasions emerging onto the provincial highway, but it had always turned out to be a false alarm. That day, though, only a minute after I'd warned the others, it appeared at the beginning of the road. Greg told me the story, and it was a touching one: all at once, those small groups of boys and girls who spent a lot of their time teasing each other had dropped their bikes and mopeds or thrown them on the kick-stand, and suddenly started chatting and smiling at each other like old friends. The sun was filtering through the trees and shimmering in the pollen raised by the wind, and some had even sat down on the grass to play with green ears of corn. It was like a scene from the Summer of Love.

The Marshal got out of his car and took a few steps along the Rocky Road.

"What are you all doing?"

Silence for a few moments. Then, from one of the groups, a voice cried out, "Making love, Marshal!"

There was a roar of laughter.

The Marshal stood there for a moment or two without saying a word, then simply turned on his heels and went back to his car, and it was as if everyone could hear applause rustling among the trees.

There were only a couple of times that the Marshal managed to get to the Rocky Road without my noticing. The first time, I had gone into the bushes to have a pee, with my back to the view, at the very moment the Marshal's car turned onto the stretch of the provincial highway that led to the entrance to the Rocky Road. Luckily, though, by the time I got back, the twins had already set off on their Vespas and Marco was checking something on his switched-off Garelli. Greg managed to warn me in time, and as soon as I spotted the twins I rushed down to the road and we had a brainwave and started gathering the blackberries that grew between the brambles on the embankment. By the time the Marshal got to us, the three of us were stuffing blackberries into the T-shirt of one of the twins. He stood there watching us with his hands on his sides.

"For jam," I said, pleased with myself. "Want some?" And I put one in my mouth.

He stared at us for a few more moments. "I'm keeping my eye on you," he said at last, then turned and walked away.

I couldn't resist. "So are we."

5

S ANDRA DIDN'T DO RACES. There was no point arguing about it: she simply had no rivals. A few guys from
a nearby village would sometimes show up at the starting
line, sitting astride highly coloured objects that you could
hear coming from a long way off but never seemed to arrive.
They'd give you a serious, fairly nasty look and say they'd
heard about a motorbike that went fast.

Whoever was there, sitting on the low wall or fixing something on his moped, would say, "Sandra".

"What?" the guy on his bike would ask.

"Sandra," the other person would repeat.

Usually the guy on the bike would lose some of his cool
and whichever of us was there would look at him with ill-
concealed boredom. "The bike that goes fast. She's called
Sandra."

The guy would look at him gravely for a moment or two.
"Bullshit," he would say.

The one of us who was there would look at the guy and
give a sarcastic little smile. "I'd wait to say that if I were you."

At this point, the guy would be told to come back a couple
of days later at a particular time.

The first few times they tried to race, but as soon as the challengers got to the end of the Rocky Road and saw Paolino and Sandra already there waiting for them they came up with all kinds of excuses: they didn't know the route and so on. One even complained that he didn't have the right gears, a claim greeted with a chorus of laughter. Their voices always sounded shriller when the race was over, and they couldn't take their eyes off Sandra as they spoke, moving their heads slightly from side to side, as if trying to extract the secret of life from that heap of metal.

Apart from anything else Sandra did indeed go like a cannonball, and after the business with the Marshal's Vespa we were afraid that some of the sports bikes that came from all over to race would sooner or later plunge down the slope and crash into the trees. After a dark-skinned young man who was in fact going quite fast took a nasty fall on a Cagiva, it was decided to stop letting anyone race Sandra.

The thing that helped us was an old stopwatch with hands which I'd glimpsed once in my dad's desk drawer a few years earlier when he'd sent me into his study to get his glasses. It struck me that we could time the races, and so I took the stopwatch up on the spur with me, along with the radio. It was a quiet revolution, but a major one, and nobody ever questioned the new system. Everyone had started to suspect that in this world an apparently freer system is simply composed of subtler but much stricter rules.

But it was Biagio who had the final, amazing idea, and perhaps for the first time I felt a touch of greatness. He asked Buti, the son of the cemetery's monumental mason, if he could drop by the Rocky Road with a few of his chisels. When Buti showed up a few days later, Biagio led him to one of the flat rocks up on the slope.

"Can you carve something on here?"

Buti moved his hand over the greyish stone. "Mmm… maybe, not too deep. I don't want my tools getting blunt."

"No problem," Biagio replied, pleased with himself.

They talked in low voices for a few minutes and made marks on the rock and took measurements. Then Biagio went back to doing what he'd been doing.

Just an hour later, when Buti had stopped hammering and evening was starting to fall, we all gathered in front of the rock. On the lichen-stippled wall was a lovely, neat inscription.

2' 10"

Welcome to the Nightmare

We all burst out laughing and shook hands with Biagio and Buti and soon afterwards went home for dinner, convinced that life could be quite amusing.

But the moment when I really seemed to sense what greatness was, and what darkness it concealed, was when, miraculously, someone who had come from forty kilometres away managed to get below the time on the inscription.

From now on, whenever anyone came to ask about Sandra, whoever was on the Rocky Road just pointed at the rock with the time carved on it.

"There it is," they said.

The other guy would look at the rock without understanding.

"Nobody races Sandra: that's the time to beat."

Nobody ever even came close, apart from that fair-haired

kid. He appeared on a day like any other, less full of himself than most and better informed: he already knew that you didn't race Sandra and simply asked if he could do the course a couple of times. He was sitting astride a shiny blue and white Honda. Although nobody wanted to be overly welcoming to this stranger, and they all pretended they weren't especially interested, they gathered around to watch.

- "Go ahead," Greg said, then grabbed the radio and informed me.

The kid finished in a time that wasn't even worth considering, but, as he was coming back to the starting point, he did something I had never seen anyone do: he was going quite slowly, looking very carefully at the ground and rubbing the soles of his feet on the asphalt. Then he simply did the course again, a bit faster, thanked us and left.

He came back a few days later and asked if he could try again. This time, he was covered from head to foot in coloured leathers.

"That's all we needed," Greg said, then picked up the radio and informed me.

On the second lap the blond kid managed to finish the course in just over two minutes twelve seconds, which to tell the truth was much less than anyone else who had tried. When he got back to the starting line, Greg was almost sorry to tell him he hadn't made it, but the boy simply thanked him and left.

The story of the mysterious blond boy soon spread, and some swore they had seen him racing back and forth like a madman along a road at the bottom of the valley.

He reappeared a couple of weeks later, which we all immediately took as an event. Now we were all rooting for him. Already on the first lap he managed to get under two minutes eleven seconds, and when, the second time, I stopped the stopwatch at two minutes, nine point three seconds, I communicated it to Greg over the radio with a sudden bitter sense of guilt. The boy, too, must have thought he'd done it, because he took the bends on the way back as if he were dancing.

When he got back to the starting line, Biagio signalled to Greg to wait: he would deal with it. The blond boy stopped and took off his helmet.

"Well?"

"Two minutes, nine point three seconds."

The boy turned to look at Biagio and smiled. In the previous few weeks, after those words were carved on the rock, we had always imagined this would be a moment of great hilarity, but I have the feeling everyone found it simply cruel.

"Welcome to the Nightmare," Biagio said after a moment, though with much less enthusiasm than anticipated.

The boy looked at Biagio, smiled for another moment or two, then hoped the black veil he could feel falling over him was only an impression. "Meaning what?"

I think that for a moment Biagio wished he had never asked Buti to carve that thing on the rock.

"Sandra's time is two minutes six seconds."

There may be nothing worse in life than cursing and sweating and suffering to get to a finishing line—only to discover that it's just the point of departure. The boy looked at Biagio for another moment or two, as if in suspense, then nodded slightly, again said thank you, and left.

Claudio is ready to swear that he met him years later on holiday: he wasn't a boy any more, he was an engineer, with a beautiful dark-skinned wife and two children. When it emerged that Claudio was from San Filippo, they got talking about the story of the bike and the Rocky Road. Apparently the engineer told Claudio that when he got home that day he had parked the bike in the garage and never started it up again. He had never sold it, in fact he even cleaned and polished it from time to time, and it had for ever become the representation of the things we don't achieve in life. I don't know if it's true: Claudio has always talked a lot of nonsense, but the story always seemed amusing to me, and I ended up believing it.

In the long run, we all paid in our own ways for Biagio's great idea. The boy and his bike and his disappointment had somewhat reduced our enthusiasm. The fact that our bike had no rivals hadn't turned out to be as exciting as we thought and, without anyone daring to say so, we were all starting to be convinced that Sandra too would become a story like any other, to be remembered from time to time to while away five minutes. Even the little races between the Vespas and the Lambrettas had lost their flavour, and after a while I even got fed up climbing to the top of the spur every time.

It was during this time that the Marshal managed to get on the Rocky Road without our noticing. He came on his Vespa and I didn't even see him. Two guys from Posta had just started off and you could hear the noise of the engines in the distance.

"You're holding races," the Marshal said in that funny accent of his as he got off his Vespa.

Tino looked at him with the same bored air as everyone else and spat out a blade of grass. "Marshal," he said, pointing his thumb at the inscription on the rock behind him, "if you get below two twenty on that old wreck, I'll give you a salami and half a mortadella."

A big roar of laughter. The Marshal made a big fuss as usual, but after seeing the boys from Posta coming back at walking pace he went away, and that was the last time we ever saw him on the Rocky Road.

Everything seemed to have taken the kind of turn typical of youthful enthusiasms, which fade as quickly as they appear.

Then came that afternoon at the beginning of August. The heat seemed to rise from the ground like steam from a teapot, and I was sitting on the spur breaking off dry blades of grass and wiping the sweat off me. I looked again at the stopwatch and casually reset it.

"Hi," I said into the radio, lying back.

"Hi," Greg's voice crackled.

"You're a prick."

The radio was silent for a moment or two. "Why?"

"You gave me the wrong start," I said, tearing off another blade of grass to suck.

The radio was silent again for a few moments.

"No, I didn't."

"What do you mean, 'No, I didn't'?"

"I didn't give you the wrong start."

"That's not possible."

"Why?"

"Because it was too fast."

"Then you're the prick."

"No," I said.

"I know it's hard," Greg crackled. "But it's just something you have to accept."

"I'm telling you no."

Silence.

"You have to get used to it."

"Idiot, I'm telling you I started the stopwatch when you said go."

Silence.

"Well?"

"I don't know."

"But how much does it show?"

"I don't know. I immediately reset it, but it was about two-five."

"That isn't possible."

"That's what I told you."

"So what do we do?"

"I don't know. Let him do it again."

"All right," the radio crackled after a moment or two.

"Don't tell him anything about the time, though. Or he'll crash into a tree."

"All right."

"Maybe tell him the stopwatch wouldn't start."

"You screwed up, I understand," crackled Greg on the radio.

I smiled and sat down again on the spur and nibbled my blade of grass. I had butterflies in my stomach, but all the same, I was convinced I'd a mistake and that very soon I'd stop the watch on a reasonable time and the world would go back within its borders.

"Are you there?" the radio crackled.

I spat out the blade of grass and checked again that the stopwatch was properly wound and was working.

"Yes, I'm here."

"Good. He's about to start."

The radio fell silent and it struck me that it had been some days now since I'd felt so excited about the start of a race.

"He's ready…" Greg's voice crackled, with Sandra's engine revving up in the background. "Go!"

I started the stopwatch, and as the radio fell silent I watched the hands move to make sure that everything was all right.

"Hey. Everything okay?"

"Yes, seems to be."

"Well, let's see."

Part of me, the sane part I think, immediately realized it was all true. All you had to do was see him come out through the Dwarf and take the S-bend. He came round the bend like a swallow, barely stirring the sand from the verge, and went like a bullet on the following lane, grazing a few blades of grass and raising a handful of leaves. The sound wasn't even like the scream of an engine, more like a cello sonata.

When he passed under the spur and crossed the finishing line, I decided to wait a few seconds before checking the time.

"Well?" Greg crackled over the radio.

I took a good look at the stopwatch. If I wanted, I could draw that white dial now, and the position of those hands.

"Two minutes, four point eight seconds."

The radio was silent for a moment or two.

"Oh. And now?"

I thought about it for a moment. "And now it's a whole other ball game."

*

When Biagio got back to the starting line and Greg told him the time, he laughed and said, "No way!"

"We thought we'd made a mistake, so we didn't tell you and made you start again. You went even faster than before."

Biagio looked at Greg for a moment and smiled. "But I wasn't even pushing."

Paolino was standing just behind, looking at Biagio astride Sandra, and for a moment it was as if she was his woman and was being taken away from him. It was just luck, he tried to say, but didn't persist with the idea.

During the first days when boredom had started to cloud our initial enthusiasm, we too had sat astride Sandra. All except Greg: he only needed to look, he said. Gradually, even I had tried my hand. At first I was scared stiff and rode her straight and slow, like a tricycle. But little by little, Paolino showed me a few tricks, taught me how to relax and, confident that it was hard to go any slower than this, urged me to put on a bit of speed. He showed me how to move up the gears, how to brake before the bends, how to shift my weight towards the inside. However absurd it might seem, as I went into a bend, I had to push the handlebars to the outside. Only years later, when revising the laws of classical physics, did I remember how it felt when I forced myself to push the handlebars in what was apparently the least natural direction and the bike leant to the inside and went round the bend as if on rails. That sense of taking a bend well is perhaps my clearest memory of my few clumsy attempts at riding a motorbike. With a bit of practice I managed to get quite good at it and, from time to time, the way my wrist increased the speed of the bike almost without my noticing it as I came round a bend gave me, at least for a moment, a surprising sensation of harmony. Usually, a bend was a frustrating jumble of things to remember: pull this lever, press that pedal, shift your weight, gun the engine, drop that lever, press that pedal again… and most of the time, all you could manage was something shaky and ridiculous. But then suddenly you saw a bend, you stretched to the outside, you shifted your weight, you pulled the brake, you pushed up two gears, spurred the clutch, gunned the engine, started to bend, pushed the handlebars in the opposite direction, aimed for the inside lane, and in a moment you slipped through. Those few times it worked I convinced myself that, when it came down to it, a bend well taken was like the current of a river: it wasn't so much how fast you went, but the elegance with which you stayed in the middle.

"I don't know what to tell you, Biagio," Greg said. "That's the time."

Biagio looked at a vague point on the asphalt in front of him. "Well?"

"Well what?"

"Let me try again."

Greg laughed and lifted the radio. "Hi," he crackled. "He's trying again."

That afternoon, before we all went home to put things back into perspective, Biagio managed to get down to just over two minutes and three seconds. I whistled to him to wait for me, and as we went back together towards the starting line, the countryside seemed to be glowing more than usual. All the others had already gone and just the four of us were left, sitting on the grass next to the bike. The sun had already sunk behind the trees at the top of the embankment and suffused the sky beyond the hills with pink. Half lying, we played with some branches and laughed about the times when, as children, on bikes or in carts, we had sped down along the paths in the grounds of Greg's villa. One day, Biagio hadn't braked in time and had ended up in the pond.

I have to admit that since everything had started to fall apart—or perhaps subconsciously, even earlier—aside from wondering where it all began, where it had slipped into that mass of confusion, another question had gradually been gnawing away at me. Was there a moment, a single tiny moment, when my life really was the way it should always have been? It goes without saying that over the course of the years, I've learnt to give short shrift to nostalgia: regretting that shrilling of cicadas and those silences and all those hormones has always seemed to me rather ridiculous. But if I have to think of one immaculate, perfect moment, that's the first useful image that comes to mind: the four of us at the entrance to the Rocky Road, next to our bike, half lying on the grass at sunset on a day at the beginning of August, the lines at the sides of Greg's eyes as he laughs and Biagio throwing a little piece of wood at him, telling each other stories, unaware that they will remain nothing but memories.

And yet, at the most perfect moment, we already had one foot on the other side. Unfortunately, in the excitement of a great turning point, you never notice what you're losing and you only think about it when it's too late. That afternoon, once we had looked beyond the wall of two minutes and six seconds, we had the feeling we could see an extraordinary world full of expectations and adventures. We liked the view so much that we climbed right up to the top without giving it much thought. Only much later, when each of us was already doing the best he could to figure out how to act in this new land, did we realize that there was no turning back and that, in our rush, we had left a lot of things behind the wall. A lot of things which, when you came down to it, could all be called childhood. But more than anything else, what we left behind that wall was the four of us, and the only one who seemed to have noticed was Paolino.

6

I T WAS GREG who first noticed the man. He mentioned him as we were walking through the village one day. It was the end of August and we had been back only a few days: Greg from one of his usual study holidays abroad and me from the terrible two weeks my parents insisted on spending in the little house in Viareggio that one of my dad's old patients let us use every summer. Those hours on the beach, that soupy, opaque water, that boiling hot powdery sand and all those bodies packed together in the sun may be the ghastliest memories I have of my youth. For the first time, Francesca had come to see me there, perhaps in the hope that far from my friends and the Rocky Road we'd finally be able to spend some time alone together. It hadn't gone exactly as hoped: every morning she'd be desperate to get to the beach and bake in the sun and I would find any excuse to stay at home reading or take a walk on the promenade. She ended up spending more time with my parents than with me.

My mum, who was usually careful to avoid the slightest comment on my life, actually said one morning, "Jacopo, perhaps you should spend a bit more time with Francesca."

"You may be right," I replied.

At night, the fact that my parents had obliged us to sleep in separate rooms hadn't proved much of an imposition.

"Did you see the man in the raincoat?" Greg asked me as we walked through the village.

I looked around. "What man in a raincoat?"

"Not here, idiot. On the Rocky Road."

"Oh. No, I didn't see any man in a raincoat."

Greg took a few more steps without saying anything. "I saw him yesterday, from a distance. He was standing there at the side with his hands in his pockets, not doing anything. Then after a while he went away. He was wearing a hat, too."

"What kind of hat?"

"How should I know? What's it to you?"

"No reason. I've always liked hats."

Greg turned to me for a moment, still walking.

"Well?" I said again.

"Well what?"

"The man in the hat."

"The man in the hat, what?"

"I don't know. You brought him up."

"No, nothing. It was just to know if you'd noticed him."

"No, I didn't notice him."

"All right, then."

A few days later, though, I saw him too. He was standing not far from the Rocky Road in his hat and raincoat with his hands in his pockets.

"Hi," I said into the radio. "The man in the raincoat is here."

"Really?" Greg crackled. "What's he doing?"

"Nothing, just standing there."

"Can he see you?"

"How should I know?"

"Hide and throw a stone at him."

"Fuck off."

"All right, get ready. He's ready to go."

The man was still standing there watching as Biagio passed on Sandra. After turning the bike round, Biagio stopped under the spur, raised his visor and looked at me.

"Two minutes, two point four seconds," I shouted. He moved his head slightly from side to side and set off back to the starting line.

The man in the raincoat glanced towards the spur—to see where the voice was coming from, I suppose. Then he walked away to wherever it was he'd come from.

Towards the end of the afternoon, when we were all ready to go home, he showed up again at the starting line. When we saw him, we fell silent and watched him as he came towards us. He took a quick look round, then his eyes came to rest on Biagio.

"Hello," he said when he was closer.

"Hi."

The man held out his hand. "My name's Lucio Torcini."

Biagio glanced at him, then shook his hand. "Biagio."

Nodding a couple of times, the man lowered his eyes and looked at Sandra.

From close up, beneath the shadow cast by the brim of his hat, you could see he had a greyish moustache, a big nose and sunken eyes. He spoke in a low, deep voice.

"Listen," he said after a while, flicking at Sandra's handle-bars a couple of times, "how would you feel about riding a real one?"

Greg, Paolino and I moved forward a little and looked him right in the eyes.

"Meaning what?" Greg asked.

The man didn't turn a hair. "Just what I said: if he'd like to try riding a real bike."

Biagio waited a few seconds. "Sandra has everything I need."

We could have kissed him, and to celebrate his repartee we moved a tiny bit closer to him, without taking our eyes off the man. Even Paolino smiled a bit.

"All right," the man said, raising his eyebrows. He lowered his head, put a hand in his trouser pocket and took out a card. "Next Wednesday we're holding trials at Mugello. Come if you can. Otherwise call me: here's my card."

Biagio took the card and checked it for a moment. There was the man's name and a logo and some numbers and a few more words I couldn't make out.

"I don't think so," Biagio said.

The man held out his hand and they shook again.

"Do what you like," the man said. "I'm not coming back here again." Then he turned to look at us. "Goodbye."

We simply nodded and watched him walk away, taking his hat and moustache and raincoat with him.

"I don't know," Greg said after a few seconds, and we simply all went home without saying anything.

The next day the rain came, washing away the summer as it did every year, and one night I heard something beating against my window again.

At first, in my half-sleep, I couldn't connect. Then the noise grew louder, and when I turned I once more saw a figure crouching on my window sill, waving at me.

"Shit," I sighed, throwing aside the blankets and getting up. "Hi," I said once I'd looked out. I rubbed my eye.

"Hi."

"Can you tell me why you never manage to do things like other people?"

"Like what?"

"Like in the daytime."

Biagio gave a not very convincing smile and shrugged.

"What time is it?"

"I don't know," he said. He started scratching at a piece of the wall with his nail.

"You woke me up in the middle of the night to destroy my house?"

Biagio took his hand away without saying anything and removed a residue of cement from under the nail of his index finger. "Listen," he said after a while, "I want to go there."

I looked at him and smiled. "I know. You're right."

"Really?"

"Of course. You must."

He looked at me, surprised—but only for a moment—then looked down again. "What about the others?"

"Forget the others, Biagio. You can't not go."

He looked at me again, a bit uncertain. "You think so?"

"Of course I do. What's the big deal anyway? It's just a trial. Go there and see what happens."

Biagio nodded slightly two or three times and threw me a couple of glances. "And listen, I don't feel like going on my own."

"And?"

He suddenly started scratching at the plaster again. "Will you go with me?"

I wasn't sure I'd understood him correctly. "Go with you where?"

"What do you mean 'where'? Mugello."

"I don't even know where Mugello is."

"Maybe we can find it between the two of us. I've heard it's the other side of Florence."

The other side of Florence. Sitting there on my window sill in the middle of the night, I felt it could have been another continent.

"And how are we getting there?"

"I thought of asking Martino for his Vespa. He owes me a favour."

"But wouldn't we get there quicker by bus or something?"

"Maybe by Christmas."

I gave a little laugh. "All right, let's go on the Vespa."

Over the next two days, taking care not to be seen by anyone, we tried to figure out how to get to Mugello.

After a while Biagio exploded behind me. "Fuck this. Mugello isn't just one place."

I continued sitting with my head on my hand at one of the tables in the little municipal library, reading the encyclopaedia. "They mention a circuit here."

"Really? Where?"

"Here."

Biagio leant over and I showed him two lines in the encyclopaedia, but he didn't seem very interested in reading them. "What about it?"

I continued reading and shrugged. "They mention it, that's all," I said in a low voice.

Biagio continued standing over me, pretending to read.

"Anyway, it's not huge," I said after a while.

Biagio turned, came back towards me and leant over my shoulder. "Isn't it?"

"No, it's not huge. If I've got it right, Mugello goes from here to here, more or less, along this river and up into the mountains as far as the passes."

"It's not that small."

"No, it's not small. But look." I picked up a pencil from the table, went to the bottom of the map, and held the pencil against the scale measurement. "This is ten kilometres, right?"

"Okay."

"From here to here is more or less thirty," I said, transferring the measurement three times across the map, from right to left.

"Is that all?"

"Yes," I said. "Of course, that's as the crow flies: it must be longer on the road. But it could have been worse."

"Of course," Biagio said, nodding gravely, then looked at the map again. "But what are we talking about? Been worse for what?"

"What do you mean, for what? For going there and seeing."

Biagio looked at me for a moment without saying anything. "What the hell are you talking about? To see what? To go up there in the mountains or to the banks of the... What's this river called?"

I looked down at the map. "The Sieve."

"... the banks of the Sieve and listen out for the sound of bikes?"

"Biagio, I don't know what to say. We can't ask anybody, because then they'll rumble us, and you don't want to call the man and tell him you're going. So I don't know: the only thing to do is go to this damned Mugello and ask someone there."

Biagio was silent for a few moments. "All right. We'll do that."

The following Tuesday evening I told Biagio to pick me up no later than four the next morning. I advised him to park Martino's Vespa not too close to the house, to prevent anyone hearing us, and to take Enzo's ladder before he called to me.

I went to bed fully dressed, so that I could get as much sleep as possible. When he came, all I'd have to do would be to get up and put on a jacket and cap and stagger outside and go back to sleep on the Vespa, resting against Biagio's back.

Actually, the coolness of the night was quite pleasant, and as I perched there, with the Vespa *vroom-vroom*ing down through the bends, everything seemed thrilling.

"What did you tell your parents?" Biagio asked me after a while, barely turning his head towards me.

"Nothing."

"What do you mean, nothing?"

"Like, nothing."

"Really?"

"Yes, I didn't know what excuse to make up. So I left them a note saying I'd be back tonight and not to worry. I'll sort it out when we get back."

Biagio smiled. "Great," he said.

After a couple of hours I took over and, as we were climbing a winding road, Biagio told me I rode well.

"Thanks," I said, feeling proud of myself.

Biagio, though, was really something else. The most natural reaction on that afternoon just a few weeks earlier, when we had taken Biagio's time as a joke, would have been to say that it was incredible, a miracle. And yet after our initial surprise, we had accepted those extraordinary times as something absolutely normal. I had been the first to accept both the times and the fact that it was Biagio who had reached them. Then, a few days later, as I was watching Biagio coming back along the Rocky Road after I'd just informed him that his new time was less than the previous one, I at last found myself wondering how the hell Biagio had learnt to ride like that, and where. And all at once a host of buried memories surged up before my eyes, memories of the thousands of times we'd raced on bicycles or in carts or on Graziano's moped around the bends of the old river bed or along the paths in the grounds of Greg's house. Greg and I were always behind, struggling to catch up, and by some strange witchcraft we never gave any thought to the fact that Biagio would be waiting for us at the end of the course every time. I'm not sure what it was: more recently, riding a beat-up old Vespa in the dark, Biagio would throw himself into the bends like a fish into the sea, and it was almost as if it weren't the Vespa that was moving, but the road. He seemed to be motionless on a pedestal, simply tilting the Vespa to one side or the other, in an almost musical rhythm, while the strip of asphalt shifted beneath the wheels.

At dawn, we stopped at the top of a knoll to see the red sun rising in the distance from the hills. The birds as usual were screaming like madmen, and a slight mist hung over the bottom of the valley.

"It's a really nice place," I said, starting up the Vespa again.

Half an hour later we stopped in a little village to have a quick bite to eat. We ordered two juices and two rolls. The thin, heavily made-up woman behind the counter asked us where we were from.

"San Filippo," Biagio replied, biting a chunk out of his roll.

"San Filippo? Where's that?"

Biagio chewed his mouthful for a few moments. "Over that way," he said, his mouth still half full, indicating some vague point outside the window with his chin.

"Oh," the woman said. She looked outside, lost in thought, and went back to cleaning something in the sink.

When we paid and left, the woman wished us good luck, and, as we got back on the Vespa, to be on the safe side both Biagio and I passed our hands over the crotch of our trousers. A few kilometres further on, we stopped to refuel at a big Agip service station just outside yet another village.

By day it was easier to drive around, and warmer, but also quite a bit more boring. After breakfast we simply rode for nearly two hours without saying anything. It was as if we'd entered a parallel zone, in which things happened by themselves, as with those mechanical cribs that Don Gianni set up every Christmas.

It was always a great moment: against the walls of the church on either side of the only nave were two wide altars, each supported by a row of four little columns beneath which, if you moved far enough back, you could almost completely disappear. When Don Gianni set up the cribs, a whole queue of children would suddenly form in front of the door of the church at least half an hour before the mass. Don Gianni always called this a miracle, and one year launched into a particularly passionate homily in which, actually dabbing the corner of his eye with a handkerchief, he confessed how every Christmas he was astounded and dazed at the power of the love of Christ, who managed in the weeks of Advent to instil such devotion in children usually so casual.

In reality, there was quite another reason for this sudden seasonal devotion: we had cut sections from a long brass pipe and Claudio provided the filling. Every figure knocked down in the crib was worth ten points, the shooting star five, the wise men fifteen and Joseph or Mary twenty. Whoever managed to get the baby Jesus, a feat only possible with a complicated blind shot—from beneath the altar opposite he could barely be seen, and you couldn't take direct aim at him—automatically won the day. The prizes changed from one Sunday to the next, but for the baby Jesus, after a bit of insistence, Marta allowed the winner to get a look inside her knickers, and if he was lucky, maybe even a feel.

It was a carabinieri car that brought us back to reality. When I saw that signal paddle waving and the carabiniere take two steps towards the middle of the road and motion us to pull over, I wasn't even sure any more that Biagio was alive.

The carabiniere who stopped us had a thin black moustache and sharp eyebrows. "Papers," he said.

Biagio and I hesitated for a moment or two, then put our hands in our pockets, and held out our identity cards.

"And for this?" the carabiniere said, indicating the Vespa with his chin.

Biagio looked at him, then to my great surprise put his hand back in his pocket and took out a blue plastic envelope. The carabiniere took it and went to his partner. We watched him as he copied something from our documents into a large notebook. They used the boot of the car as a desk and from time to time said something to each other. Then the carabiniere who had stopped us finished writing, talked in a low voice for a moment to the other one and came back towards us.

"Where's this place you come from?"

"A long way from here."

"How long?"

"Quite long."

"How long?"

"I don't know, quite long. A few hours."

The carabiniere gave us back our papers, and as he studied us the other one came up behind him.

"How many kilometres?"

Biagio looked at him for a moment, then glanced at the clock. Vespas didn't usually have them, but Martino had installed one. It was small and round.

"Oh, I don't know," Biagio said. "A hundred and fifty."

"And you've done a hundred and fifty kilometres on this old wreck?"

"Yes. Maybe more."

The carabiniere turned to say something to his companion, and was a bit startled to discover him already behind him. "He says they've come a hundred and fifty kilometres."

"Yes, I heard."

"Or even more," Biagio said.

"Or even more."

"Yes, I heard."

The first carabiniere looked at us for another moment. "And where are you going?"

"To Mugello."

"Mugello?"

"Yes, Mugello."

"To do what in Mugello?"

"To ride a motorbike in the trials."

"To ride a motorbike?"

"Yes, to ride a motorbike."

The first carabiniere turned his head slightly and exchanged glances with his partner, then turned back to us. "There are two of you."

Biagio turned his head slightly and threw me a puzzled glance. "Yes," he said. "There are two of us."

"So what are you going to do?"

Biagio was silent for a moment. "Well, there are two of you too."

"So what?"

"We could play a game of bridge."

The second carabiniere, the one who was behind, laughed. But the first one just kept looking at us without moving. "Is it a good bike?"

"Apparently," Biagio said. "But I wouldn't bet on it."

Even the first carabiniere couldn't help smiling.

"All right, you can go. And just hope that nobody else stops you."

"Thanks, Captain," Biagio said, then hit the pedal and sped off before they could have second thoughts.

As we were riding away, I turned and threw a glance at the carabinieri: they were standing there watching us leave, shaking their heads slightly, but with half-smiles on their lips, and I'm convinced that part of them would have liked to have been in our place.

*

Not long afterwards, having passed a dreary little village and a long tree-lined avenue, we saw a sign saying *Florence*. As I tried to guide Biagio in the right direction with the map in my hand, I kept looking around but I didn't recognize anything of the Florence I had visited two years earlier on a school trip. Not a single sighting of anything resembling an old palace, not the slightest inkling of a bit of history: only a horrible spider's web of wide avenues and apartment blocks and cars overtaking us and making us skid. In the middle of all that, the noise of the Vespa suddenly sounded like the crying of a baby. Fortunately, after a couple of halts to take a closer look at the map, I managed to find some secondary roads that took us back to the countryside and up a slope and through a wood.

About an hour later, coming round yet another bend, I tapped Biagio on the shoulder.

"We're here," I cried. "If I'm not mistaken, we're in Mugello."

I continued looking at the map and the trees around us. They were no different from the trees we'd been seeing all along, but everything looked that bit darker and gloomier.

"Really?"

"Yes, really. Let's stop and ask."

At the top of the rise there was a snack bar with wooden benches outside, and beyond the snack bar the road curved and again descended out of sight.

Biagio put the Vespa on the kick-stand and stretched. "Jesus," he said.

It was hot and we both tied our jackets round our waists. We went into the snack bar, and a fat grey-haired man told us to take a seat. We ordered two more rolls. We felt tired and neither of us had the courage to ask for directions: by now we were convinced that nobody would be able to give us the slightest information and everybody would take us for madmen, and we would ride round and round like idiots for hours and even if we made it we would go back to the village shattered, with our tails between our legs. We sat there in silence taking chunks out of our rolls and chewing and every now and again sipping at the water.

We'd paid and were at the door when I decided to take the initiative. "Listen," I said, turning towards the fat grey-haired man. "Do you have any idea where they hold motorcycle trials?"

He stopped cutting the bread and looked at me. "What?"

"The circuit," I said unconvincingly.

"The circuit?" the host said again. "You're on the circuit."

"I'm on it?"

"Yes, the circuit used to pass this way. But what are you looking for?"

I looked at him for a moment and felt more tired than ever. "I don't know, I only know that the other day we were at the Rocky Road and this man in a raincoat showed up and asked Biagio if he wanted to ride a real one and Biagio said no and the man said, 'Do what you like, but if you have second thoughts, there are trials at Mugello on Wednesday,' and they said goodbye and then Biagio really did have second thoughts and I told him he was doing the right thing and so we asked Martino for his Vespa and we left at four o'clock this morning and came to Mugello but we don't even know how big this damned Mugello is and we don't even know where the trials are and Biagio didn't want to call and now we don't know where to go."

If it weren't for the fact that every cell of my body had been struggling for the past few months now to become a man, I would certainly have burst out crying.

The host had kept still all this time, listening to my monologue, his knife halfway through a slice of bread. "The race track," he said.

I looked at him and snorted. "Yes. The race track."

The host lowered his eyes and started cutting the bread again. "Straight ahead. Keep going down the road, stay on the left, and after three hundred metres you'll see the signs. You can't go wrong."

I watched him cutting his bread for a moment. "Thanks," I said. "Have a good day."

"You're welcome. Have a good day yourself."

As we were on our way out, Biagio gave a slightly bewildered look.

"Straight ahead," I said, getting back on the saddle.

7

WHEN WE GOT to the top of the hill and started the descent, Biagio slammed on the brakes as if an animal had crossed our path. The rear tyre squeaked for at least twenty metres and the Vespa veered slightly to the side.

Beneath us on the left, beyond a high concrete wall and a thick metal fence was a long downhill bend, with red and yellow stripes on the inside and at a couple of points on the outside. In the distance we could see a few other stretches of the track, and farther down, a long, square, coloured building. At the end of our road, in the hollow, there was a massive gate, covered by a huge wooden roof.

After a few seconds we saw something dark come round the bend, beyond the fence, screaming like a hyena and going like a bullet.

"What was that, a bike?" I asked with a smile on my lips when that thing had disappeared again behind the wall.

Biagio continued staring at the point from which it had disappeared. "Yes, I think it was."

For a few moments we kept looking at that stretch of black road half hidden by the wall.

"I don't know," Biagio said at last, then got back into first gear and slowly descended towards the large gate with the wooden roof.

A tall, thin man holding a radio came out of a small square hut. "It's closed," he said, holding his hand up.

"What do you mean, 'it's closed'?"

"Just that," he said, jutting out his chin. "It's closed."

"So what are you doing here?"

He looked at us impatiently. "I'm here to say it's closed."

"It doesn't look closed."

"It's closed to the public."

"Oh," Biagio said. "We're looking for the motorcycle trials."

"The trials are here."

"So it isn't closed."

"Listen, what do you want?"

"To ride in the trials."

"I said it's closed."

"But didn't you say the trials are here?" Biagio said, opening his arms wide in irritation.

"Yes, that's right, the trials are here."

"Well?"

"Well what?"

"I don't understand any of this." Biagio turned his head slightly towards me. "Can you talk to him, please?"

"Listen," I said, "we've come a long way because a man told us to come here today for the motorcycle trials, and the only place where they're holding trials, so I've heard, is here."

"Yes, the trials are here."

"So it's all right, then."

"No, it isn't."

"Why?"

"They aren't public trials."

Biagio ran his hands through his hair. "Fuck this, I'm going crazy."

"But if someone told us to come…" I said.

"And who was this man?"

"How should I know? He was a man in a raincoat and a hat. I don't remember his name." Then I had a flash of inspiration. "He gave us a card!" I said excitedly. "Hey," I tapped Biagio on the shoulder, "give him the card."

Biagio searched through his pockets, then finally brought out the card that the man on the Rocky Road had given him. It was all crumpled.

The tall thin guard took the card and looked at it. His hands were rather funny: thin and knotty. He raised his eyes and looked at us, then lifted his other arm and brought the radio up to his mouth. "Hello."

"Go ahead," the radio crackled after a moment.

"I'm here at the entrance. There are two young guys with a card from Team Torcini."

"What about it?"

"They say they've been invited to the trials."

The radio was silent for a moment or two.

"I'll check," it finally crackled.

The man lowered his arm and gave the card back to Biagio. "They're going to check."

We nodded without saying anything, and Biagio put the card back in his pocket. We stayed like that for several minutes, without moving and without saying anything, looking away from each other.

"Hello," the radio crackled again.

"Yes?" the man said, bringing it closer to his mouth.

"Let them through."

"Okay." The man looked at us and moved aside. "Go ahead," he said. "Pit sixteen."

Biagio hit the pedal hard to start the Vespa again. "What?"

"Pit sixteen."

"Oh," Biagio said. "Thanks." Then he got into first and set off.

After a few hundred metres, coming out of a kind of tunnel, we saw a red iron fence with big gates in it. Behind the fence, on the left, there was a long square red and yellow building. In front of the building was a vast car park with some lorries covered in writing and a few vans. We went slowly through one of the gates. The sound of the Vespa seemed to drown in all that space. After a few metres we saw a young guy coming from behind one of the lorries wearing a shirt with the same colours and writing, but in miniature.

"Excuse me," I called to the young guy when we were almost level with him.

Biagio stopped the Vespa and put one foot on the ground. "Do you know where pit sixteen is?"

The young man looked at us and our Vespa, then smiled and shook his head. "Fifty metres on the left. You can see it—there's the number." He was already continuing on his way towards the square building.

I took a good look at the building: every few metres there were huge red shutters with numbers on them, in ascending order.

"Thank you," I said.

Then Biagio got back into first and at walking pace, trying not to look in the other doors, we rode towards number sixteen. He seemed intimidated and I knew him well enough to know that he was wondering what the hell he was doing here, in this place full of signs and colours, where everything seemed fake.

Thinking about it now, I can't help wondering if Biagio had realized something: if in some way the cells of his body had already sensed that he was coming to one of those moments when life takes an unexpected turn and you feel you're losing control. I don't know if I've ever really understood how these things work, but it's as if, while your insides are pulling you one way or another just so as not to have to make a decision, you let the world drag you along. Then you always find something you weren't expecting, and you wonder if, in the end, it's true that the world knows more than you do.

When we got to number sixteen, Biagio stopped the Vespa in front of it and put one foot on the ground. After a few moments, the man who had come to the Rocky Road appeared from the half-darkness of the entrance. He was in his shirtsleeves, no raincoat, no hat. He had short grey hair combed back, and his moustache, unshaded by any hat, looked bigger.

"You've come," he said with a half-smile as we came level with him.

"Yes," Biagio said, "I've come."

"On this?" the man asked, putting a hand on the clutch of the Vespa.

"Yes, on this."

The man laughed and shook his head. "All right, put it somewhere and let's see what we can do."

Inside, mechanics dressed in yellow and black T-shirts with lots of writing on them were bustling around three motorbikes mounted on hydraulic hoists. I had never seen bikes like

97

that: so shiny and clean and bright. They looked as if they had never been used. I remember wondering if they were really used in races or were just there for show. The tyres of the bikes had these strange cloth covers on them attached to an electric wire. The mechanics were going backwards and forwards, carrying spanners or sometimes just screws. There was someone checking papers and saying something into a radio. At a table over to the side, two young guys in the same yellow and black T-shirts were marking something on big blocks.

The man who had invited us called a girl and told her to see if they could find something for Biagio to wear. The girl smiled, said, "Of course," took Biagio by the arm and led him away. As he was going towards the lorry, Biagio turned to look at me, shrugged, then disappeared outside. The man told me to make myself at home and even to look around, and asked me if I wanted anything to eat or drink.

"Maybe a little something," I said.

The man called to another girl and told her to give me something. She had big red hair and blue eyes, and was one of the few not wearing the same colours and T-shirts as the others.

"Come," she said. "What would you like?"

Lots of things, I'd have liked to say, but in the end I settled for a coffee. I also had some biscuits filled with honey and fig paste that were really terrific.

I didn't see him at first, but there was a guy sitting in the corner who looked even younger than me. He was in tight-fitting leathers, again yellow and black and with lots of writing on them. He was talking in a low voice to a man who was sitting next to him, half turned away. The young guy kept sipping something from a big beaker through a straw. When he saw that I was watching him, he raised his eyebrows slightly and gave a little nod with his head to say hello.

The red-haired girl told me she had a couple of things to take care of, and that I could take whatever I wanted and make myself at home. Every time I was told that, I found it hard to associate all that coming and going and those colours and that nervous tension with the silence of my parents' living room. But I thanked her anyway and grabbed another couple of those delicious fig biscuits, then realized I was exhausted and went and sat down on a canvas chair. Everyone was still working on the bikes, and one of those with covers over the tyres was taken down from its hoist and taken over to the other exit from the pit. Every now and again, beyond the entrance, you could hear the roaring and screaming of engines behind a wall. I thought for a moment of going to see what was happening, but then I told myself to take things easy, and I sat there quietly on my chair. I saw the man with the moustache call one of the mechanics and point at me. He told him we had come from some remote place in the countryside on an old wreck that was parked outside the pit. He also told him to take a good look at it before we left, because he didn't want us on his conscience. Then he came up to me and asked me who the Vespa belonged to.

"A friend."

"And he gave it to you to come all the way here?"

"He doesn't know we came all the way here."

"I see," he said. "Good idea."

When Biagio reappeared, I couldn't help laughing. It didn't look like him any more. He was wearing tight leathers, like the young guy sitting in the corner, and they made him look hunchbacked, with twisted legs.

"It could have been made for him," the girl said to the man with the moustache.

"Excellent," the man said, putting a hand on Biagio's shoulder.

Biagio gave me a bewildered, slightly irritated look.

"How can you walk?" I asked him, smiling.

"I don't know," he said, stretching his arms a little. "It's pulling everywhere."

The man with the moustache laughed and slapped Biagio on the shoulder. "When you're riding you don't even notice. Let's see how the helmet fits."

The girl handed the man a big brand-new helmet and the man told Biagio to put it on. When Biagio had put it on, the man checked to make sure it was okay, grasping it by the chin strap and tugging at it to try and shift it. Biagio swayed backwards and forwards like a puppet.

"Perfect," the man said, adjusting the binding under Biagio's neck. Then he led him over to the bike that had just been taken down from the hoist. "All right, now, take it easy, ride as it comes. Don't think about going fast, just think about riding and gaining confidence with the bike. It'll be different, it may seem strange to you, but go on and ride, we have time and petrol. Try and get a good idea of the course. It's quite a hard track, so take it nice and easy. For now, use only third and fourth gear, go into sixth only on the home straight. Then we'll see."

When Biagio and the man were near the bike, one of the mechanics got on it and, pushed by one of the others, went forward a few metres to start it. The bike screamed and belched blue smoke. As he came back to the man and Biagio, the mechanic continued to gun the engine and look at something on the side.

The man was still talking to Biagio, but I couldn't hear what he was saying. He was making the gesture of putting his hands on the handlebars, bending his arms and legs, moving as if he were riding. Then he held out his hand and motioned Biagio to get on. Biagio placed his left hand on the handlebars. Just before lifting his leg and getting on, he turned to look at me. He was very serious. I smiled and nodded and raised my thumb. He looked at me for another moment, then also nodded, gave me a little, not very convincing smile and mounted the saddle. It was only a split second: if only they prepared us for this kind of thing, life would be quite different.

As Biagio continued to rev up, the mechanic who'd started the engine leant over the frame to make sure that everything was all right, then placed a hand on the rear tyre and gave a signal: yes, everything was fine.

The man with the moustache moved his head closer to Biagio's and told him something else. Biagio nodded again, then the man stepped backwards and patted him twice on the back. Biagio raised his foot and got into first. The man smiled and patted him again, then we watched him go in that little cloud of blue smoke.

The man turned and smiled at me. "If you like, you can go up on the roof. You'll see better from there."

From the roof of the building you could see the whole of the home straight: it appeared at the end on the left and climbed on the right, towards the top of the slope. As it rose it curved slightly, and at the end seemed to lead to a kind of hairpin bend. I saw Biagio pass a couple of times. He raced past below me, hunched over the bike, which seemed almost to disappear in the middle of all that asphalt.

The man with the moustache was leaning on the low concrete wall with a stopwatch in his hand. He stood there with his elbows on the wall and watched the bikes passing. When Biagio zoomed past he gave an imperceptible jerk with his hand, then raised it to check the stopwatch. After a few laps, one of the young guys with the T-shirts full of writing approached him, carrying a square black instrument. The man with the moustache looked at the young guy and the instrument, then spoke for a moment and the young man went back into the pit.

One lap later, the man signalled to Biagio to come back in. I saw him leave the track and slow down beneath me. As soon as he arrived, the man with the moustache leant towards him. They talked in low voices for a while, then the man mimed something and watched him leave again. After another couple of laps, the man stopped the stopwatch just as the same young guy as before came up behind him. They looked at the time together, then the young man lifted that square instrument again and showed it to the man with the moustache. The man put one hand over it as if to shelter it from the light and leant forward to get a better look. He stood still for a few moments, perhaps a minute, then again moved away, said something to the young guy, then put his hands back on the low wall.

Once more, he made Biagio come back in. This time, though, he made him get off and take off the helmet and drink a bit of water. Biagio was bathed in sweat, but looked calm, and the leathers now seemed less ridiculous on him.

After a few minutes, the man made him get back on and watched him drive away.

A little while later, I was aware of the man joining me. He had come up behind me and put his elbows on the low wall.

"Everything all right?" he asked.

I glanced at him again.

"Yes," I said, "not bad. And you?"

The man smiled. "Yes," he said. "Not bad."

After a couple of seconds Biagio passed below us.

"And how is he?"

The man watched Biagio vanish round the bend at the top of the slope at the end of the home straight.

"He's not bad," he said, shaking his head slightly. He didn't seem very convinced.

I nodded and said nothing. I didn't know what to say.

"What kind of person is he?" he asked me after a while.

I thought about it for a moment. "I don't know. Quiet, I'd say."

Then we looked down again without saying anything. The bikes of the other two teams passed, and so did the young guy who'd been sitting in the pit earlier, sucking from that big beaker.

The man with the moustache looked at his stopwatch another few times, then got to his feet and started looking at the exit from the bend before the home straight.

All at once, from the big square to the left of the circuit, a siren sounded and an ambulance set off.

"Shit," the man said, running towards the stairs.

TWO

Initiation

1

THE MOMENT we were perhaps closest was also the one at which we were most distant. And what brought us together, as is often the case where men are concerned, was sex.

I was halfway through my second year at the University of Glasgow, and had just recently moved from the Mathematics Department to the Physics Department. I'd ended up in Glasgow in an unexpected way. Everything had started in my last year at the Fermi high school, on an ordinary rainy morning in the middle of February, during a very boring technical drawing class. I'd already finished all the equations in the maths book and was leafing through it to see if I could find an exercise to amuse me for five minutes.

When you came down to it, that had always been my relationship with maths, the same relationship my aunt Giovanna had with crosswords: it was a hobby.

All at once, three quarters of the way through the book, I came across a card. It was green and purple, with a couple of logos I didn't know in the corners. In the middle, in big letters, the words:

CAN YOU SOLVE IT?

Beneath them was a strange, complex equation that struck me as less obvious than most. I turned the card over: *If you think you've solved it, send the solution, and how you reached it, to this address*, followed by the details of something called the Cirri Foundation, based in Mantua. I spent two whole days on that damned equation, tearing up whole exercise books and sometimes desperately fishing the discarded pages out of the waste paper basket. There was always something that didn't quite fit. I even went to the little school library to see if I could find a book that might help, but that wasn't much use.

Then, three evenings later, as I was sitting on my bed, tired and drained, wondering whether or not to clean my teeth before trying to sleep, an element of the equation that had so far eluded me suddenly loomed up in front of my eyes and seemed, if I could twist it around in a different way from how I'd been stubbornly doing it up until then, as if it might lead me in the right direction. Actually, I'd had quite a few of these revelatory moments in the past couple of days, and the intervals at which they were recurring was in inverse proportion to the enthusiasm I felt for them.

So I got up lazily from the bed, collapsed like a sack onto the wicker chair by my desk, reached out my hand and pulled the waste paper basket, decorated with English hunting scenes, towards me and slowly started to unfold and flatten the screwed-up pages as best I could and then drop them on the floor. When I recognized the right page I didn't feel any particular quiver of excitement: I simply turned towards the green desktop, picked up a couple of books that lay open on it, threw them on the floor, adjusted the beam of light from the lamp, opened a large exercise book at random, tore off what I didn't need from that page of scrap paper and stuck the rest to the top of the blank page of the exercise book with a piece of Scotch tape. At the point at which the idea I'd just had, sitting on the edge of the bed, connected to the previous draft, I simply continued writing as if I'd never stopped. It was as if the way to go on came all by itself, every step a natural consequence of the previous one, and was being transferred automatically to my hand and from there to the tip of my blue ballpoint pen. It was like looking from the outside at someone solving an equation, but that someone was me.

After a while I started to feel excited, as if instead of simply watching myself work, I had finally decided to participate. I got into a better position at the table, leaning well forward, getting through pages at a frenzied rate. Yes, sometimes I had to tear off a page and roll it into a ball, but these were only small hitches, brief oversights or moments of creative madness, which actually made me smile for a moment. At 1:20 in the morning I finally arrived at a fairly elegant solution. I stretched and finally leant back in my chair. My face felt shrivelled, my neck and back were stiff, and yet those few letters remaining on the page were like the beautiful view you see at the end of a long hard climb in bad weather.

I took more than an hour to copy out the solution so as to make it presentable, slipped it, along with my details, into an envelope taken furtively from my father's study and finally wrote on it the address indicated on the card found in the book. The next morning, before going to school, by arrangement with Ada, the postmistress, I decided to send it by recorded delivery.

A month and a half later, at the beginning of April, my

mother told me when I came back from school that an envelope had arrived for me from abroad.

"What is it?" my father asked me as he served himself a plate of pasta and I sat down at the table lost in thought, reading the letter.

"I've been invited to Glasgow to compete for a scholarship."

"A scholarship? In Glasgow?"

"Yes, they've even included the plane tickets." I showed him one of those old blocks of red carbon paper. There were, in fact, several letters in the envelope. One was from the University of Glasgow, in which they informed me that they had the honour to have selected me to compete for one of their most prestigious scholarships, promoted by something called SETEC. The second letter was from SETEC itself, in which I was again informed that—through the Cirri Foundation of Mantua, to which I had sent the card—my name had been selected as the Italian representative. A third letter was signed by somebody named Kinda Lowell, director of student relations for the University, and explained how to get to Glasgow and how to orientate myself once I reached the campus. Attached were a number of maps and leaflets, full of stone spires and smiling young people.

"That's nice, that's really nice," my father kept saying. Ten days later, at Fiumicino airport, before I joined the long queue waiting to go through security, he simply wished me good luck, then added perhaps the only useful thing you can say to an eighteen-year-old who's leaving to face one of the most important challenges of his life: "Don't worry."

As they kept telling us the evening of our arrival in Glasgow, shut up in an old wood-panelled room that smelt of wax and mildew, the scholarship was promoted by SETEC, an international association based in Munich which had been providing the best opportunities to the best talents in Europe for more than sixty years. The organization promoted scholarships for all the main courses of study, and in each case the system was the same: about fifteen countries were chosen, then for each country and each course the competitors were selected, often through affiliated local foundations. Finally, the various candidates were put through a number of tests and a shortlist was drawn up, from which only the first three were selected. These three were offered complete scholarships, which included accommodation and monthly expenses for food and books. A member of the staff from the department—in our case the Department of Mathematics and Statistics—was then appointed as guarantor: he would be the person the chosen students would turn to if there was anything they needed, and at the same time would have the task of establishing whether the students continued to deserve the scholarship.

Those three days were killing, and even now they are still a bit of a blur to me. I shared a bare room near the university with a rather grumpy young German. We were given a decent breakfast, and at lunch we had time to go somewhere for a quick sandwich. The rest of the day we spent closed up in two or three different rooms, together or alone, solving equations, answering questionnaires of various kinds and being subjected to long interviews. Some of these were quite strange. Not knowing the level of our English, a student from our country had been assigned to each of us, to act as interpreter and help us out any time we were at a loss. Mine was named

Tommaso. He was a kind but standoffish boy from Parma in his third year of mathematics, who seemed not to have any clear idea of where Tuscany was. The selection board, on the other hand, were all too interested in my native region. Unlike in the first interview, where we did actually talk just about mathematics, in the two that followed they seemed more interested in finding out about my life in the village. Signora Rossi, our teacher, hadn't done a good job with our English and, even though she loved to give everyone good marks, I had never before realized quite how poor the results of her teaching were. The Scottish accent, although fairly refined and moderate, obviously didn't help. So when they asked me about Italy and San Filippo and country life and agriculture and olives and summer heat and the right time to plough or harvest, I kept turning to Tommaso to make sure I had understood correctly. The third interview did not improve matters all that much: luckily, the board seemed to have lost interest in my personal life, but the questions became even stranger.

"Tell me what comes into your head when I say the word 'bicycle'."

I stared at them for a moment, then turned towards Tommaso.

"Bicycle?" I asked him.

"Yes, bicycle."

"Bicycle bicycle?"

"Yes, bicycle bicycle."

"What do they want to know about bicycles?"

Tommaso turned towards the table where the board sat. "He's asking what you want to know about bicycles," he said in English.

"Whatever comes into your head," he translated.

I stared at him for another moment or two, dumbfounded.

"Whatever comes into my head? Well, what comes into my head is spokes, wheels, pedals, chains, cogs, gears, slopes, rates of incline, Gino Bartali, effort, mineral salts, Ivan Lendl, heat, friction, work, hard graft, water, steak, dust, molecules, hydrogen, vectors, centrifugal force, groin pain, sunshine, cyclists' hats, plastic marbles, petrol, refineries, factories, fumaroles, the baths of Petriolo, sulphur, rotten eggs, magma, an erupting volcano, the…"

Tommaso was going mad trying to keep up with me.

"Thank you, that's fine," one of the members of the board stopped me with a smile. Then he asked me what I thought about clouds.

"You mean—again—whatever comes into my head?"

Tommaso asked for elucidation.

"No, they're actually asking what you think about them, what your opinion of them is."

Jesus, I thought.

By the time we got back to the room in the evening, I was exhausted. I tried to ask Fredrick, the German boy I was sharing with, how it had gone for him, but he pretended not to understand, and I found myself simply staring up at the bare white ceiling, wondering once again what kind of place I'd ended up in.

The board also seemed quite curious about my way of solving the exercises, the way I was always tearing off pages and sticking them together with Scotch tape, the way I was always surrounded with rolled-up balls of paper. When, on the first day, at the end of the morning's tests, I approached the table where the board sat with the exercises copied in a fair hand, they asked me if I could also leave them the other papers. In my left hand I was holding a pile of pages all crumpled and stuck together as best they could be.

"These?"

"Yes, those."

"Are you sure?"

They smiled. "Yes, we're sure."

I put the papers down on the table. As I was leaving the lecture room, I saw two of the board members leaf through them and laugh. Two young guys who were there with me for the tests also said something to each other and laughed. I really didn't think it was nice of them to laugh at me: I might have been a foreigner, I might have been a fish out of water, my native village and my clumsy way of solving equations might have been remote from this place, but there was no need to be laughing at me. This cold city might well have great centuries-old universities carved like monuments in stone, but where I came from we had something called politeness. I gradually started to feel that I was somewhere sinister and inhospitable, somewhere I needed to escape from as soon as possible.

On the last afternoon, the board retired to draw up a shortlist, planning to announce the names of the three winners before dinner. So we had a few hours free and Tommaso asked me if there was anything in particular I wanted to see.

"The underground."

"The underground?"

"Yes, the underground."

In the small amount of free time they'd left us, Tommaso had already shown me the central complex of the university with its towers and its courtyards and its spires and its sinister fifteenth-century arches, but they meant nothing to me now, they were just monuments to this dark, repulsive place. The previous day, though, while looking for something to eat, we had walked through the area surrounding the campus, and Tommaso had pointed out a large opening and told me, as if it were the most normal thing in the world, that it was the entrance to the underground.

"But there's nothing to see. The Glasgow underground is horrible."

I shrugged. I had never seen an underground railway and to tell the truth, ever since I'd heard that word, I hadn't been able to get it out of my mind.

"All right," Tommaso said, shaking his head. "We could take it to the centre of town and maybe go for a walk there."

I shrugged again without saying anything. It was, as I had anticipated, one of the most extraordinary things I had ever come across. A man in a blue uniform sold us some tickets from inside a steel cage, and with them, along with various other people, we went through the mechanical turnstiles. We then all went in single file down a long escalator and onto the platform, which had tunnels at either end. The whole station was covered in brown and cream tiles, with a number of posters. After a couple of minutes we felt a gust of wind and gradually heard the muted din of an electric train. It appeared all at once from the darkness of the tunnel, and for a moment it seemed to me to be rubbing against the walls, so exactly did it fit the circumference. Once it had stopped, the doors opened automatically. Through the nearest one, two or three young men and an old lady with a dog got out. The carriage was rather low, and the perfectly cylindrical shape was reminiscent of a worm. Inside, two rows of upholstered seats faced each other. Everyone was silent and motionless, doing everything they could to keep their eyes away from anywhere that wasn't either up at the ceiling or down on the ground. Actually, compared with all the underground railways I would later discover around the world, the one in Glasgow was somewhat ridiculous. Small and low, narrow, worn and dirty: a dishevelled worm that simply went in a circle round the centre of the city. On the seats, the remains of sandwiches and empty beer cans. And yet that river of people walking in silence underground and going round corners like a single snake and the shuddering of the train over the rails and the neon lighting and the seats on either side of the carriage all seemed to be telling secret stories of a civilization that might have been in a desperate state but that suddenly seemed much more attractive.

I love underground railways. For some time now, I've been forcing myself to walk whenever I can, to be in the open air as much as possible. There have been times in my life when I was either indoors reading by lamplight or stuck in an underground train and never saw sunlight and rarely breathed fresh air. My skin ended up wrinkling and taking on a surreal, translucent colouring, and my mood was like the surface of a carpenter's rasp. So when I can, I walk. And yet, every time I set foot in an underground, I sink back into that strange sense of peace, that paradoxical feeling of respect for the human race. There we all are, together, underground, all trying in our clumsy, stubborn way to give meaning to our lives.

All right, let's go and take this tooth out, I thought, when my turn came to hear the results of the selection process. I walked in with Tommaso, assuming a nonchalant, even bored air, and sat down. I wondered who would laugh this time, and what bizarre new questions they would ask me. I didn't mind: if nothing else, I'd have something to tell my friends when I got back.

The man who spoke was the one who had probably spoken least during those three days. If I'd understood correctly, his name was Jones and he was SETEC's internal guarantor for the scholarship. He had floppy grey hair that almost completely covered one eye and his nose was red and swollen, as if someone had blown inside it with a straw.

He seemed very serious and spoke very slowly, and for the first time I got a fairly clear idea of what was being said. As he spoke, he rolled an orange-coloured pencil between his fingers.

"Dear Mr Ferri, I want to tell you right away that as of now you are one of the three candidates chosen for a scholarship."

The muscles of my face fell and I turned for a moment towards Tommaso, but he didn't seem to react much. He had grown a bit distant towards me since I had asked him to stay on the underground for two whole circuits, not saying a word.

"We really liked some of your solutions, and the way you arrived at them. They did contain a number of naïve elements which occasionally led you astray, but it'll be our task to help you overcome such frivolities. We believe that if you learn to control yourself and find a better method, your impulsiveness may bring you great satisfaction. We also like the way in which you're able to abstract yourself from what you do. I confess that you share this with a number of your compatriots: you Italians can be quite vague and confused, but often, we have to admit"—here Dr Jones glanced quickly round at the other members of the board, some of whom smiled—"you have really brilliant ideas. I've worked with a number of Italians in the course of my life and I've come to the conclusion that your brilliance depends on your capacity to look around you and be surprised. But anyway, that's another matter. We would be very happy to have you studying here with us. However, we're not very satisfied with your level of English. It's quite unacceptable for a serious course of study. So I have to inform you that we're going to keep a fourth candidate on standby. Apart from the TOEFL, which you're expected to pass in order to be admitted to the university, we'll be giving a supplementary language test in September, before the beginning of classes, on the basis of which, whether or not you have the TOEFL, we'll decide if we're going to accept you for the scholarship."

Then at last the whole board stood up and smiled at me.

"Congratulations Mr Ferri. We'll see you in September."

When I got back home and told my parents all about Glasgow and the scholarship, my father looked at me for the first time with that mixture of pride and mistrust which over the course of the years would always leave me somewhat bewildered. Ever since I was little, I'd had the vague feeling that for my parents having a son was a strange experience. There were small signs I would dredge up from my memories and put together only long afterwards: a way of looking at me, of serving me my food, of taking me by the hand and walking me to school. There had always been some kind of mistrust there. Yes, that's what it was: they treated me with a vague but unmistakable degree of mistrust. It was as if one day they'd found an already well-formed child outside their front door, four or five years old perhaps, that somebody had abandoned. As good Christians, they'd decided to take that child into their home and treat him as one of their own. And yet they appeared to feel completely unsuitable. To a large extent, they managed not to let it show, but this small creature that was growing before their eyes and scurrying about the yard, with a passion for little red pencil cases, and who'd one day sprouted longer limbs and facial hair, must have constantly surprised them. Not to mention when he had started solving impossible equations and winning big scholarships to study abroad. An alien in the house. I think the few times my parents—especially my dad, out of medical deformation if nothing else—considered that the alien was in reality the product of their own secretions and humours, it had caused such a short circuit that they had preferred not to think about it. One day a friend of mine at university asked me if I had brothers or sisters and why my parents hadn't had more children. "It would have been unthinkable," I found myself replying. That was another reason the usual quarrels, conflicts and dramas between parents and children were completely unknown to me, and my dad had always been able, even at the most difficult moments, to behave like a reasonable person: it was as if I didn't belong to him. My life choices were no concern of his, any more than they might be the concern of a pleasant uncle who likes you a lot. He is, and has always been, wonderfully free of all those complexes that govern the frustrations and successes of parents and children. Since I was very small, my parents had had their life and I'd had mine. The fact that we might share part of it was, all things considered, accidental.

To solve the problem of English, my mum suggested a new DeAgostini course she'd seen in Piero's tobacconist shop the day before and had also, she seemed to remember, seen advertised on TV. I didn't think it was such a great idea. Then Dad remembered Mrs Hampton, a massive Englishwoman with skin as smooth as an apple who'd bought a little house in the area a few years earlier. It was around the Easter holidays and apparently he had met her a couple of days before at the Coop. The previous year he'd treated her for a nasty and foul-smelling intestinal infection and had refused payment for it. He was sure Mrs Hampton would be really happy to give me a hand with my English.

Mrs Hampton had made her Italian dream come true along with her husband. They had bought the property and had sacrificed a great deal to refurbish it, doing much of the work themselves. Mr Hampton must have been dazzled by his own tanned skin and reinvigorated physique, and had suddenly run off with the female owner, also English, of the agency through which they'd found the house. It was assumed in the village that she was a younger and more attractive woman than poor Mrs Hampton, but in fact, when she appeared with him in the local bar one day, everyone found it hard to hold back their laughter when they saw that she was equally bulky and equally smooth, and not necessarily younger. A kind of clone of Mrs Hampton. Obviously there had been some idle speculation about the new partner's hidden qualities, but for the rest of their days, everyone would use Mr

Hampton and his wife and his new partner as the basis of any sensible conversation on the delicate subject of marriage and the longevity of relationships.

Once the final exams were over, my summer with Mrs Hampton proved to be a real trial. I had never found anything as hard as learning English: it had never cost me so much effort before to get something into my head. Or to keep it there. I spent every afternoon at Mrs Hampton's studying irregular verbs and trying to write and make decent conversation. She was very understanding of my difficulties, but eventually yielded to moments of obvious exasperation. At first I had the terrible suspicion that behind her willingness to help me there was actually a touch of mischief, but gradually this was transformed into more than a hint of annoyance.

"I don't understand how you managed to win a scholarship!" she cried one afternoon early in August, getting up and disappearing into the kitchen. I sat there in the living room without saying anything, wondering if this put an abrupt end to our lessons, but five minutes later Mrs Hampton reappeared carrying a tray.

"Let's have a nice glass of iced tea," she said, recovering her usual amiable smile.

I went back to Glasgow feeling very nervous and for the first and only time was aware of the kind of nausea most students report when they have to take an exam. The fact was, I had never felt any kind of panic about exams. My character, I think. The coldest, most rational part of me would say that I was simply aware of my own preparedness and my own abilities, but I've had dozens of companions who were just as capable and well prepared as I but felt an overwhelming desire to vomit before every exam.

But not this time. No, this time my blood was anything but cold, and my gastric juices were seething so much that it was impossible for me to eat. Fortunately, the internal English test—I had already passed the TOEFL in a language school in Rome at the end of August—was just the day after my arrival in Glasgow, otherwise I would probably have died of starvation. Obviously what made it all worse was my lack of confidence in my English, but it was, above all, a matter of aesthetics: here I was, one step away from the most important opportunity of my life, an opportunity any reasonable student would give his eye teeth for, and that big train filled with equations and functions and dreams of glory was about to crash, derailed by a stupid English test. As I placed my hand on the brass door handle of the lecture room, repressing a great desire to throw up over it, I imagined an older and dustier version of myself telling a class of spotty-faced kids about the time I'd been selected for one of the most prestigious international scholarships, and how fate had played the most sinister of tricks on me by depriving me of the slightest talent for languages.

2

T HE DAY I FELT CLOSEST to the others, even though we
were many thousands of kilometres from each other,
I was with Trisha in the attic room I'd been using for a few
weeks thanks to Leonard. The evening I discovered it, I'd
been working at Leonard's Lodge for more than a month.

One morning, walking along Ashton Lane as I did every
day, I'd seen a hand stick up a notice in a window. I turned
left into the alleyway and then towards the steps that led up
to the university, which always reminded me of the steps
in *The Exorcist*. My foot was just coming to rest on the first
step when I stopped and let another student overtake me. I
stood there at the foot of the steps, in a daze, then turned
and walked back as far as the window where I'd seen the
notice. *Help Needed*, it said.

A bell rang softly as I opened the door. Beyond it, a narrow
staircase led directly to the first floor. I'd been in that bar
a couple of times the previous year. It was furnished like
somebody's house, not very tidily, with a red carpet and sofas,
a few framed posters, table football and a counter. By night,
if I remember correctly, the lights were as red as the walls; at
the moment it just looked very scruffy. A man with a droopy

Mexican-style moustache and wearing a lumberjack's shirt over a T-shirt came through a door behind the dark wooden counter and put a box down next to the sink. He threw me a glance and started taking bottles from the box.

"Yes?" he said after a while.

"I saw the notice downstairs."

He finished taking out the bottles and threw the box aside, then crouched behind the counter and said something incomprehensible.

"What?"

He repeated what he had said, more slowly, but it was still a jumble of sounds.

"I'm sorry, I don't understand."

He reappeared from behind the counter, put his arms, which were as thick as tree trunks, down by the sink and stared at me. Then he looked around, picked up a pint glass, moved it closer to the mouth of one of the taps and mimed pulling it.

"Beer," he said, slowly. "Know how to pull pints?"

"Yes, of course."

Sometimes, at the fair in San Filippo, I had spent hours in the evening filling glass after glass from the demijohns of wine and the beer kegs.

"Good," he said, putting down the glass and going back behind the bar. "You're hired. Thursdays, Fridays and Saturdays, from six till closing time. Four pounds an hour. When you go down, take the notice off the door. See you Thursday."

I stood there looking at his thick hand as it appeared every now and again from behind the bar to grab a bottle.

"See you then," I said at last as I turned.

"Hey," I heard him say behind me. He'd reappeared from behind the bar and was holding out his hand. "I'm Leonard."

I turned back and gave his hand a good shake. "Jacopo."

He looked at me and smiled. "Italian?"

"Yes, Italian."

He nodded. "Fingers crossed, then. Welcome to Leonard's Lodge, Italian."

From the start, working at Leonard's was a real life saver. Not that the scholarship left me wanting for much, but it was useful to have a bit of extra money in my pocket, and at least I got out of the house and saw people—if standing behind a bar and pulling pints for drunken students could really be called seeing people.

The previous year I had moved into a hall of residence on the other side of Kelvingrove Park, near Argyle Street, in that section of the city over which the main complex of the university towered like a mediaeval castle. Not that I was exceptionally sociable, but at least I had ended up in a mixed apartment and for some reason Mathías, a Brazilian guy in his final year who lived with us, had decided I was interesting. He would come into my room from time to time and ask me what I was studying. He seemed quite fascinated by the fact that I or anyone else could find a meaning in all those numbers and letters, and always said that he really envied me. He also very much enjoyed my stories about San Filippo and my friends down there. He was about to graduate in sociology and was working on a thesis about microcredit. Sometimes he'd simply appear in the doorway and ask me if I wanted to go out for a drink.

"I have to finish studying."

"Don't piss me off. Let's go."

125

Then, on the way out, he'd knock at the other doors and yell at the others to follow us.

Living with us were a well-built Danish girl named Krista and Ricardo, a weird Spanish guy who never left his room. Krista wasn't studying at the university. She'd found the room in that hall of residence through a friend who was engaged to a guy and now spent all her time at his place. Apparently they had agreed to a sublet that was little more than symbolic, which suited both of them just fine. Krista had found work in a clothes shop in the centre of town. How she had come to be in Glasgow in the first place remained a mystery.

Ricardo didn't understand why on earth we could never respect the shelves of the refrigerator. In fact, almost all my fellow students spent most of their free time complaining about the difficulties of living with other people, and how other people never seemed to respect their space. They often mentioned dividing the bathroom into different areas or assigning the various shelves of the refrigerator, or complained about this or that flatmate's passion for fish or mature cheese. All of these things were unknown to me. As early as the second day, Mathías had come in without knocking, as usual, and told me that he and Krista were going shopping and asked me if I needed anything.

"I don't know. I hadn't thought about it."

"Come on, drop those books and come with us. We can keep each other company for a while."

We returned home with six bags of stuff and put it wherever we could in the fridge and in the cabinets. Whenever any of us was hungry, we'd simply start cooking and call the others. Mathías did a lot of the cooking, but Krista did even more. Among other things, she was a dab hand at Oriental cuisine.

In a quarter of an hour she could make a dish of noodles, rice, chicken and vegetables that was a real masterpiece. I usually just did the washing up. I found I could rustle up a decent sauce—a pomarola or a carbonara—and everyone was very happy with the jars of ragù that Mum occasionally sent me from Italy. Ricardo wasn't keen on such promiscuity, and after a few complaints we discovered he'd made himself a little pantry in his room: the Scottish cold made the windowsill an excellent refrigerator. And yet, every time we went out, Mathías continued knocking on his door to let him know. One evening, when the three of us were in the kitchen cooking a few pieces of meat and washing the dishes that had been left in the sink , Ricardo appeared with his hands down at his side and his eyes fixed on the floor.

"Mathías, I'd appreciate it if you stopped constantly knocking at my door."

Mathías looked at him for a few moments without saying anything, then got up and went into his room. He immediately came out again holding a magazine, which he placed against Ricardo's chest, and sat down.

"Ricardo, go and have a wank please."

On the cover was a big blonde with her legs open and a sticker over the spot. Ricardo moved the magazine away from his chest and looked to see what it was, then without saying another word, took it with him into his room and closed the door behind him. We looked at each other and laughed. I held out my hand to Mathías.

About the middle of December, Mathías decided to organize a party. As Christmas was coming, we found our apartment invaded by Santas and reindeer. Two guys even showed up in a plastic sleigh with holes in it for their bodies. About two in the morning, Mathías saw me sitting on the kitchen counter with a glass in my hand and came and joined me. We clinked glasses and toasted the party.

"You're a good guy," Mathías said, looking at me for a moment.

I laughed. "You too."

We clinked glasses again.

"Hey, what happened to Ricardo?" Mathías asked.

"No idea. He must be in his room, contemplating suicide or a massacre."

Mathías smiled and looked at me for a moment, deep in thought, then raised his head and looked around, as if searching for someone. For a while, he continued looking among the guests, then put his hands around his mouth and called, "Charlotte!"

He laughed and grabbed the sleeve of a guy with reindeer antlers full of little lights on his head.

"Hey, can you call Charlotte for me, please?" he said, motioning with his chin behind the guy's back.

The guy with the antlers turned, reached out a hand and pulled the arm of a big red-haired girl, who now also turned and looked at him impatiently. The guy simply pointed at Mathías and went away. The redhead smiled and came towards us. Her face was covered in freckles, she had a big gap between her front teeth and a long Father Christmas hat was falling halfway down her back. She was wearing a red blouse with a low neckline, and her huge breasts were supported by a push-up bra with lace trimmings.

"Hi, darling," Charlotte said, coming closer.

"Hi, Charlotte. Let me introduce my friend Jacopo. He lives here with me."

"Jocopo?" Charlotte said, mispronouncing my name. "Where are you from?"

"I'm Italian."

"Oh, Italian," she said with a smile, coming closer and leaning against my leg. "Hi, Italian. Nice party."

She was holding a big plastic cup, from which beer was overflowing slightly, and she looked quite drunk.

"Listen, Charlotte, we need a favour. Or rather, not us, a friend of ours. The other guy who lives here."

"Where is he?"

"Well, he's had a bit of a hard day, and he's alone in his room."

"In his room? Alone? Why?"

"I don't know. He's a bit down. He's quite shy, and finds it hard to meet people. Between you and me, I think he's also a virgin."

"A virgin?" she asked, moving her head forward.

"Yes, I think so. In my opinion he needs someone to console him."

"I'll console your friend!" Charlotte said, raising her arms and spilling some of the beer.

"Good old Charlotte," Mathías said, laughing. He got down off the kitchen counter, took her by the arm, led her to Ricardo's door, opened it abruptly and pushed Charlotte inside. Mathías and I gave each other a high five and then forgot all about it.

Late the next morning, we were in the kitchen, having breakfast. There was me, Krista and Jane, a girl who had spent the night with Mathías. After a few minutes, Mathías also appeared. His hair stood on end and his eyes were puffed up like rolls. He came up behind Krista and gave her a kiss on the cheek, then kissed Jane on the head and sat down. Krista was making scrambled eggs and toast.

"We all love you," Mathías said to Krista.

We were already sinking our forks into the eggs when Charlotte emerged from Ricardo's room, taking care not to make too much noise. Her curly red hair was like an explosion around her head and with her red blouse and miniskirt and those big breasts and thick swollen legs she looked like a whore from a low-class brothel. We had completely forgotten about Charlotte and when we saw her come out of Ricardo's room we sat there and stared at her, our forks in mid-air.

"Virgin my arse, Mathías," Charlotte said. "Your friend wrecked me."

Mathías and I looked at each other for a moment with our forks at half-mast, then burst out laughing, spitting out a few pieces of egg as we did so.

From that day on, Ricardo was nicknamed the Oracle. Our curiosity aroused by the fact that he appeared to accept whatever was offered to him, we started leaving dishes or bowls for him in front of his door, and half an hour later we'd find them picked clean.

One day a few weeks later, I tried approaching him in his room to make conversation, but he simply told me he had no time for chitchat. We became convinced that he was a superior but alien being, whom we couldn't help venerating and occasionally propitiating with an offering of some kind.

Almost every week we went to a basement club called Nice & Sleazy in Sauchiehall Street near the centre of town. Monday was open-mike night: you could get up on stage and sing whatever you liked, covers or songs of your own. In return you got a free beer. The ones who weren't so good had the sense to sing something amusing or sing in a funny voice, and we always had a bit of a laugh. Usually they were the ones who got the most applause. All the times I went there in my four years in Glasgow, most of them in that first year with Mathías, I never heard anyone being booed. There were a couple of really good guys who sang their own songs and we often saw them in other clubs. One was called Liam. He wore thick glasses and had a mass of frizzy hair plastered down in an improbable way on one side. He looked like a caricature of a student from my department. And yet, every time his turn came, he'd pick up his guitar, sit down on the high stool in the middle of the stage and launch into these terrific songs, a bit country in style, in a moving, light-toned voice. Another guy with long smooth dark hair falling over his face, whose name I can't remember, always surprised us with his choice of songs. We would wait for Liam with the same kind of excitement you feel waiting for a song from an album you know by heart, and for the other guy full of curiosity to see what he would come up with. During covers, Mathías would start to clap his hands even before the musicians opened their mouths and tell me the name of the song, recognizing it just from the opening chords. From time to time he'd tell me a few backstage stories: the tragedy of Syd Barrett and how the rest of the group had once left him at home, the morning Paul McCartney woke up with only a vague memory of having written "Yesterday" during the night, or how Brian Wilson, convinced he had written the best album in the history of modern music, went crazy after hearing *Sergeant Pepper*.

One young guy was like a vocal photocopy of Mark Knopfler.

"He's from here," Mathías said one evening, applauding the start of an arpeggio.

"Who's from here?"

"Mark Knopfler."

"Here where?"

"Glasgow. He lived here until he was seven."

Since then, every time I've happened to hear Dire Straits, I've always been surprised: I've never quite managed to digest the fact that those very American rhythms, that very American voice, which seemed to be talking about the desolate prairies of the Midwest and country fairs in fields of corn, actually came from that cold, grey, working-class Scottish city.

The little I know about music I owe to Mathías. For Christmas he gave me a Sony Walkman, black and full of buttons, and was always giving me cassettes to listen to. I would put on my headphones as I went back up Kelvingrove Park towards the university, with the facade of the main building seeming to look me straight in the eyes and tell me to behave. That was how I learnt to love Black Sabbath, the lesser-known songs of the Beatles and the Rolling Stones, Miles Davis, Lou Reed and the Velvet Underground, Tracy Chapman, Nirvana, Iron Butterfly and Creedence. It was there, sitting on a bench with my headphones on, that the music and lyrics of Pink Floyd started to shine an obsessive searchlight on the the darkest, sharpest side of me. On cold, snowy days I also liked to listen to Joni Mitchell, or the guitar breaks of J.J. Cale. But if it was sunny, nobody could beat the Grateful Dead, especially "Bertha".

When Mathías graduated at the end of the year and we

said goodbye—he already had his simple knapsack on his back—he threw his three black boxes of cassettes on my bed. I stared at him with a mixture of fear and emotion I would not have expected.

"They're yours. Treat them well."

I looked at him, stunned. "Are you mad? All of them? What about you?"

"I have the originals at home. I can tape them again."

I got out of my chair, walked slowly to the bed and opened one of the boxes. I knew them well, and yet the idea that this row of cassettes was suddenly mine—transparent TDKs with the names of the bands and the songs written neatly on them by hand—was astonishing.

"Are you sure?" I asked again as I lifted *L.A. Woman* and turned it over in my hands.

"Yes," Mathías said, "I'm sure. And don't spend too much time in your room next year."

I promised him I wouldn't, and we hugged and said we'd see each other soon.

And it was music that always kept us connected. From time to time, a cassette or a CD by this or that new band Mathías had got to know on his travels around the world would arrive wherever I was living at the time. As early as my second year, he was the one who sent me my first Pearl Jam cassette, with the words "Listen to these people" written on it. That was how I also got to know Nine Inch Nails and Faith No More, and later Radiohead, Beck and Elliott Smith. One day Mathías called me from some remote place in Brazil or Peru to tell me he'd seen a funny-looking monkey that had reminded him of me.

"Fuck off," I said with a laugh.

There was a great din in the background, but we still somehow managed to have a bit of chat. I asked him if he'd heard Wilco yet.

"Look at him now, he can walk on his own two feet," he said, and you could tell from his voice that he was smiling.

Then he yelled that he had a helicopter to catch and hung up.

Only months later would I discover that at the time Mathías was on the border between Peru and Brazil, shooting a documentary on an Amazon tribe that had only just been discovered and was seriously threatened by the mining industry in the Brazilian state of Acre. There had always been something about Mathías I'd never quite understood while we were living together. There were signs during the year we shared the apartment in Glasgow, but I just took them as eccentricities: a certain carelessness about his appearance, the fact that he was spending his final year in a bleak hall of residence, even the choice, for a Brazilian, of a Scottish university. Only years later, when I got to know both his story and the world better did I realize what Mathías was trying with all his might to run away from: his fortune.

Yes, along the way Mathías had been bitten by the bug of authenticity. He was the son of a banker in São Paolo, and being the son of a banker in São Paolo meant living in villas with armed guards and barbed wire on the walls and going around with bodyguards in armour-plated cars. Mathías could have had anything he wanted from life, or at least from life in Brazil. And yet, from a certain moment on, he had become convinced that nothing he ever obtained would really be his. That was why he had chosen a Scottish university: was there anything farther from the beaches of Brazil with their skimpy bikinis? And there was also that affected scruffiness of his, the need he seemed to feel to always be sloppy, that simple backpack, those improbable haircuts, and then, after a while, that almost completely shaved head.

But life is clever, and the net result of all this was to turn him into an even more attractive character, which made him feel as if he were a walking cliché. Wherever he escaped, Mathías was haunted by the knowledge that he would always somehow manage to be fascinating, and for reasons independent of his will. He was fascinating *despite himself*, and those two words had blighted his life.

That was why he started making documentaries. After university he had worked for various humanitarian organizations around the world, always looking to make peace with his past. He had been in African villages and the outskirts of South American cities and in earthquake zones of India and Indonesia, until, in Sudan, he found an old 16mm Arriflex and some reels of film left behind by a young surgeon from Médecins sans Frontières, and he amused himself filming the building of a well. When the project was finished, he went to see a friend in London and decided to develop the reels, convinced it would all probably have to be thrown away. The laboratory put at his disposal a room and a projector to view the films. A thin man with greyish skin explained to him how to put the film through the projector and left him alone in that small dark room. Apart from a few scenes, the lighting and focus of most of the images were fine and Mathías was as excited as a little boy to see the silent black and white images of those young Africans and those volunteers working hard and smiling and sometimes play-acting for the camera. There was no sound, but for almost every scene Mathías imagined a musical background: the Prelude to Charpentier's *Te Deum*, "Money" by Pink Floyd, a long extract from "Jessica" by the Allman Brothers. As he went from one reel to the next and that trembling beam of light projected its grainy, silent images on the screen, Mathías realized that he was starting to see the broader picture. When he left the little projection room, the thin man with the grey skin asked him how the films were.

"Beautiful," Mathías said, lost in thought, then thanked him and headed for the exit. He was just about to open the door when he turned and walked back. "Listen, if I wanted to put all this material together in a single film, how would I go about that?"

"A single reel?"

"Yes."

"If you like, we can do it for you."

Mathías looked at the man for a moment, then lowered his eyes and picked up a blunt pencil stub from the counter.

"What if I wanted to shorten a few scenes, cut others completely and so on?"

"You mean, edit them."

"Yes, edit them."

"Well, either you find an editor to work with or you learn to use a Moviola and edit it yourself."

"And who has a Moviola?"

"Actually, we have. We can let you hire the room by the hour."

"What about the sound?"

"These films don't have sound."

"Yes, I know, but what if I wanted to put sound on them?"

"That's a bit complicated. You have to make a magnetic track and either keep it separate and synchronize it every time you project the film, or you transfer everything onto super 16 and add an audio track."

"Is that difficult?"

"Expensive more than anything else."

So Mathías stayed in London. His friend Junior told him with a laugh that if he wasn't going to be too much of a pain in the arse, he could crash in his living room for as long as he wanted. Mathías found work in a Caribbean restaurant near the flat, and every penny he put aside he spent on renting the Moviola by the hour. It was an old light blue Steenbeck with six decks. The thin man with the grey skin from Dolly Films, whose name was Marlow, showed him how to pass the film through the machine and how to mark the points where you wanted to cut with a yellow wax crayon.

"You have to be very careful," he told him. "These films are developed directly as a positive. They're the only copies you have. If you make a mess you'll have to throw everything away. So think carefully before cutting."

He gave him a roll of transparent tape riddled with holes and showed him a small black metal machine with supports for the film and a paper cutter with springs. He explained how to cut the film and join the ends with the tape.

"The scenes you cut, mark with a small piece of white tape and a title or with a number and attach them here." Marlow led to him a funny-looking trolley that resembled a coat rack with a canvas laundry bag beneath it. Attached to the horizontal bar at the top were dozens of little metal hooks on which you could hang the scraps of film by their sprocket holes.

So Mathías started spending all his free time in the dark with the Moviola, and some years later he would tell me that it was probably the purest, cleanest period of his entire life. He spent hours on end by himself, looking again and again at his scenes, looking for the right frame at which to cut, imagining the music he would insert. In his new-found enthusiasm, he decided to walk around the city and shoot more images: water flowing, puddles, lights, the coming and going of people, neon, traffic, refuse, and so on. At a few points in the film he even decided to use colour film for various apparently insignificant details, which gave an unexpected and very effective sense of alienation. When he told me about the idea, I have to confess I found it rather pretentious, one of those spurious film festival tricks that always left me with a false taste in my mouth. But when I actually saw the finished documentary, I was surprised to have to admit that they worked and, even though I couldn't explain to myself why, I knew that without them everything would have been weaker and more slipshod. He called the documentary simply *Water*, and once it was finished dragged Junior to see it. When he switched the lights back on, Junior turned to Mathías and told him it was a masterpiece.

"You think so?"

"You should enter it for some competitions."

"I think so too," Marlow said, leaning in the doorway of the projection room.

"Really?"

"Yes, really."

He had ten or eleven prints made of the documentary and sent it to a few festivals. The film caused something of a stir and even won a few prizes, including one in Brazil.

Years later, as we sat in a large black car on our way to a restaurant at the top of a skyscraper in São Paulo, Mathías told me, with a touch of sadness in his voice, that he would have preferred to be one of those reclusive directors who kept filming in 16mm, and at that moment would have liked to be in the dark, editing them on an old Steenbeck. But in the meantime he had became quite a famous director and formed a company with his producer.

For a moment or two I looked at him as he gazed out vaguely at the cars gliding past the window. My studies on cosmic radiation and the possible destiny of the universe had already made me somewhat cynical and blunt.

"Fuck off," I said to him, and fortunately he laughed.

3

R IGHT FROM THE START, my second year at university proved to be much greyer. I had moved to a small new building in Witton Court on the other side of the campus, beyond the Botanical Gardens and the River Kelvin, a building so bleak as to be positively numbing.

The previous year, crossing the park and passing the red stones of Kelvingrove Museum and the facade of the university's main building, I'd learnt the meaning of words like "awe" and "gratitude". Walking towards the Mathematics Department every morning, I couldn't help feeling all that stone and those massive five-hundred-year-old buildings lowering over me and somehow protecting me. I would feel that I was part of a centuries-old granite dream, a dream that became reality every day thanks to all of us, and I would be overwhelmed by a surge of pride. On better days, I also liked to sit for a few minutes facing the statue of Kelvin and look at him with his notebook in his hand and feel a bit as if I were his grandson. Walking to Byres Road from the new hall of residence, though, I didn't feel anything at all, except maybe an insidious wave of depression. I couldn't get used to the direction the cars were going and I always had the impression that they were about to run me over. The river was nothing but a thin stream with a rusted lock-gate, and the terrible state of Kibble Palace always put me in a grim mood.

I also looked awful. During the summer in San Filippo, which I spent mostly on my own listening to the cassettes Mathías had left me—for various reasons, my friends had barely shown their faces—I'd started to grow my hair so that it fell over my face like the fur of an Afghan hound. On returning to Scotland I also decided to grow a beard, but I didn't have much facial hair and it grew quite sparsely, making me look as if I were ill. I fell in love with a velvet jacket I'd found in a second-hand shop in Byres Road: in order to keep wearing it when the cold weather arrived, I had to cover myself with at least four or five layers, which made me look clumsy and ridiculous. I was also crazy about a synthetic plum-coloured scarf that these days I wouldn't give my worst enemy. I always walked stooped and with my head down, rarely talking, savouring that dark, anonymous air I had started to indulge in.

If requested, the university was supposed to guarantee students single-sex accommodation. For whatever reason, a student could ask not to live in a mixed flat. I've never completely understood why, but the various students who demanded single-sex accommodation were never put together—perhaps in order not to ghettoize them—and were always put with people who would have been more than pleased to see members of the opposite sex passing in the corridor or the kitchen. I was one of these. A young Muslim fundamentalist, the son of Lebanese Shi'ites but brought up in England, had been forced by his parents to demand single-sex accommodation, and I was the one who was put with him. Although Hamal, this Muslim boy, wasn't a bad person, he was very shy, and the fact that his presence made it impossible to bring women or alcohol into the building didn't exactly endear him to us—especially not to Mark, a skinny Irishman who considered the four years of university nothing but an unrepeatable opportunity to sleep with as many girls as possible. To be honest, he wasn't much different in this from most male students, except for the fact that many of them succeeded, while Mark wandered around the campus and went to parties in a desperate and futile search for someone to get off with. Sharing a single-sex flat obviously didn't help. The fourth flatmate was a certain Georg, a politics and economics student as big as a wardrobe, who divided his time between his room and the gym. He was always shut up in his room, like Ricardo, though without Ricardo's strange, obscure charm. Mark would unfortunately learn the hard way that Georg was of uncertain sexuality. One evening, just a month after the beginning of term, Georg went to Mark and asked him if he wanted to go out for a drink. Mark wasn't very keen on Georg's bulk or his American-style caps, but he accepted in the end. On the way back, apparently, as they were crossing the bridge and talking about women, Georg made a clumsy pass at Mark, who retreated and started to laugh nervously. Two days later, coming back from his classes, Mark had found his room turned completely upside down and the door smashed in and a sperm stain on the sheets. For the next few nights Mark asked me if he could move his camp bed and stay in my room—as if I could possibly do anything against Georg's bulk—then went back to his room and for the rest of the year slept with the bed against the door.

Georg, for his part, continued dividing his time between the gym and the university as if nothing had happened.

Fortunately, I sometimes managed to talk to Greg. The hall of residence had a telephone in the kitchen, which everyone was expected to use sparingly. When I had a few minutes I called Greg on one of his mobiles and if he was able to he called me back. One day I told him I didn't mind paying for a call once in a while, but he told me he didn't know what to do with all his money and preferred to make this small contribution to science.

In those few years, Greg had changed into something more abstract. It was as if he had evaporated. I didn't think much about it, but I always told myself that the first true signs of his transformation had manifested themselves a couple of days after his eighteenth birthday, at the end of our penultimate year at school.

On his birthday the chauffeur had dropped him in front of the school as usual and he had walked in through the gate as if everything were normal.

"Hi," I said. "Happy birthday."

"Thanks."

"How about doing something this evening?"

He threw me one of his ironic glances. "Forget about trumpets and shooting stars."

"Christ, how boring, Greg. You're eighteen, let's think of something."

"Like what?"

"I don't know, let's have your chauffeur drop us at Biagio's and we'll all go somewhere together."

Saying nothing, Greg continued walking into the school, but I was sure he was tempted by what I had said.

"Look, I don't know. Let's talk about it later," he said as he turned left towards his class.

"Many happy returns!" I yelled after him.

He hated it when anybody shouted at him in public, and he raised a hand behind his back and gave me the finger.

Later, on the way out, I suggested the plan again, or at least the intention to celebrate in some way. Greg told me he wasn't sure and we'd talk later.

He disappeared for two days running. He didn't come to school, didn't answer the phone, and was nowhere to be seen. When he reappeared, he seemed tired, as if he hadn't slept: he was paler than usual and there were deep circles around his eyes.

During the break, I went to find him in his classroom. Apart from two girls who were laughing as they leafed through thick diaries chock-full of captions and cuttings, Greg was alone in the room, sitting at his desk doing nothing.

"Hi," I said.

"Hi."

I sat down at the desk, facing him. "Well?"

"Well what?"

"You look terrible."

"Look who's talking."

"Have you been ill?"

"No, I had to talk to the lawyers about Dad's inheritance."

"Your dad's inheritance?"

"Yes, the inheritance: you know, that thing you're entitled to when a family member dies."

"And?"

"And I had to talk to the lawyers about matters connected with the inheritance."

The word "inheritance" conjured up in my mind images of gold doubloons and safes. The mere fact that a friend of mine was an heir was incredibly thrilling.

"And how is it?" I asked, all emotional.

He raised his black-circled eyes and stared at me. He seemed to look through me, and I couldn't help noticing a hint of resigned annoyance. "Let's just say it's not what I expected."

Gregorio's father had died when we were eight. A virulent cancer had carried him off in less than six months. The memories I had of Giulio Mariani were quite vague. From when I went up to the villa as a small boy to play with Greg or a few times at the village fairs, I remembered a somewhat elderly man, tall and slender, his greying hair combed back, always dressed in elegant suits and waistcoats.

"Look," we children said to each other whenever we saw him, "Greg's dad."

If, in the years following the count's death, you had asked anyone in the village what kind of person he had been, they would always have used the same words: a real gentleman. It was never actually said, but I'm sure that anyone in the village or the surrounding area would have taken it for granted that the wealth of the Mariani family was derived from their property and the general estate. Things, to use Greg's words, were in fact a bit different.

Coming home from school on the day of his eighteenth birthday, Greg had had dinner with his mother, unwrapped his present—a gold Montblanc pen—then gone up to his room and some time later, he confessed to me, had been on the verge of coming down and making arrangements with the chauffeur for our escapade with Biagio. Instead, the butler had knocked at his door and told him that Signor

Rastello was waiting for him in the small drawing-room downstairs.

"Rastello?"

"Yes, sir."

"And what does he want?"

"I really couldn't say."

Massimo Rastello, the so-called trustee, was a mysterious figure who, for as long as I could remember, had always been involved in the life of the Mariani household. As a child, Greg had seen him trailing his father like a shadow, and since his father had died he had reappeared from time to time to give a few directives. Greg had never liked him very much, especially since the day he had decided, out of the blue, to dismiss Maurizio, the estate manager, whom Greg was always visiting to play with his electric train set. Greg had always found the presence of this individual somewhat sinister, but the word "trustee" and his father's blunt words to his wife at table, barely a month before he died, "Just do as he says," had stopped Greg from thinking too much about it.

Rastello turned when he heard steps at the entrance to the drawing room. "Hello, Gregorio. Happy birthday."

Greg would have liked to act calm but he found himself swaying, his heart beating faster.

"This is a very important day for you, my dear Gregorio. More than you might imagine."

Greg did not like that grave tone and all but imperceptible smile one little bit. "It's a day like any other," he said, trying his best to maintain his usual sharp tone.

Rastello raised his eyebrows and smiled with an unbearably paternal air. "Not really. Maybe it's best if we close the door and sit down for five minutes."

The so-called "small drawing room" had two doors, and, as Greg closed the door he had just come through, Rastello went and closed the other. To be on the safe side, he even turned the key in the lock. Greg went and sat down on the big brocaded couch he had always found uncomfortable and rather ugly, while Rastello sat down in an armchair on the other side of the narrow room, facing him.

"Where do you think all your wealth comes from, Gregorio?"

I realize now that, in all probability, much of this conversation must have taken place before the time of the motorbike and the tarring of the Rocky Road. That explains the first signs of Greg's transformation two years earlier, the slow emergence of his cutting remarks and his disenchantment.

Greg swallowed his saliva. "I don't know... From the estate, I suppose."

"From the farm?"

"I suppose so."

Odiously, Rastello gave another paternalistic little laugh. "Gregorio, the farm is fortunately well managed, but it's a miracle it manages to pay its way and we can still afford a few improvements from time to time. The summer rents have brought in a bit of money in the past couple of years, but I assure you that if we only had the estate, things would be every different."

"You once told me about one or two businesses we invested in, if I'm not mistaken."

"Yes, that's right. They also form part of the package. And I didn't invest in them. They're yours."

At this word, *yours*, Greg felt a strange shudder run right through him, from his heels up to his neck. "What do you mean?"

"I mean the whole thing is a bit more complicated, Gregorio. Your father was one of the richest men in Italy."

Greg remained motionless and swallowed more saliva.

"Do you remember his trips to South America?"

Greg nodded. More than the trips, he remembered the photograph albums, the sense of admiration and pride he'd felt for that younger version of his father, in khaki trousers and shirt with a machete in his hand or with his arm around the shoulders of an Indian, surrounded by the gigantic leaves of a tropical forest. Over the years, poring over the pages of these albums, he'd felt as if he had got to know both his father and the meaning of the word "adventure". Apart from that, all he remembered were long absences, and an undeclared sadness over his mother's loneliness.

"Why do you think he went to South America?"

Greg sighed and for the first time since he had entered the room managed to regain a little self-control. "Signor Rastello, I don't think I want to spend all afternoon on guessing games."

Rastello looked at him and smiled. "Zinc, Gregorio."

Greg continued to stare at him without saying anything.

"Your father bought a zinc mine. He went down there just after the war to follow a friend on an expedition to the Amazon, but on the way he ran into the owner of an old mine. This person was an eccentric American gold prospector who hadn't been very successful in his own country and had gone down to Peru because he'd heard there were large unexplored deposits. He'd bought some land where he thought there might be a deposit, but all he'd found were some greyish metals. Nobody in the area knew what to make of these minerals, and the mine was a burden on the American's back. Your father always told me he bought it more to amuse himself than for any other reason. He was young and innocent, and had simply been fascinated by the idea of owning a mine. But I think he must have seen something in it."

"And then?"

"And then it turned out to be much more than an amusement. The mineral was sphalerite, or blackjack, the main source from which zinc is extracted. It was a very rich seam. In partnership with a German he found a way to refine it, and he was among the first to market it by air. At first, they sold it as anode for navigation. These days, our zinc is used mainly as a protective industrial coating. Our mine... your mine, is one of the largest deposits in Peru. Up until about twenty years ago it was the biggest, then people woke up and started exploring other seams. He and the German split up at the end of the Sixties. Your father kept the mine and his partner kept the extraction centre on the coast."

Rastello looked at Greg for a moment, then continued. Once production had started and people had been found to run the mine, he explained, it had more or less taken care of itself, and his father, with a huge amount of capital suddenly at his disposal, had invested in various other sectors, buying and selling large shares in companies around the world. Apparently he had a great nose for such things and, apart from a few rare disappointments, had managed to multiply his capital and become quite a powerful figure. Rastello then paused again briefly.

"When he was told that his cancer was incurable, he devoted every remaining minute to arranging things for you. I well remember the evening he called me. He had me sit down in the armchair in front of his desk. 'Massimo,' he said, 'it's quite likely that I have less than four months to live.' I swear,

Gregorio, I almost fell off my chair. Your father was a quiet person, quite aloof, and yet I had never before realized how much I was in his debt. Everything I was I owed to him and all he'd taught me in his quiet way. He told me he was planning to wind up most of his companies and that he was spending a lot of time with his lawyers laying the groundwork for when he was no longer around. 'But I need someone I can trust to keep the show on the road,' he said. I don't think I've shed a single tear since I was twelve, but I was so struck by your father's dignity in the face of death that I had to strain every muscle of my face and body in order not to burst out crying like a baby. I set up a holding company, GMH, comprising the mine, the farm, the properties, the foundations and those few companies he couldn't or wouldn't wind up. And he made me managing director of the holding company. He had watertight contracts drawn up, to which he devoted all his remaining energy. He was very worried about the fact that this would fall on you so early, but for technical reasons that was very difficult to avoid. So here I am, Gregorio: from today you are the sole official president of GMH, the owner of more than 60% of the shares. In accordance with your father's wishes, I remain, at least for the moment, the managing director."

So Massimo Rastello was no longer that sinister, ambiguous figure who turned up from time to time to shake things up a bit, but the man to whom Greg's father had entrusted their lives. He was good, though, and without venturing into large operations—Greg's father had ordered him to be cautious and had appointed three different lawyers as guarantors—had continued increasing the capital. Some time later it emerged that the reason the famous estate manager had been quietly asked to leave was that he was caught pocketing money from the estate's coffers.

"What about Mother?"

Rastello looked at Greg for a moment, his lips pursed slightly in what seemed to be a hint of embarrassment. "Gregorio, your father always sensed she wouldn't be up to it." For a moment, a kind of shadow fell over the room. Then Rastello unfolded a sheet of paper he had been holding in his hand from the start and held it out to Greg. "This is a draft prospectus of all you own, apart from the turnover and net profits for the past year. The data isn't exact, but it'll give you an idea."

Greg took the piece of paper and as he ran through all those numbers he felt a series of kicks in his stomach, forcing it up into his throat. That sense of nausea, of disgust, stayed with him for months. He rarely came to school, often said he was ill, and headaches prevented him from sleeping well. My father visited him, and simply prescribed sedative drops and decent sleep. "He's not sleeping enough, that's all it is," he said that evening at dinner. He was hardly ever seen in the village that summer, and on all the occasions I went to his villa to see him, he was available only a couple of times.

Apparently one evening at the end of July he called Rastello and told him he had to talk to him. When they were in the small drawing room again, with the doors closed, Gregorio looked him straight in the eyes. "I want to know everything," he said.

"About what?"

"About everything. I want to see the mine and find out how it works. I want to know where the money is and how to invest it and how the markets work and all that stuff. I want to know everything."

Obviously I wasn't there, and I never heard this for certain, but I'm sure Rastello smiled.

That was the moment when Greg really started to evaporate. The first symptom was quite simply his disappearance: he was nowhere to be seen, either in the village or school. While he was learning everything there was to learn about his businesses and his history and about zinc and the markets, while he was constantly at Rastello's side, posing as his new young assistant, he was also, with the help of tutors, studying for his final exams as an external student at a private school in Rome.

The couple of times I managed to see him, he was displaying the second symptom of evaporation: his appearance. He wore only dark, elegant suits, grey or black, presumably made to measure, and with his fair hair and pale face had the mad, remote look of an Andy Warhol. Only a few months had passed, but he wasn't like my old friend any more: he was a colder, more rarefied version of him. Nobody in the village ever saw him again in person, and the only signs of him were the dark cars or the helicopters that came and went.

Even though looking down at that vast terraced hollow in Peru had given him an unexpected quiver of pride, he wasn't very interested in the mine, let alone in the farm. What really fascinated him were the fluctuations in the international markets, and gradually discovering that the world was a lot smaller than he had imagined.

"It doesn't take much," he said to me one day on the phone, after telling me about a killing he'd made with a Japanese transport company and confessing that he didn't know how he did it. "It's a bit like playing Monopoly, but with real money."

"I'd die of anxiety."

"To be honest, all you have to do is take away a few zeros and then just stop thinking about it."

After a while, he really did disappear. At the beginning of my first year at university, he vanished into thin air, and apparently nobody knew what had become of him. He told Rastello to keep things going on his own, and that he needed to be by himself for a while. Nobody heard from him for nearly seven months, at the end of which he drove up to the gates of the villa in a dark car as if nothing had happened.

"Where have you been?" I asked him the first time we talked on the phone.

"In the Far East."

"The Far East?"

"Yes, the Far East."

"Where in the Far East?"

"All over. I spent quite a bit of time in Mongolia."

The idea of Greg in Mongolia just didn't fit the image I had of him.

"What's it like?"

"Cold."

Years later, it emerged that he had actually spent a few weeks in a monastery, but he always seemed reluctant to talk about that journey and those weeks.

So, from time to time, we would talk on the phone. That was what Greg had become more than anything else: a voice. A voice suddenly filled with a wonderful, keen sense of humour. Surrounded as I was by the ridiculous dreams of all those students, listening to him talk was like looking out again at the world for a few minutes, or at least at the most overt and glittering part of it. The idea that behind that voice there was also a body, a person of flesh and blood, had gradually ceased to be of any importance.

4

THOSE OCCASIONAL phone conversations with Greg were, as I've said, the only pleasant note in my second year in Glasgow. So it was no surprise that I clung to the work at Leonard's and that old attic room like a shipwrecked sailor to a tree trunk.

As storeroom, Leonard used a small attic at the top of a narrow wooden staircase you reached through a dark door at the far end of the club. The door of the attic was on the left at the top of the stairs. On the right there was another door, which it had never occurred to me to open.

I opened it for the first time one day in mid-December, after taking a box of drinks and cans from the storeroom to fill the fridge. I dragged the box outside, and as I bent to pick it up, my eye fell for the umpteenth time on the white wooden door on the other side of the landing. I was in something of a hurry. Whenever I went up to get the drinks, the fear of being bawled out by Leonard had always stopped me from yielding to my curiosity. That day, though, Leonard, after sending me upstairs, cursed and yelled up the stairs that he was going to the electrical shop for a moment. So I turned and looked for a few moments at the mysterious closed door.

I looked around as if I were being watched, then went closer and put my hand on the handle. The door opened with a creak, and I barely had to force it. Beyond the threshold there was another attic: completely empty, the floor of rough dark wood, a few damp stains on the walls. And yet, all things considered, it seemed in good condition, and at the far end of the room was a small brick fireplace. Light from the neon sign of the club opposite filtered through a skylight in the ceiling. I stood in the middle of the room for a couple of minutes, and suddenly imagined myself there, studying and working, by candlelight if necessary, next to a lit fire.

When Leonard came back a bit later, I was still arranging the drinks in the fridge. He went to the box room, messed around with something and came back with a small screwdriver in his hand and then went over to the blender and started taking the plug off.

"I saw the other room upstairs," I said after a while, placing a bottle of tonic water on a shelf.

"Mmm," Leonard replied, trying to force a screw that was holding the plug together.

"Whose is it?"

"It's mine. Whose should it be?"

"Don't you do anything with it?"

"At first I thought..." He broke off, his face contorted with the effort of trying to turn the screw, which finally moved with a creak. He extracted it, opened the plug and took a good look inside, then glanced at me. "... I thought of making it my office, but it was too cold so I left it the way it was."

"And don't you have any intention of doing anything with it?"

"I don't know. Not for now."

Leonard finished fixing the plug and I finished filling the fridge and shelves and the evening continued as usual. I didn't mention it again, but the image of that damned attic continued to haunt me, and every day when I went back to sleep in the hall of residence I felt like throwing up. I now hated everybody and everything: my flatmates, the endless bustle of students, the winks, the knowing looks, the cold, the hard-edged light and the eighteen hours a day of darkness, the cars driving on the wrong side of the road and Kibble Palace and the greyness and the whole of Glasgow. The only salvation seemed to be the shelter of that little attic above Leonard's Lodge. When I got to the club the following week, I couldn't even wait until I had taken my jacket off and hung it up.

"Listen, Leonard, I've been thinking about this a lot, and I was wondering if you'd be willing to rent me the attic."

Leonard was cleaning the low tables and sofas with a cloth. He stopped and turned to look at me. "Rent you what?"

"The attic."

He stood there looking at me without saying anything and after a moment or two a slight sense of unease crept up my back. I felt awkward, and didn't really know where to look or what to do.

"All right, I understand. Forget it," I said after another few moments, unable to keep a hint of irritation out of my voice. Actually I had no desire to forget it, but I didn't know how to get out of this uncomfortable situation. I went to the door of the box room, opened it, hung my jacket on the usual hanger, took off my plum-coloured shoes and a couple of sweaters, went behind the counter and crouched on the floor to see what drinks we were missing. In the meantime, Leonard had gone back to cleaning the tables with his cloth.

"And what would you like to do with it?"

I stood up slowly, my heart pounding in my chest, and for a moment I thought I could hear the sound of an orchestra from somewhere.

"I don't know. Stay there, I think. Study, spend time there, do my own thing."

"Can't you do all that where you live?"

"I hate where I live, Leonard. I'm living with an idiot who's always in the gym, a Shi'ite who stops us from doing anything, and an Irish loser whose greatest ambition seems to be to make porn films."

"Porn films?"

"Yes, he'd like to get laid but nobody will have him. I tried fixing him up with a friend of a friend, a pimply girl who's fucked just about everyone, but he says she's a loser too."

Leonard laughed and continued cleaning the two remaining tables, then the battered old jukebox and all the shiny surfaces. He did this every Thursday. The bottles behind the counter, on the other hand, he dusted on Tuesdays.

After watching him move the cloth around for a while and waiting in vain for a sign from him, I dived under the counter again, finished checking what was missing, brought the usual crate from the box room and headed upstairs to collect juices and bottles. Before coming back down, I opened the door of the attic again for a moment, just to have another glance in. It seemed even cleaner and more welcoming than when I'd seen it the week before and I almost had the impression that I could see myself, lying there reading on cushions in front of a lit fire, a beam of moonlight illuminating part of my face.

When I went back down, Leonard was beating the cushions on the sofas into shape, the cloth over his shoulder like a barman in a film. I went behind the counter and started getting out the bottles.

"And what will you do about the cold?" He had suddenly appeared behind the bar and startled me.

"Jesus," I said, catching my breath for a moment. "I talked to Larry, the owner of the pub opposite. I asked him where he gets wood for their fireplace. He says someone brings it every Wednesday morning from out of town. I asked him if I could also take some and he told me he didn't think there'd be any problem. In fact, he also told me that we could get it together and maybe they'd charge us a bit less, or at least give me the same price."

Leonard gave a slight smile. "And when did you ask Larry all this?"

"Two or three days ago, something like that."

Leonard shook his head, smiling, and continued looking at me for a moment or two. "It'll cost you at least half what you're earning."

"No problem."

"And you'll have to come and give me a hand on Tuesdays too."

"No problem."

"And you can only be there when I'm also around. I don't want any trouble."

"No problem."

"And you'll have to come and clean the club and the toilets every day."

"Don't overdo it, Leonard—I'm not that desperate."

Leonard laughed, then gave me a little slap on the face with the cloth and went back to arranging the sofas.

So I had the attic. It didn't seem true. The following

Saturday I spent the whole morning and afternoon there with a bucket and rags, trying to remove all the dust and make the place look at least slightly respectable. The skylight was half caked with dirt, and in my attempt to open it I was afraid for a moment that I might break it. Then fortunately it moved, icy air came rushing in through the wide-open pane, and I seemed to feel the room starting to breathe again. The wooden floorboards were loose or warped in several places, but, once cleaned, the deep, dark veins of the wood looked like the lines I'd have liked to have on my face as an old man. I also thought of buying paint and giving the walls a coat, but all things considered, those two or three damp patches didn't bother me too much for the moment. Around the middle of the afternoon, I had to go down and warm my hands and body with a big steaming cup of tea. I was all wrapped up in my jacket and my layers, with a woollen fisherman's hat on my head.

The next morning, I bought a bit of furniture from a bric à brac stall in the Barras Market. For me, that market was like an adventure on a new continent. I should make it clear that when I talk about Glasgow I'm basically talking nonsense. Glasgow is quite a big, complex city, whose tortuous history stretches from the Celts up to the most recent industrial unrest. The granitic Scottish identity and the recent collapse of big industry, especially the shipyards, have left a kind of strange urban swamp in which an extraordinary variety of life forms manage to grow. Sometimes I'd hear about places like the East End, Ibrox, Maryhill, places where terrible things were said to happen: stabbings, gang fights, robberies. When Carlo, one of my fellow students, was questioned one day on the way out of an algebra class as to why he had a black eye and thick glasses patched together with tape, he told Dr McKenzie, me and two other classmates that he'd ended up in the middle of an Orange parade in the East End wearing a green jacket. Some policemen had seen Carlo wandering brazenly in the middle of the road. They'd watched him as he stopped suddenly and stared in astonishment at the crowd, which was already pointing at him. Carlo told us that when he saw that formless mass of huge men dressed in orange he had frozen. Then he had felt himself being yanked strongly to one side, thrown to the ground, crushed by what seemed like dozens of hands, his arms twisted unnaturally behind his back. He'd tried to look around, but all he remembered were dark clothes and incomprehensible cries in Scottish and the asphalt crushing his face. He'd been taken and handcuffed and even a bit manhandled by policemen in riot gear, who lifted him up and threw him into a van. Bewildered and terrified, Carlo kept asking what had happened, what he was doing in that van, why he had been beaten and arrested. In his confusion, he even mentioned the Italian ambassador and, giving great autistic movements with his head—he did this sometimes in class too—kept repeating that it was unacceptable, completely unacceptable… A young policeman, perhaps the only one who had figured out what was really going on, gave him back his broken glasses and apologized. It had taken quite a while and quite a lot of shouting to clarify that Carlo wasn't a fanatical Celt carried away by heroic delusions and convinced that he could face an Orange parade by himself, but simply an innocent Italian student who deserved, at most, mockery and a bit of compassion. Once the parade was over, the policemen had let him get out of the van, advised him to turn his green jacket inside out and told him how to get back to the university. Carlo had set off with some trepidation along one of the wide, desolate streets of the East End, with his jacket turned inside out and half a black eye and his thick glasses held on by only one arm, constantly looking around as if entering an uninhabited house. The three remaining policemen must have watched him for a few seconds, then probably nudged each other and laughed and drove towards him. One got out and told Carlo to get in again.

"Again?" Carlo said, on the verge of tears.

"We'll take you home."

So Carlo got back in the van and, while the ride lasted, felt for the first and last time in his life what it was like to be a criminal. When the policemen dropped him outside the main gate of the university, they smiled and asked if he could find his way home from there.

"Yes, thanks," he said.

"You're welcome," the policeman at the wheel replied. "And keep away from the East End. In fact, try to keep away from anywhere that isn't the university campus."

When the story was over, we all laughed and told Carlo it wasn't bad advice.

Dr McKenzie shook his head and smiled. "It may also be time to throw away that green jacket," he said as he finished putting his books back in his leather briefcase.

"But it's a gift from my mum."

"Precisely."

In four years of university, I heard quite a few stories like this. To me they all seemed as exotic as night battles on the outskirts of Baghdad or journeys along the Yellow River. I never went to the East End or Ibrox or any other area of the city that wasn't either the centre or Hillhead, the university area. Going as far as the end of Queen Margaret Drive to have dinner with a couple I knew who lived in the area—no more than ten minutes on foot—was quite enough travelling for me. In every city I've ever lived in, I've been able, in a surprisingly short space of time, to establish a restricted but solid network of places where I could find the basic necessities and feel at home, and to go outside it as little as possible. For some time, this deep-rooted rejection of novelty has been another of those tiresome elements that lead people to make all kinds of insinuations about me, but previously it was never a great problem. Under the pressure of other people's arguments I began to wonder about myself, but in the end I simply decided that it wasn't about unresolved issues, and it wasn't a phobia: it was more like a simple lack of interest. I've lived in several places, and have always lived in a small part of them. What's wrong with that? I can well understand the charm of new landscapes, I know how excited people get about them, and I respect anyone who decides to devote a lot of time and money, maybe even the best moments of their lives, to such activities. But if I'm not like them, what can I do about it? From time to time, over the years, I've been dragged into pointless discussions over this. Some people smile, some drop the subject, some get annoyed. They can't understand how it's possible for someone not to like travelling: that's usually the more or less explicit subtext of the conversation.

"I don't know," I've learnt to answer. "I don't like aubergines either, but I've never had to argue about it."

I've discovered that this sentence often manages to silence even the most pigheaded.

*

The day the previous year that Mathías had suggested we go to the Barras, I'd felt as if I were venturing into the unknown. It was a cold Sunday morning and I was quietly reading under the blankets, minding my own business.

"Come on, get up, we're going to the Barras," said Mathías, entering as usual without knocking.

"Where?"

"The Barras. How come I never catch you having a wank?"

"Where's the Barras?"

"Here in Glasgow, just past the centre. It's a market."

"A market?"

"You know, those things where people have stalls and put things on sale and hope someone will come and buy them."

"And what will we do in a market?"

"Have a look at it, whatever. Don't piss me off, just get a move on."

"I don't know, Mathías... it's cold, I'm reading. I opened the bathroom window to let a bit of air in and I couldn't get my hand off the handle."

"Get dressed. Its cool, the Barras. It's like another world. You see a bit of the real Scotland."

Maybe that's the point: real places. We always think where we are is less real than other places. It's as if we're each living on an island, as artificial as a stage set, and the neighbouring islands seem more authentic. Not to those who live there, of course: to them, our island is more authentic, which makes the whole thing rather ridiculous and paradoxical. Until not long ago, it had never occurred to me that my life might not be authentic, and to tell the truth, whenever I heard that idea expressed I always treated it with a certain sarcasm.

Before we left, Mathías knocked at Ricardo's door and told him we were going to the Barras: there was no answer.

I had already been to the centre occasionally and had got quite accustomed to the square stone buildings and the lights and all the shop windows. At the end of Argyle, however, where there was an old tower that looked like the bell tower of a ruined church, a completely new landscape suddenly opened up: low and in some cases dilapidated buildings, iron bridges, obese men in torn track suits, street vendors, fish and chip shops. It was as if, just by going a few steps further, we were entering one of those dubious areas on the outskirts of town I had often heard about but had never felt any urgent desire to venture into. Mathías was happiness personified. He kept looking around and pointing out apparently insignificant details that seemed rather seedy to me, but extraordinary to him: an old woman's hacked-off fingers, a young boy's patched-up crutches, a group of three men with red faces and swollen bellies, two young men in black T-shirts and broken shoes, and so on.

"Can't you feel life?" Mathías asked, all excited.

The Barras Market was the essence of all this, its most intense, most crystallized expression. A sinister individual with a noticeable scar across one eye, standing behind a stall full of T-shirts and pants and trousers, was screaming incomprehensibly, accompanied by a little boy who was like a scale model of him; another man, fat and with only three teeth in his mouth, was also screaming behind a stall of used records and cassettes; a thin old man close by was laughing and rubbing his hands; small groups of elderly men with red unshaven faces waved lottery tickets and yelled at passers-by to try their luck. The smell of tar and incense and rottenness, the reddish tinge of the light, the impression of being in some strange mythical place at the ends of the earth. On both sides of the main thoroughfare there were three large sheds, also full of stalls. Second-hand drills, tea services, LPs, dolls, books, videocassettes, toy pistols and rifles, broken typewriters, entryphones, military helmets and caps, hooks, chairs, sagging armchairs, bicycles—probably stolen—wooden beams, toy clowns, old telephones, propellers, binoculars, curtains, ornaments and trinkets of all kinds.

When I went back now by myself, a fat woman with hair stuck to her forehead sold me, for half the original price, an old worm-eaten table and two rickety chairs, two oil lamps, one in aluminium and one in brass, and then congratulated me and told me I was a tough customer. I asked her if by any chance she also had a mattress.

She thought this over for a moment, then shook her head.

"No, I'm sorry, I don't have a mattress." She turned towards the back of her stall. "Hey, do we have a mattress for this boy?"

I didn't see where it was coming from, but a voice that sounded like a motorbike with a broken carburettor said something I didn't understand. With the woman too, I'd had some difficulty communicating at first, but we'd managed in the end.

She turned back to me and shook her head, but after a moment she stopped and, making a sign to me, came out from behind her stall and told me to follow her. She was wearing a horrible hairy pink jumpsuit and her bottom swayed inside it like a straw case on a dirt road. We passed another couple of vendors and walked outside the shed. The woman then started calling someone in a loud voice. A huge shaven-headed man dressed in military green turned and said to wait a minute. He was stabbing his index finger into the chest of a thinner man, who jumped slightly at every blow. The thin man did not seem very pleased at that index finger being stabbed at his chest, but before long he went away without saying anything. The man with the shaved head turned towards the woman and smiled at her and they shook hands. Then the woman pointed at me and said something. It was pointless for me even to try to understand them. The big man looked me up and down. At the sides of his mouth he had two long scars rising towards his ears. The previous year, Mathías had cheerfully explained to me that they called this a Glasgow smile and it was caused by a beer glass thrust in the mouth as someone was finishing drinking. A typically nice Scottish custom. That face and that lopsided smile weren't a pretty sight at all. Then the man addressed me directly.

"I'm sorry, I don't understand," I replied, looking at the woman for help. Luckily, she supported me with some words I didn't understand either. The man shrugged and gestured to us to follow him. He went around the outside of the shed and stopped in front of a rusty little van. Inside it, there were various pieces of furniture: tables, chairs, an armchair, a crystal chandelier, a basket full of cutlery that might have been silver. And stuck in on the side, two mattresses. The man jumped into the van, and with extraordinary ease, holding one upright, pulled out the other. It was a decent double mattress, apparently in good shape. When I moved my face closer to it to smell it, the man and the woman both laughed. He said something to me too, sniffed and passed a finger under his nostrils, but I thought it was best to keep silent and just smile. Then I asked the woman how much the mattress cost. In the end, with a bit of difficulty and, I have to admit, a certain amount of courage on my part, we arrived at a figure. I asked if it was possible for them to take my purchases up to

Hillhead. The man and the woman discussed this a bit and in the end we came to an agreement that he would bring the stuff directly to the club on Tuesday morning.

When Leonard saw that huge, dubious individual come into his bar and go up the stairs, helping me to carry the things, he wasn't very happy. Before he left, the big man shook my hand and once again said something I didn't understand.

"What did he say?" I asked Leonard when he'd gone.

"To drop by and see him in the Barras. But who is he?"

"A new friend of mine," I said to Leonard, and winked. "He's a good lad."

From a little shop in the area, I bought two pillows and some sheets and blankets, and when the following afternoon, having gathered firewood that morning before going to the university, I lit the fire in the attic for the first time, I felt as if nothing could happen to me now. At last, the world could even disappear: I had my refuge, and as the heat from the fireplace was enough to let me push aside the blankets and take off a couple of sweaters, it honestly seemed to me the most beautiful refuge in the world.

I went there every afternoon and every evening, and the main room of Leonard's Lodge became a bit like the hall and front room of my home. Leonard discovered that it was quite convenient for him to have me there, and very soon, instead of my working fixed shifts, we decided that he would call me when he needed me. All he had to do was climb the stairs and knock at my door. For my part, I assured him that if some evening I had to study more than usual and couldn't give him a hand, I would tell him in advance. In return, for half the pay agreed at the beginning, I had my attic. I would have worked for free.

5

I T MAY HAVE BEEN thanks to—or the fault of—the excitement of my newly regained freedom and the crackling of the fire and the light of the oil lamps on the worm-eaten wood of the little table that the idea of moving to the Physics Department had started to grow inside me. But if I think about it again now, seeing the bigger picture, it was more to do with productivity, in the most industrial meaning of the word. The ease with which I understood numbers and functions had started to exasperate me without my realizing it. In reality, the first shoots of this future evolution had appeared much earlier. I was in middle school, and one morning, as our teacher Signora Scarpelli was explaining exponentiation, I suddenly raised my hand and asked what the point of it was. It was a question I'd already asked a couple of times over the previous few months. Signora Scarpelli, who had always singled me out for praise if not actual affection, snorted, "Jacopo, if you ask me again what the point of it is I'll throw you out and give you four out of ten."

Unlike some of my classmates, I wasn't used to such harsh words from a teacher—or from anybody, to tell the truth—and the violence of that reply must have triggered a small trauma in me. My brain, which was not yet very flexible, must have automatically pigeonholed that "What's the point?" as something not to ask, especially to a maths teacher, and I pretty much forgot all about it. It wasn't difficult: I enjoyed maths and I was good at it, so why should I ask what the point was? If nothing else, it helped to reassure my teachers and parents, which was already quite something. And it helped me pass the time pleasantly enough. And when school was over it had taken me to another country and helped me win money and scholarships and discover Frank Zappa and Talking Heads. And yet that question always hung over my head like a dark shadow. True, not everything came as automatically as it once had, and on a few occasions I felt a vague sense of frustration: when you came down to it, it was the same frustration we might feel faced with a complex rebus we can't solve. Once solved, it's only the key to more ambitious puzzles. But in the meantime, that same inescapable question hovered over me like a vulture: what's the point?

Now, aware of the risk and with my heart pounding in my chest, I tried once again to ask one of my teachers. This time, though, I asked it in a less arrogant way, with a slight touch of sadness in my voice.

I was sitting on a bench in the botanical gardens, next to Dr Jones. We'd met by chance. From time to time, as I walked from the hall of residence to the university or Leonard's Lodge, I liked to go through the park and take a look in the greenhouses. I particularly liked the tropical house. It was a small circular section, with a concrete pond in the middle, and was very hot and humid. There were ferns drooping on all sides and small aquariums with seaweed and tiny fish. In the central pond, which was two or three metres in diameter, curious catfish stuck their mouths out on top of the water and sucked at the surface. There was almost never anybody there, and the silence and the drops of moisture hanging from the leaves and the slight hissing of the water made me feel for a few minutes like an adventurer in a South American rainforest. Sometimes I also liked going to the succulent plants section, where the air was very dry and there was a smell of dust.

As I was walking along one of the paths in order to get back to the street, I spotted Dr Jones sitting on a bench, facing the big lawn with Kibble Palace in the background. He was staring into the distance, with his hands together on his lap, as still as a statue. His big nose was redder than usual and his floppy hair was moving slightly in the breeze.

"Dr Jones," I said, approaching and bowing my head a little.

He looked up, and for a moment his eyes had the unseeing gaze of a newborn baby. Then they lit up and he raised his eyebrows.

"Ah, Mr Ferri. You here too?"

"Yes, I sometimes come in here on my way to the department."

I propped my rucksack against one of the legs of the bench and sat down. We both looked at the lawn and Kibble Palace, he leaning back against the bench and me with my elbows on my knees. He asked me how my second year was going.

"I don't know… last year was better."

Out of the corner of my eye I saw him turn his head slightly towards me. "Why's that?"

"No particular reason," I said. Then I told him a bit about Mathías and Krista and the new hall of residence. I also told him that luckily I'd found a job in a club two or three evenings a week and I even mentioned the attic, where I could spend my free time, which at least distracted me a little.

"And the course?"

"What about the course?"

For a moment I played with a chipped nail, then said, "I sometimes wonder what the point of it is."

Inside me, just under the surface, there was another face contracting its muscles and screwing up its mouth and eyes, as if expecting to be hit. But nothing happened, and after a few seconds I turned and saw Dr Jones simply sitting there, quite still, looking at me with a grave, nostalgic gaze.

"I know," he said after a while, leaning forward and also putting his elbows on his knees. "In the long run, mathematics isn't as comforting as it seems."

I wasn't quite sure I knew what he meant, but, encouraged by his unexpectedly melancholy reaction, I decided to risk going a bit further and see what happened.

"I'd like to have the feeling that what I study might one day be of some practical use. Help people in some way. I'd like to know I didn't do all this just to solve puzzles and because I liked it. I don't know how to explain it... I'd like to study something that enters the world and changes it. That enters people's lives."

"For example?"

"I don't know. Physics, for example, astronomy... whatever. To study something concrete."

Dr Jones leant back again and looked at me for a few seconds from behind. "You could try."

I turned to look at him. "What do you mean?"

"I could talk to some of the staff, arrange for you to follow a course, to see if you like it."

"What about the scholarship?"

"I said, try. And then if you really like it, we can find a solution. You could graduate in mathematical physics, but in any case, if you changed departments and maintained your standard, we could easily carry on with the scholarship. It wouldn't be the first time. A few years ago, an Indian boy did the opposite, moving from physics to pure mathematics. Obviously he wasn't all that interested in the world."

"Was he good?"

"He was brilliant. Very strange, though. I think he's back in India now. He went to Chicago after he finished here, but apparently the classes started to scare him and in the end he had a breakdown. Another half-Indian boy who was studying with him went to see him and said he never goes out: he spends all day in his room reading and solving equations in piles and piles of exercise books."

"Jesus."

"Yes, a strange business."

Dr Jones looked at his watch and said he had to go, but that he would talk to a few people about my situation and let me know.

A couple of days later, Dr Jones came to see me in one of the classrooms.

"I've talked to Dr Marker," he said in the doorway. "Go tomorrow morning just before the lesson. This is the time and the room. In the Physics Department, obviously." He handed me a sheet of paper and winked. "Good luck."

Perhaps it was just an impression of mine, but I'd never seen him look so cheerful. He even seemed a bit rejuvenated.

*

Productivity: that was the word. Related to it was the thrilling feeling that overcame me the following morning as soon as I went in search of the room indicated by Dr Jones.

The Mathematics Department was on the street which led from the steps behind Ashton Lane to University Avenue and the main building. It was a shabby grey pebble-dashed building next door to the Boyd Orr Building. It was everything you'd expect of a Mathematics Department: precise, simple and boring. The linear structure had none of the age-old charm of the university's older buildings, let alone any hint of the boldness of the Department of Medicine. It was a plain, dull block of concrete stuck there with no apparent thought. The interiors were similar: emergency door bars and upholstered armchairs and large formica tables. Sobriety. "This is the kingdom of numbers," every corner of the building seemed to say. "Nothing else matters."

The Physics Department was another matter entirely. In order to get there that morning, I didn't go in through Botany Gate, as I usually did, but walked a bit further on and went in where the cars did. A narrow road wound between old buildings and more recent buildings with large shiny air ducts. It looked like the entrance of a factory, and if I listened carefully I could almost hear the clatter of production lines. Not that the Kelvin Building, which housed the Physics Department, was much more intriguing from the outside than the Mathematics Department building, but when I went in and looked for the staircase that would take me up to the third floor and the room I wanted, I caught glimpses of strange machinery and electrical wires and metal pipes through a few open doors. I went down a couple of corridors very similar to those of my department, and through a massive door, and found a broad wooden staircase, which for the first time seemed to be telling me the stories of all those who had gone up and down them over the decades or centuries. Even the students seemed different. Everyone you came across in the corridors of the Mathematics Department seemed grim and sad: people who would put you to sleep before they finished a sentence. Here, though, the two or three students I passed looked quite lively. They had bright shirts and crazy hairstyles and the way their bodies tilted forward made you think they were on their way to do something exciting. To do something. There they were, the magic words. The pipes, the machinery, the age-old wood: everything suggested a world where you didn't rack your brains for nothing, but where you did something, you produced, you somehow entered the world fully.

Room 12 on the third floor was a rather dark room full of upholstered armchairs similar to those in my department. Dr Marker turned out to be an attractive woman of no more than fifty with fluffy dark hair, covered in necklaces and rings and bracelets. She was looking through some papers in a disorganized kind of way, and when I approached and told her who I was and that Dr Jones had sent me, she didn't seem to understand at first. She stared at me without saying anything, as if I were transparent and she was looking through me at something behind my back.

"I'm sorry?"

"My name's Jacopo Ferri. Dr Jones from the Department of Mathematics sent me."

"Oh yes! All right, take a seat," she said simply, then went back to searching among her papers. About ten minutes later, when the room seemed to have filled, she finally gathered the papers together, looked around, picked up a pair of eye-catching red glasses, put them on and looked at the class, waiting for everyone to quieten down.

"Good morning," she said.

The class replied more or less in unison.

"So, how were the exercises?"

A murmur and some laughter went through the class.

"All right, we'll see about that later."

She paused and took a long look around, first at the last rows, then slowly all the way to the front rows. When she got to me—not sure where to go, I'd sat down right in front—she stopped. She stared at me for a moment or two and I started to feel a bit embarrassed.

"And who are you?"

I wondered if there had been some hitch, and it took me a moment to reply. "My name's Jacopo. Dr Jones sent me," I said in a low voice, leaning forward slightly.

"What? Speak up, boy."

I felt everyone's eyes on me, and for a moment I would have liked to curse and run out. "My name's Jacopo Ferri. Dr Jones sent me here."

After staring at me for another moment or two, Dr Marker's face seemed all at once to open wide. "But of course, Dr Jones... our doubt-ridden mathematician. Ladies and gentlemen," she said, addressing the rest of the class, "our friend here is a student from the Mathematics Department who seems a little confused in his ideas. My friend Jones asked me if he could follow our course and see how it goes." I heard some chatter and a few more laughs behind me. "I told Dr Jones it might be a bit ambitious to start with a course on relativity, but it appears that our friend in the front row is quite brilliant, so we'll see."

What was she trying to do, make me look like a swot? It might have been better to stay in the silent sobriety of the Mathematics Department.

"But I need a volunteer to give him a hand and monitor him a bit."

Her gaze started to wander over the rows behind me, but apart from some more murmurs, nobody seemed to give any signs of life.

"Ladies and gentlemen, I can't believe it," Dr Marker opened her arms wide. "Haven't we progressed beyond that point? You're at university, or hadn't you noticed?"

More murmuring, but obviously no arms raised.

"All right, you, over there."

The noise of heads and bodies turning.

"Yes, you."

A few laughs.

"I can't remember your name."

"Trisha," came a weak, expressionless voice from the back of the class.

It seemed the right moment for me to turn as well. In the corner on the left, a tiny girl with a funny button nose was sitting sideways in her chair. She was wearing a broad woollen hat with a little brim and hadn't taken off her coat.

"Trisha. Will you give him a hand? Study together. If he has any difficulties you can guide him."

Trisha shrugged without saying anything.

"All right, then. Thank you, Trisha."

Trisha limited herself to nodding and forcing her mouth into a thin, vague smile, then started to scribble something in an exercise book. At last she raised her eyes to me. I tried to smile and wave a hand in greeting, but she replied with that same false smile and immediately looked back down at her exercise book. More laughter came from the class. Trisha turned towards someone and showed him her middle finger.

Outside the room, as the other students passed us, still laughing, I shook Trisha's hand awkwardly and again thanked her and asked her how she wanted to do this.

"I won't come to your place, and I don't study in the library."

"Oh. Then I'll come to yours. When's okay for you?"

Trisha shrugged, but in the end we managed to make some kind of an appointment.

She lived in a small flat with two other girls she hated, but the rent was quite low and the place was nicely furnished. When one of her flatmates saw me come in and disappear into Trisha's room, she ran to the third girl's door and told her something in a low voice, laughing.

"Forget them," Trisha said, once inside.

Even indoors, she still had that funny big woollen hat on with the narrow brim, and was wearing a number of layers, one over the other. She sat down at a little desk and told me to sit wherever I liked. Not that there were many places to sit, and in the end I settled for the floor. That's how it was, with my back resting against Trisha's bed and my feet pointing to the sides of her desk, that I at last entered the magical world of physics.

Every time I asked Trisha to explain something, she reacted with hints of ill-concealed irritation, but she was very clear in her explanations, and even though she always seemed to be making a great effort to summon up the necessary energy, she managed to make me understand what she wanted to in the end.

That first day, when I asked my fifth question, Trisha sighed and paused for a moment. "All right, let's do something," she said, turning towards a bookshelf over her desk. "Take this… and this… and while we're about it, this too." She handed me three thick tomes, one after the other. "Look at them, and if you like them we'll start studying together. Otherwise we'll never get through this."

"All right," I said, then sat there for a moment in a bit of a daze, not quite sure what to do.

"Now go," Trisha said, resuming her work without even looking at me. "We'll see each other in class."

In a week, sleeping at most four hours a night and spending as much time as possible in the attic with the headphones on in order not to hear any noise coming from the club, all the while continuing with my mathematics course, I went through the whole tangled history of modern physics, from Galileo and Newton, through Maxwell and his colleagues, to the Lorentz transformation and the special theory of relativity.

It was one of the most intense weeks of study in my life, and perhaps the one that more than any other would turn my life upside down. Some of the mathematical functions I encountered were hard to figure out, but as soon as I did so I was plunged into dark corners of the universe, surrounded by electromagnetic waves, heavenly bodies and tiny particles whirling around me like ballerinas until they made me dizzy. Those letters and numbers hid stories about the world, something I could observe, or at least try to imagine, and more than once, overwhelmed by a sudden ecstasy while music roared in the background, I found myself lying on my mattress, arms open wide, with the clear impression that the magnetic fields were vibrating inside me and all around me.

In class the following week, after reluctantly greeting me, Trisha was surprised to see me already giving her back the books and thanking her.

"Already done?" she said, unable to repress a clear hint of scepticism. "Are you sure?"

"Yes, I'm sure. Shall we see each other tomorrow at your place?"

She nodded in bewilderment, said, "All right," and continued scribbling in her exercise book.

The next day, she tried to set a few traps for me. She talked about this or that complex aspect of the Michelson-Morley experiment that I wouldn't have been able to grasp if I hadn't really studied them, and the fact that I followed everything in an apparently relaxed way must have really surprised her.

There were a number of small signs that showed her new-found consideration for me: the brief but spontaneous greeting when she saw me in class, the quick kiss she allowed me to give her when she opened the door of her flat, the simple gesture of clearing the corner of the bed so that I could sit comfortably. In other words, she manifested her respect for me by admitting my existence, which when you came down to it was already something of a coup.

One day, when we were in her flat, both working on one of the exercises set by Dr Marker, but separately—one of the few occasions when I was able to do without the satisfaction of explaining something to Trisha—in the next room one of her flatmates and a few of her friends were listening to disco music at full volume and shrieking incomprehensibly. After a while Trisha leapt to her feet and went next door, and I heard her say something.

"What?" one of the girls screamed.

Trisha spoke again at the same volume as before. The girl turned down the music and again asked Trisha what she wanted.

"Could you make it a bit softer, please?"

Even without seeing her, I could hear in her voice her efforts to remain calm. From the little I knew of her, I was sure she was looking down at the floor as she talked, or maybe throwing just brief glances at the other girl.

"Oh, of course, I'm sorry," the other girl said, laughing.

By the time Trisha came back, the girl had turned up the music again. The volume was definitely lower than before, but still fairly annoying. Trisha sat down again at the desk, put her elbows on it, took her face in her hands and for the first time since I had known her made a small confession.

"God, how I hate them."

I looked at her for a few seconds. From behind, with that big hat of hers and the colourful sweater, she looked like an extraterrestrial.

"If you like, we can go to my place."

"Yes, to play cards with your Muslim friend," she said pulling herself together and picking up the thread of the exercise with a sigh. One day, laughing, I had told her about Hamal and how, a few weeks earlier, I had tried to teach him how to play *scopa* (I'd also had to explain to her what *scopa* was). It had gone rather well until, just I was showing him a particular trick to liven up the game, he opened his eyes wide and asked me what time it was.

"Twenty past four."

Hamal had sighed as if somebody were dying and rushed into his room, came out with his doormat, turned it to face southeast, and started saying his prayers.

"Bloody hell, Hamal, we can't even finish a game of *scopa*!" I said in Italian to avoid a diplomatic crisis. It was the first time I saw a real attempt at a smile appear on Trisha's face.

"No, I have an attic room all to myself."

Trisha half turned. "An attic room? Where?"

"Above Leonard's Lodge, the bar where I work. It's small and there isn't any lighting or heating, but there's a good fireplace that gives off a decent amount of heat, and I have a few oil lamps."

"Why didn't you say so before?"

"You said you didn't want to come to my place."

For a moment Trisha looked at me reprovingly. Then she gathered her books and exercise books, put them in her bag, stood up and put on her coat.

"So, are we going or not?"

The fact that I was going up to the attic with someone— and that this someone was actually a woman—filled me with embarrassment, and when I got to Leonard's I hurried straight to the door at the back of the club.

"Hi. I'm going up," I said quickly.

Leonard smiled as he watched us rush past. Luckily, Trisha's reticence protected me from further embarrassment and, as we passed, Leonard and I simply nodded at each other.

It was the first time I had let anyone in there, and I was a bit nervous. All at once the attic seemed shabby and untidy, and colder than usual. I wished I had a bit more furniture, even if only another couple of chairs, anything to give it a slightly more domestic appearance. I went straight to the fireplace and started heaping logs on it.

"It's cold now," I said, "but it gets hot quickly if we stay close to the fire. You'll see."

I struck a match and lit the two oil lamps. I left one on the table and put the other one down next to the bed. As the fire started to crackle, I moved the table closer to the fireplace.

"If you want, you can sit here. I'll sit on the bed—I've got used to it."

I tried to smile. I felt like a big idiot, worried and embarrassed about the place where he lived. And yet I couldn't do anything about it, and I couldn't find a way to shrug off my awkwardness. Trisha looked around her and for some reason approached the ceiling at the point where it came down almost to head level, near the skylight. She stared intensely at one of the beams and after a while passed her index finger over it.

"It's nothing much," I said.

"No, I like it."

There was a different note in her voice, a slightly warmer tone, which convinced me that she was sincere. She went to the fire, warmed her hands a little, and after a few minutes took off her coat and put her things on the table.

She started spending time in the attic. The next time we met by chance outside Botany Gate, we said hello with the usual tinge of embarrassment. Then, as I was leaving, Trisha called me back and told me that her flatmates were doing something or other that afternoon and asked me if she could come and study at my place.

So in the end, she would often arrive even without warning me, and surprisingly it never bothered me. After the first few times, Trisha started to look with a certain envy at the way I'd arranged myself on the bed. She started with little glances, before asking me one day if I would prefer to be at the table. Actually, I'd developed a taste for lying on the mattress, and had even found an arrangement of pillows and blankets that kept me in the ideal position.

"All right," I said.

That day, about a month later, an icy Arctic wind was inching its way through the skylight. We both obviously had little desire to study and were looking for any excuse to distract ourselves. As I was poking the fire, Trisha asked me what life was like in my village.

"I don't know, really," I said, throwing another log of wood on the fire. "Like life in the country: lots of crickets in the summer and lots of bare trees in the winter."

"It must be beautiful."

"Yes, I suppose it is."

Trisha looked at me for a moment or two as I crouched by the fire, watching the flames lick the new log and slowly start to turn it brown.

"And do you have a girlfriend?"

"I had one."

"Aren't you still together?"

"No."

"Why?"

I shrugged. "No particular reason."

I thought about it for a moment, then picked up the old steak fork Leonard had given me to use as a poker and stirred the logs. A cloud of reddish sparks rose and disappeared into the flue.

"To be honest, I don't even know if there was a particular reason to be together."

"When did you break up?"

"I don't remember. The last year of school, I think, just before the exams."

"And did you ever do it?"

I glanced at Trisha to make sure I'd understood correctly. I smiled. "Of course."

I gave another poke to the wood with the fork and watched the cloud of sparks rise again towards the flue.

"If you like, I could show you mine."

I turned. Her lips were twisted in an unprecedented smile that still seemed to bear a trace of embarrassment. I felt my heart beating slightly faster and a rush of saliva filling my mouth and throat. She stared at me for a few seconds, I think to make up her mind whether to really do what she'd said or to laugh and throw a pillow at me and tell me she was joking. Then she pulled herself up into a sitting position on the mattress, rolled down her colourful knee-length socks, unhooked her skirt and slipped it off, swaying slightly as she did so, then unhooked and slipped off a second one, which was purple. She put her thumbs in the elastic of her black tights and in a single movement, shifting her lower back, slipped them down to her calves and off her feet. There was something vaguely sad about her as she did this, as if she had lost a bet, and for a moment—before it was too late—I felt like telling her to stop. On top of the tights, where she had thrown them aside, I also caught a glimpse of her knickers. She put her knees together and placed her hands on them, then turned and looked at me with a shy air I would perhaps never again see in her. Part of her was definitely rebelling and wondering what the hell she was doing.

"Should I go on?"

I still couldn't quite believe it was really happening.

"Wait a minute." I pushed the lamp in the corner of the table closer to Trisha and turned it slightly in order to lengthen the wick and give more light, then turned the chair properly to face the mattress and compose myself, trying—to simplify matters—to muster all the detachment I could. "Go on."

Trisha sighed, rolled over on to her buttocks, keeping her heels together, and laid her back and elbows on the pillows. Then she opened first one leg and then the other. For a moment, as she was doing this, I wondered how I would behave once I had her parted legs right there in front of me. I liked the shamelessness with which Trisha had made me her offer, as well as the surgical detachment with which I had greeted it. But what next? In a moment we would be there, me sitting like an idiot on a rickety chair and she half dressed, with her legs parted, and we wouldn't know how to get out of it.

In the meantime, there it was. I was as rigid as a block of marble, unable to breathe, while a wave of calm heat invaded my stomach and chest.

"Jesus," I said.

It was nothing like that strange and at the same time disgusting thing that I'd seen in a few magazines, or in Marta's knickers, or that Francesca had reluctantly given me a closer view of two or three times as we embarked on that cold, clumsy operation we insisted on calling love. This was something new, something soft and round and alive, which seemed to look you straight in the eyes and smile at you. Something that had more to do with the universe than with the world. I leant forward a bit and moved the chair slightly closer. Trisha raised her eyebrows a little and smiled and seemed all at once to become convinced that she hadn't been wrong to do what she did. I continued to stare at her, moving my head slightly from side to side. I couldn't take my eyes off it. It was like a powerful magnet, the beginning and end of the world, and all at once I was overwhelmed for the first time by the one true drama of every man: how can an ordinary fragment of human flesh turn your life upside down like this?

I threw Trisha a glance: a mixture of innocence and desperation, I suppose. "Can I?"

She smiled and nodded. I let my knees drop straight from the chair onto the edge of the mattress and gradually, with my gaze held spellbound, I reached out my hand. I don't think I had ever touched anything softer. It was almost as if I could feel it breathing in my hand, and as I asked again for permission and Trisha laughed and said yes and we rubbed noses and mouths and I felt the urging of her lips and kissed her and smelt her and opened her and licked her and tried to sink inside her and Trisha let her head go back and sighed, I thought it was the most incredible thing that had ever happened to me and that I could never again do without her and that without her I would die and that I would be her slave for life and that I was scared and that I wanted to live and die inside her.

Trisha started unbuttoning the first of the sweaters she was wearing. I helped her, and when it was unbuttoned, she sat up again and slipped off the others too. For the first time since I had met her, she took off her thick woollen hat. She grabbed the little brim and simply pulled it back, freeing a great mass of wavy hair, dyed plum-red, which suddenly gave her an unexpectedly adult and sophisticated air. I smiled, and another wave of excitement took my breath away. At last we kissed: her mouth too was very soft, and her breasts and her hips and every inch of her skin. The whole of her was extraordinarily soft: the softest creature I had ever come across.

When, some time later, we lay naked under the blankets, side by side, half entwined, looking up at the beams of the ceiling, I asked how come.

"How come what?"

"How come you always keep your hair hidden in that hat?"

She paused for a moment, and with her hand, which had been around my neck, played with my cheek and the hair of my goatee.

"I don't know. I just don't think my hair is something that should concern other people."

6

THE WORLD BEGAN and ended at the door of the attic, and Trisha and I seemed like the only people on the whole planet. Everyone outside appeared ugly and stupid and useless; our skin was the border of our world. When we went out, we wrapped ourselves in all our layers, me with my sweaters and jacket and scarf, Trisha with her coat and skirts and woollen hat. It was like putting on a mask: we were no longer that frank, naked version of ourselves, we concealed ourselves beneath our clothes and our silences and our apparent solitude. We parted before going into the class and treated each other in public with the same awkward composure with which we had always treated each other. The thought that nobody knew about us, that nobody knew what we were made of, filled us with great excitement.

What I found overwhelming was the strange experience of discovering, moment by moment, another human being. I liked to stand aside and watch Trisha as she moved, as she studied or wrote or looked around her or walked in the street. She had a great, unconscious passion for details, and liked to feel them at her fingertips. On the coldest days, when the icy mist clung to the branches of the trees or the wrought iron lamp-posts on the streets of Glasgow, Trisha would bend down to get a closer look at the crystals, and after a few seconds reach out her index finger and touch them lightly. She did the same with the sequins or stitches of a dress, the button on a sofa, the surface of a sugar cube. It was the same gesture she had made that first day in the attic, with the sloping ceiling beam and its deep veins: she would look at something from close up, bending or leaning forward slightly if she needed to, and after a few seconds move the tip of her index finger over it. She couldn't stop herself and, ever since I had pointed it out to her, every time she discovered me watching her she burst out laughing and told me to go to hell. Trisha rarely laughed, but when she did, her laugh, short as it was, was unusually deep and infectious.

"I never imagined it would be like this. It's really incredible," I said one day on the telephone to Greg, sitting at the kitchen table in the hall of residence.

"All right," Greg said.

"Biagio found a girl too, apparently."

"Yes, I met her."

"Oh, what's she like?"

"Dubious."

The day we'd gone to the motorcycle trials, Biagio had fallen coming round the Savelli, the second bend in the downhill S which led to the Arrabbiata. By the time I arrived, Biagio was already sitting in the ambulance. He seemed fine, but was complaining of a lot of pain in his left hand. The paramedics didn't want to take off his glove on the spot, but preferred to take him straight to hospital. I turned and looked at Torcini, the man with the moustache who had invited us to Mugello. He looked at the ambulance driver and asked him where they were going to take us.

"The trauma unit," the other man replied.

Torcini turned to me. "Go with them. We'll join you later."

"What about his clothes?" I said, indicating Biagio.

"I'll bring them. Go."

So I also got in the ambulance, which—even though Biagio did not seem in a serious condition—tore round the bends with sirens blaring. Biagio was simply lying on the stretcher supporting one hand with the other and looking at the transparent tubes swaying at every bend.

"How are you feeling?" a dark-skinned young guy who was sitting with us asked him occasionally, and each time Biagio nodded in silence.

It was only ten minutes later, as the ambulance slowed down, presumably for the traffic lights, that he said, "What a stupid idiot!" and shook his head.

"Forget it," the young guy said. "We see all sorts when we're at Mugello." He laughed and tapped Biagio's leg, then started telling stories about people who'd skidded at two hundred an hour and exposed fractures and broken helmets. The one effect of this was to make me feel like vomiting.

"And now what do we do?" Biagio asked me just before we arrived.

"I don't know. I think we should call home."

He nodded and looked again at those tubes dancing. "My mum will kill me."

When we got to the hospital they rushed him into a long corridor full of people moaning and left me in a large waiting-room with a floor of shiny reddish tiles, like a huge garage. In a corner of the room, behind a pane of glass, a short nurse with thick hands gave abrupt answers to questions from people who came in. I sat down for a few minutes, unsure of what to do. Next to me, an elderly man was turning an old felt hat round and round in his gnarled and cracked hands, which seemed to belong more to San Filippo than a big city. In the end I made up my mind, dug some coins out of my pocket and went to one of the public phones in a corner of the room. To be on the safe side, I put in a thousand lire's worth of coins. It was just after one o'clock.

"Hello?"

"Hi, it's me."

"Where are you?"

"Listen, Dad, we got in a bit of mess."

"A bit of a mess?"

"Yes, I think so. It's just that this morning Biagio went to the motorcycle trials and he slipped and hurt his hand."

"But where are you?"

"In Florence."

"Florence?"

"Yes, Florence. The trials were in Mugello."

"Mugello?… How did you get to Mugello?"

"On Martino's Vespa."

Dad paused for a moment, as if putting the whole thing together. "I'm sorry, where are you now?"

"At the hospital."

"Which hospital?"

"They said something about a trauma unit."

"Oh, yes, the trauma unit at the Careggi. And how's Biagio?"

"He hurt his hand quite a bit. They brought him here in the ambulance and he went inside and I haven't heard anything since."

"And how are you? Did you hurt yourself too?"

"Oh no, only Biagio fell."

"Mmm. But whereabouts in Mugello? The race track?"

"Yes."

Dad paused again. "All right, I'll see what I can do. You wait there. Someone'll come."

"Dad, I'm sorry."

"Yes. Stay there."

I sat down again on one of the plastic chairs in the waiting room, and after a while Torcini showed up with his assistant.

"How is he?"

"There's no news yet."

Torcini didn't seem angry, but all the same, I felt I had to say I was sorry. He smiled and passed a hand through my hair, as if I were a child. "Don't worry, it happens. The important thing is that he hasn't injured himself badly."

"What about the Vespa?" I said after a while.

"It's there, in the pit. We'll find a way to get it back to you, don't worry."

After a couple of hours, just before Biagio came out, my father showed up. Part of me would have liked him to act like any other parent, to slap me or something like that, but he came up to me as if everything was fine and asked me if there was any news.

"No," I replied.

"Hello," Torcini said, approaching and holding out his hand. "Lucio Torcini."

Dad shook his hand and introduced himself.

"This is the gentleman who let Biagio ride in the trials," I said.

Dad nodded, and for a moment I thought Torcini would

be the one he got angry with. But all he said was, "Is it true he hurt himself?"

"I don't know. He was holding his hand."

"Did you see him fall?"

"No, I was with your son on the other side of the circuit, just above the finishing line. Apparently he slipped coming out of the Savelli. Do you know Mugello?"

Dad shook his head slightly. "Not really."

"It's a downhill bend. But I don't know exactly what happened."

Dad nodded, then looked at the glass door that led to the wards. After a few moments we all sat down.

"You could have told me," Dad said after a while, glancing at me. "I would have taken you."

For a moment I thought of telling him that we had wanted to go by ourselves, that it was a kind of escape, that it was difficult to explain but that journey at dawn on the Vespa with Biagio, in search of a place we didn't know and that might have been on another continent, had perhaps been one of the most beautiful moments of my life. But then I changed my mind, especially because my dad might have said something like: "Yes, I understand."

"I know, Dad. I'm sorry."

When Biagio reappeared through the big sliding door of opaque glass, the colourful leathers had been lowered to his waist, with the stiff sleeves floating at his sides like wings, and on his left forearm was a big plaster cast. With him was a doctor.

"Are you the father?"

"No," Dad replied. "They couldn't come. But I'm a doctor."

"Ah." The hospital doctor held out his hand. "Nannucci."

"Ferri."

"Well, it's nothing too serious. A fracture between the metacarpal and first phalanx of the little finger. It's likely he'll lose some functionality, but that's quite common in motorcyclists. He'll feel right at home." The doctor smiled and gave Biagio a clip on the ear. "Maybe come back in about a month, and we'll take off the plaster and see how you are." Then the doctor looked behind us. "And you are?"

"I'm the head of the team," Torcini replied behind us.

"Ah, hello. No more races, please, until we see how his hand is."

"Of course," Torcini said, cutting him short.

I saw Biagio bow his head and for a moment I felt annoyingly embarrassed for him.

Outside, in the car park, Biagio took off the leathers and put on the jeans with which he had arrived in the morning at Mugello. I placed the jacket over his shoulders and took his shirt and sweater.

"So long, then," Torcini said and held out his hand. "Now let's see how to get you back your Vespa."

Biagio nodded and quickly shook his hand. It could have been taken for impoliteness, but I knew it was only shame, and that he didn't want to do anything but leave and go back to his life and forget this business, and probably never again sit on a motorbike.

Torcini again passed his fingers through my hair, then gave me a pat on the head. "Hey, it's okay."

I simply shook his hand and thanked him.

We honestly thought it was all over at that point. The whole village never missed an opportunity to pull Biagio's leg, Betta gave him a good few slaps and grounded him for a week, and we were convinced it would simply remain a great story to tell in the years to come. The fact that I had been present also filled everyone with a great deal of envy, and I gradually learnt, in telling the tale, how to time the pauses in order to get the most laughs.

Then, one evening a couple of weeks later, the phone rang and my mum came running into my room and told me that Greg was asking for me. That urgency on my mum's part every time it was Greg always made me uncomfortable.

"Hi," I said into the receiver in the hall.

"Hi. Let's meet in ten minutes outside Biagio's house, on the road."

"Why?"

"Just come." And he hung up.

"Mum, I'm going out for a moment."

Mum came to the door of the kitchen. "Going out? Where?"

"To Greg's for a bit. He says he wants to show me something."

"All right, then."

I left the house and went down towards the end of the village as far as the old houses. I then climbed along the ridge, and even before I got there I saw Greg in front of me, clambering over the low wall and hiding on the other side of the road.

"Hey!"

Greg turned, put a finger to his mouth and gestured to me to be quiet, then waved at me to join him behind the wall.

"Look," he whispered when I reached him.

He was crouching behind the wall and pointing to the other side of the road. It was the window of Biagio's kitchen. Inside, we could see Biagio sitting in silence playing with a napkin, his parents and, with his back to the window, a man in a raincoat.

"The man in the raincoat," Greg whispered again.

"Torcini."

"Is that his name?"

"Yes," I whispered. "What's he doing here?"

"How should I know?"

Then I thought about it for a moment. "How did you find out he was here?"

"I saw him by chance."

Inside, Torcini seemed to be speaking and Biagio's mum and dad were listening with great attention. Biagio kept twisting the paper napkin. His dad said something, and so did his mum; then they listened some more. After a while they looked at each other, then turned to Biagio, who seemed to nod, even though he was still looking at the napkin. At this point Biagio's dad stood up and disappeared from the window. After a few seconds he reappeared with a bottle of wine in his hand, poured some for everybody, laughing all the while, and proposed a toast. Biagio's brother Graziano also appeared: he looked unamused, as he always did, but even he was drawn in. About ten minutes later, Torcini came out of the house and shook hands with Biagio's parents and Biagio and went away smiling and saying, "All sorted then." In order not to be seen, Greg and I slid down until we were sitting on the ground, our backs against the wall.

"What was that all about?"

"No idea."

Nobody ever completely managed to explain the whys and wherefores, but Torcini had gone back to San Filippo to offer to take Biagio with him to Rome. He told his parents that he would put him up in his apartment and enter him for a school in the city and in the meantime try and get him some races.

197

Nothing was certain, he said, but the boy might just have what it took and it would be a pity to see it wasted like that.

So the doctor had been a prophet, and that hooked finger on his left hand did indeed become the first mark of Biagio as a motorcycle racer. He ran in a few minor championships, Italian and European, 125cc first, then 250cc, and just two years later Torcini decided to let him make the leap and entered him for the World Championship Grand Prix. Biagio was inconsistent. He fell often, he often screwed up a race completely, but he still managed to attract quite a bit of attention and was much loved by the sponsors. The experts said that it was because of how he rode: yes, it was true that he made lots of mistakes and sometimes seemed to be totally out of it, but when he got it right he was a sensation. He would throw himself into the bends and fast lanes like a young boy on a 125cc, his rear wheel raised every time he pulled hard on the brakes, and you wondered how a human being could get so close to the ground without falling. "Luckily, he often makes mistakes," a French journalist wrote once, "because otherwise he'd have to race alone."

One day, years later, when I was a guest in the pit at a Grand Prix at Laguna Seca, in the United States, I asked Lucio why on earth he had taken such an interest in Biagio, to the extent of taking him with him to Rome.

"You didn't seem very enthusiastic at Mugello," I said, as both of us leant on the low wall, waiting for the bikes to be ready.

"No. In fact he hadn't impressed me much." Lucio moved his mouth forward and made a strange noise. "I don't know. Maybe it was the accident. Or something in his eyes. I liked him, and every time I thought about him, for some reason

I felt kind of bad. A few evenings after the trials I found in the camera the footage that Manuel, one of the boys who worked for the team, had shot at Mugello. When I realized it was footage of Biagio, I felt a strange mixture of affection and pity and decided to take a look at it. To be honest, I found my opinion hadn't changed much."

"But then you went to see him and suggested he come with you."

"Yes." For a moment Lucio played with a little stone from the wall. "Look, I don't know if I can explain this properly. It was a momentary thing. I got up to go into the kitchen and out of the corner of my eye saw something that aroused my curiosity. If I'd got up two seconds earlier, I'm convinced we wouldn't be here. Manuel had filmed the exit from the Correntaio, before the Biondetti, the S-bend that leads to the last bend in the circuit. I stopped, went back and rewound the tape for a few seconds. You could see Biagio coming out from the Correntaio, not very well, but then he went into the Biondetti like a cannon and was out in a flash. I remember I went back one more time, to be sure it wasn't my other rider."

He broke off.

"What of it?"

"Only a real rider could get through the Biondetti that way. At Mugello, if you ride a bit and have a modicum of talent, sooner or later you learn how to take the bends. I've seen riders as thick as stones learn how to come out of the Savelli and climb the Arrabbiata the right way, just by doing it over and over. The Biondetti, though, is another matter. If you take it correctly, you can cut two or three seconds off your time. So I wound back the whole tape and looked at it more closely. It was true, Biagio was making lots of mistakes, but now they seemed more like mistakes of inexperience, the mistakes of somebody who hadn't raced much, if at all, and it struck me they could gradually be corrected. I don't know why, but in a moment that sense of unease and pity had vanished, and I decided I wanted to give him a go."

The real baptism was in Jerez in '92. It was the year of the Italians: Cadalora dominated from beginning to end on the Honda as he had the previous year, and Reggiani and Chili had taken most of the other victories, both on Aprilias. The Spanish Grand Prix was the fourth race of the season and Biagio, with a fall in the first race, eighth place in the second, and the third abandoned because of a problem with the clutch, had only gained a handful of points. At Jerez he started out fairly well, and by the third lap was fifth, immediately behind Cardus, who was struggling a bit and seemed to slow him down. Behind him, hot on his heels, Alberto Puig. At the sixth lap, at the entrance to the bend going into the home stretch, Puig did a nasty thing: he got on the inside of Biagio and hit him. In order not to fall, Biagio went straight into the sand. I saw him get off his bike, turn it with the help of the commissaires and set off again, making angry movements with his head. It was madness. By the time he got back on the track, he was in thirteenth place. He bent low behind the windshield, braked hard ten metres after anyone else, his rear wheel always a centimetre or two off the ground, and put on speed at least two seconds early. On the bends, there was barely a crack between his body and the ground. He was exploiting every available millimetre of asphalt, and at each bend you prayed he wouldn't end up on the ground.

Lap by lap, position by position, slipping into every gap, he came up again behind Puig, who was fourth behind Reggiani and Cadalora and someone else I can't remember. He tailed him for a couple of laps, then on the third lap, at the start of the bend after the home straight, got on the inside, touched Puig without making him fall, overtook him, and as he was tackling the second tight bend on the right, already tilting, he raised his left hand and gave him the finger. He then got into third place—it may have been Bradl he overtook—and up until one lap before the finish, battled it out with Cadalora for second place. At that point he must have realized he had given more than enough for one day.

The following day, in the *Gazzetta*, under the photo of the three Italians on the podium, Candido Cannavò began his piece like this: "Call it, if you like, emotion." I still have the article, framed.

In my opinion, what grabbed the attention of the sponsors—despite his results, which were patchy to say the least—was partly the way he'd grown his dark hair so that it always covered one of his blue eyes. And also those absurd interviews of his. You kept wondering if he'd understood the question or was actually answering something else, and yet you couldn't help feeling that there was something magnetic about that vague air and those half laughs, and you ended up thinking that maybe his answers hid more subtle meanings.

The following year the season began in Australia, at Eastern Creek. The evening before the Grand Prix, the team threw an opening party in the pits, inviting the sponsors and a couple of managers from Honda, who provided the engines. Biagio always told me that these public relations shindigs were probably the things he found hardest to bear. To tell the truth, Lucio didn't like them much either, but couldn't do without them. After half an hour Biagio went to the lorries parked behind the pit to smoke what I had always imagined to be a cigarette. A few minutes later, one of the hostesses hired for those three days in Australia came along. She was very tall, with fluffy brown hair and fine, slender features that made her look like someone in a painting. She was wearing a miniskirt and a shirt with the colours of the team.

"Oh, hi," she said, hiding something behind her back as soon as she realized she wasn't alone.

"It's pointless your hiding it," Biagio said, sitting on the metal steps of one of the lorries. He raised the joint and held it vertically between his index finger and middle finger. The girl laughed, then skipped towards him.

"Then I'll keep you company," she said with a smile, snapping her fingers excitedly and taking the joint from him. She sat down and let the smoke out of her mouth, then held out her hand. "Kate," she said.

"Biagio," he replied, holding out his.

"I know who you are."

Biagio laughed. "Good for you."

Lucio's assistant Laura found them an hour later, inside the lorry. He was half lying on a camp bed, red-eyed, and she was standing up telling him something, tears of laughter streaming down her face. For a moment, Laura tried to figure out what they were laughing about, but couldn't, so she told Biagio that he had to go back to the pit, and that they were all looking for him because they wanted to propose a toast.

Biagio let his head fall back. "Jesus," he said. Then he got up with difficulty and gently took Kate by the elbow. "Come," he whispered, "give me a hand."

The next day, before the Grand Prix, Biagio looked for Laura and asked her to find something for Kate to do for the rest of the championship.

"What do you mean 'something', Biagio? Everything's planned in advance. The hostesses are all provided by the various circuits."

"Anything, Laura. My nurse: make her my nurse. I'll pay. You just have to find an excuse for her to go with us. She's a good girl."

Laura pursed her lips. "I'll see what I can think up," she said.

So Kate was offered a job for the whole season as part of the hospitality for the team. She wasn't really very keen on work and the few times she was given any responsibility she made a complete mess of it. Biagio, though, seemed calmer, and even raced more consistently at first. "I don't know what I'd do without her," he said to me not long after meeting her.

To tell the truth—I'm not sure why, just something in the way he talked about her—I got the idea that the relationship between Kate and Biagio was more one of friendship than passion. At first, when I told him about Trisha and he told me about Kate, I had the vague feeling that we were united by very similar emotions. But then gradually I told myself that maybe it wasn't like that at all, and that Biagio didn't feel that sense of vertigo I felt every time I found myself alone with Trisha and her skin.

The first time I met Kate, in London, the year Biagio made his debut in the 500cc, I couldn't help thinking she was the devil incarnate. At first glance, everything would have suggested the opposite: her smile, her blue eyes, that sprinkling of freckles over her nose, her laugh. Even her amusing inability to keep still for more than ten seconds.

And yet, without any apparent reason, I told myself that the devil, if ever he had to disguise himself as a woman, would have donned her clothes.

"What about you?" I finally asked Greg, as I sat at the pale blue table in the hall of residence.

"What about me?"

"Women."

Greg paused for a moment, as if wondering what to reply. "Two days ago I was in Tokyo, being completely oiled and massaged and penetrated by three Japanese men as fat as sumo wrestlers."

The image of Greg's tiny body, naked and oiled, surrounded by three sumo wrestlers, in a completely white room—not quite sure why I thought the room had to be white—made me feel dizzy for a moment.

"I'm exploring the depths of perdition, Skinny," Greg went on. "I don't think Don Gianni would be very proud of me."

If anyone else, at any other time, had mentioned a scene like that, I think I would have fallen out of my chair. Instead of which it didn't strike me as odd at all. All I felt for a few seconds was the sensation of unknown pieces grinding into place.

"Well, I did tell you."

"What?" asked Greg.

"That with your character you'd get it up the arse sooner or later."

Greg—maybe for the second time in his life, and one of the very few—exploded with laughter over the phone.

THREE

Doubt

1

"TO HELL WITH YOU AND YOUR CULT OF THE DEAD. I already did all I could for Biagio. Now it's up to you."

There it was: that damned sentence, those simple words which, like an earthquake, would gradually bring down everything that up until that moment I believed I'd built with my own hands.

I'd already been in San Filippo for a month, which was something that hadn't happened in a while. Over the past few days I'd spent most of my time planting nasturtiums. Nasturtiums don't require too much attention and can take root in any kind of soil. They should be watered often and, when they bud, helped from time to time with a high-nitrogen fertilizer. When they flower, though, it's best to use a fertilizer with more potassium. They require sun, but not too much: the ideal would be in the shelter of a tree that isn't too thick. In the shade they produce a lot of leaves, but not many flowers. Excessive sunlight, on the other hand, strips them at the base and makes them wilt. That was why my mum had chosen to plant a fine patch of them to the right of the front door of our house, in that flower bed she'd amused herself adapting from part of the lawn, together with Enzo. She had designed several of those flowerbeds, surrounding them with chipped grey stones and old bricks. In one—at the back, beyond the kitchen—she'd planted herbs, in another, rambling roses. When Enzo had died a couple of years earlier, struck down one morning in September by a heart attack, Mum had decided, in agreement with Dad, not to hire anybody else and that they would tend to the garden themselves. Dad would take care of cutting the lawn and the heavier work, and Mum would deal with the flowers. For that year, in the two or three free beds, Mum had decided to concentrate on small, colourful flowers: nasturtiums, petunias and pansies. She had planted the nasturtiums at the end of February in small black pots, to protect them while the nights were still cold. She'd left them in Enzo's old shed at the bottom of the garden and took them out every morning to put them in the sun. She should have planted them in April in the flower bed to the right of the front door, but then she'd come down with that strange illness, and when I arrived she had asked me if I could see to it.

It had begun as a simple little cough, apparently. Dad had first given Mum syrup, then antibiotics, but it had persisted and he'd started to get worried. He'd taken her to get various tests, but neither he with his specialization in geriatrics nor the professor at the Fatebenefratelli hospital in Rome had been able to figure out what exactly was wrong with her. The professor had even asked Mum if she had been in a tropical country. Both Dad and Mum had thought this a somewhat curious question, and for a moment the image of them dressed in little straw skirts with garlands round their necks must have silently amused them.

"No," they'd replied.

For me, it had been a good excuse to go back home for a while. Over the years, as I had been pursuing my academic ambitions around the world, the familiarity with which I'd learnt to treat the laws that govern the universe had grown in proportion to my irritation with my native village. Suddenly, though, the idea of that calm, tranquil life seemed to me, perhaps for the first time, like a secure roof beneath which to take shelter. So I'd moved back into the room I'd had when I was a boy, left more or less as it had been the day I'd left for Glasgow sixteen years earlier, and I had assumed the role of the good Italian son I'd probably never been. In the morning I would prepare a cup of tea and two rusks for Mum, give the kitchen a bit of a clean if it needed it, go shopping at the Coop and chat to the cashier and the old ladies who would ask me with a gleam in their eyes about America, making comments about it as if they knew it. Somehow we always ended up agreeing that, when you came down to it, all the world is a village. I took care to inform everyone about my mother's state of health and I would listen to their *God bless her*s. I went to mass on Sunday and found myself reciting the *Mea culpa* and the *Pater Noster* with a vigour of which I'd never have thought myself capable. Dad and I always occupied the end of the third row on the left, and there too the ladies were always very pleased to see me. On the way out, full of Sunday fervour, they usually lingered over the times when I was small and ran around the village. I didn't remember running around the village all that much when I was small. They smiled at me, then placed a hand on Dad's arm: "I've known this boy since he was born," they'd whisper, before winking at me and walking away with their nice flowered dresses and their handbags over their forearms and their bandy legs. On the second Sunday, Don Roberto, the parish priest who'd replaced Don Gianni four years earlier, came up to me and asked me why it had taken me so long to put in an appearance in church.

"I live abroad, Father."

"Yes, I know. But you come back from time to time."

"Maybe I was a bit confused."

"Well," Don Roberto concluded, taking my hands and squeezing them, "the Lord is always here, waiting for us."

After dinner I would watch TV in the living room with Mum and Dad, all three of us sitting comfortably on the old yellow velvet sofa, watching a variety show or an episode of a detective series. When there was a pause on TV and Mum wasn't coughing, I could hear the muted ticking of the big grandfather clock that Dad loved to rewind every night. I felt, quite pleasantly in the main, as if I were in one of those absurd minimalist films from northern Europe that my girlfriend Amanda liked so much—and I had always hated absurd minimalist films from northern Europe.

When it came to New York, though, against all my wishes and all my predictions, I had fallen in love with it from the first moment. In my first weeks at Princeton for my post-doc, whenever anyone started talking about the nearby metropolis and the weekend they had just spent there or were about to spend there, I started to feel a slight but sharp sense of irritation, which I had to make an effort not to let develop into anger. To hell with New York, with its skyscrapers and its brokers and its movies and its strolls in Central Park and its clubs and its money and all those artists and the shops-you-can't-find-anywhere-else and its stars who walk the streets as if it were quite normal and its "guess who I saw today?"

and its Villages and SoHos and TriBeCas and other ultra-cool acronyms and that whole mass of indigestible clichés.

Then one day I made up my mind. One Saturday, when my friends had decided to take advantage of the last sunny day and go to a beach resort in New Jersey, it struck me that the time had come—though mainly because the thought of spending even five minutes on a beach was a lot worse than a whole day wallowing in a big city with all its stereotypes. Nor was I crazy about being alone on campus that day. Yes, I suppose my enthusiasm for the warmth of that unexpectedly sunny autumn day had even overcome part of my increasing cynicism. So I would finally go to the Big Apple, I would come out of the station, I would have a nice day walking around the city and I would once and for all amass all the reasons I had to hate it.

It didn't go quite like that, although it would take me quite some time to admit it. When we hooked up again in the evening, the others—sun-reddened and unbearably excited about their day by the sea—asked me where I'd been and what I'd done. When I told them I'd taken a trip to New York they cried, "At last! So, did you see it?"

"Yes, I saw it."

"Well?"

"I don't know if I was all that convinced," I said with a shrug. The others shook their heads and went off to the showers, giggling and hitting each other with their towels like little boys.

And yet, as soon as I could, I went back to the station in Princeton and took that damned train again for Penn Station. I didn't get out immediately: every time, like a greedy little boy faced with a huge cream cake covered in coloured sugar,

211

I couldn't stop myself taking the blue line, going all the way up to Lexington and 51st Street, then catching the green line farther north and getting off at the next stop. As an intolerable chorus of voices rebelled inside me, muttering that all this was childish and stupid and that I had spent the best years of my life trying to free myself of certain kinds of shallowness and elevate myself to more noble and refined thoughts, that dazzle of height and glass opened up above me and I stood motionless on the sidewalk, with my head thrown back and my eyes on the sky. The skyscrapers seemed to sway as the clouds moved in the wind, and a flurry of electric shocks made me lose my senses for a moment. When I then walked for hours on end around every corner of Manhattan, always trying to discover new ones and occasionally venturing into quite dubious neighbourhoods, my legs seemed to move by themselves, driven by that first electrical charge at the intersection of Lexington Avenue and 59th Street.

However hard I tried to silence all those voices barking inside me, I couldn't ignore the fact that the idea of living in Manhattan had become my greatest obsession. The opportunity was offered to me by my lack of consistency. I was on the phone, making my usual weekly call home, talking to Dad. Usually I talked to Mum: she would ask me how things were, she would pretend to listen, she would monotonously repeat out loud to Dad what I was saying, and after barely two or three minutes would ask me if I needed anything. I would say no thanks, she would tell me to look after myself, I would say of course, we would say goodbye and each go back to our own business. That day, however, Mum was out shopping: a pipe had burst in the house, which had annoyingly delayed her trip to the Coop by two hours, upsetting her whole afternoon schedule and probably also dinner. So I found myself talking to Dad, who, if nothing else, asked me different questions than usual. At first, when I was studying the laws of physics, which he was in a position to understand because of his medical training, he would actually ask me about my studies, but that hadn't lasted long—mainly, to tell the truth, because I didn't really feel like explaining anything. That day, he was interested in knowing how I found America, if it was really the way you saw it on TV and in films.

"Yes, I suppose it is," I replied.

Then came the glorious question: "What about New York?"

Yes, what about New York? God, there were so many things I could tell him about New York, so many things with which to hit a virgin imagination: all the smells and the tastes and the tiny details I loved to immerse myself in whenever I had half a day free.

"It's interesting."

"Oh. Is that all?"

"I don't know if I was all that impressed by it."

"It looks great in the photographs. All those skyscrapers…"

"I don't know… I'd like to live there for a while, to see what everyday life is like. You know, until you live in a place…"

"Of course."

"Maybe find an apartment, even a small one."

"Would you like that?"

"Oh God, *like* is a big word. Just to see how it is."

Dad paused for a moment. "Why don't you do it, then?"

"Where would I get the money?"

Dad paused again. "Listen, Jacopo, there's something I've been meaning to tell you for quite some time. I know you've made a big effort never to ask us for anything, and that does you credit, but with all your scholarships you really haven't cost us much at all. I'm not saying I'm rich, but when you're a doctor, even a country doctor, you manage to put a few lire aside, and I'd always thought of giving you some of that money for your studies or some other activity of yours... I don't know. I don't want to make you uncomfortable, but if you needed money for rent, we could see..."

It was the typical moment when a man is called on to fight the great battle of consistency. No more than two evenings earlier, talking in the campus cafeteria, a Korean friend named Kim and I had boasted to each other that we had never asked anything of anybody: indeed, we claimed that it was almost our mission in life. In fact, I had stopped to consider more than once that there were few sensations that filled me with the same reassuring warmth as my beloved and hard-earned independence.

"Well, there *is* a great two-room apartment with a kitchenette and a wooden floor that would be just right for me."

After a while, in my wanderings around the city, I'd started going into the various real estate agencies I came across to ask if they had anything small and nice to show me. I knew I couldn't afford it, and yet entering those patches of the world for a moment and imagining sitting there with a book in my hand, or working at my desk, or making myself a coffee in the kitchenette, always gave me a thrill, which unfortunately soon subsided in a wave of sadness. Every day I spent away from that city, every morning I didn't wake up in one of its bedrooms and every lunch I wasn't served in one of its restaurants seemed like irreparable thefts of my precious and all too brief existence.

The previous Saturday, walking down 34th Street on my way back to the station, I decided on impulse, as I was crossing Broadway, to follow it uptown. I stopped for a few minutes to take another look at the hustle and bustle of Times Square. Bumping into a couple of passers-by, I walked between the Midtown skyscrapers with my head tilted back and my mouth half open. I crossed Columbus Circle, almost getting knocked down by the traffic, and continued farther north. I turned my nose up at the ugliness of Lincoln Center and, seeing a sign for the New York City Ballet, felt the desire to go and see a good show for once. Then, at that long intersection at 72nd Street, where Broadway crosses Amsterdam Avenue, I suddenly felt a wave of warmth rise from my stomach and spread through my back and neck. It might have been the slightly British appearance of the area, a bit reminiscent, if not exactly of the centre of Glasgow, then maybe of part of the Strand in London, but the overwhelming excitement of New York gave way to something calmer and more reassuring. I noticed the sign of a small real estate agency and without thinking twice went in.

A slim young man with a sharp demeanour named Josh greeted me as if I were an old friend and told me about a little place nearby that would be perfect for me: if I wanted, we could actually go and see it immediately. As we walked, after asking me if I had a girlfriend, Josh told me with a tiresomely knowing air that I was doing the right thing moving to New York—a city full, as he put it, of available girls. To quote his exact words: "You're doing the right thing, bro—there's a truckload of chicks within easy reach." He winked as he said this and made a sucking noise with his mouth. A couple of blocks further uptown, we turned into a quiet side street lined by low three-storey houses with steps up to their front doors. On the second floor of every building were wonder-fully large semicircular windows. The apartment he wanted to show me was in fact on the second floor, and the larger part of the two rooms that composed it faced this window. At the far end of the room there was a tiny kitchenette and beyond it a small bedroom with a huge glass door. On the left, opposite the kitchenette, was a small bathroom so small that anyone overweight would have found it hard to turn round in it. The floor was of light-coloured wood, and I hadn't felt the same irresistible attraction to a place since the days of my beloved attic. I could already see the couch, probably brightly coloured, on which I would spend my afternoons reading, the desk in the corner on which I would study and work, the bed and the bedside table I could fit into the little room beyond the glass door.

As we were walking down the narrow brown-carpeted stairs a few minutes later, a tiny, shrivelled lady came out of the door on the ground floor. She locked the door, then turned and asked who we were.

"I'm Josh, madam, from the agency. I've been showing this young man the apartment."

The lady squinted at me. Her blueish hair surrounded a face that was a spider's web of lines swamped in thick foundation.

"And who might you be?" she asked.

"I'm not anybody, madam, I've just come to see the apartment."

"Oh. And what kind of work do you do?"

I instinctively thought of simplifying things and aiming a bit high. "I teach physics at Princeton."

The lady's face immediately lit up. "A professor!" she cried.

"And so young! How wonderful. Come in, both of you, let's have some tea."

And then when we were in her living room on the ground floor, improbably covered in brocades, and it emerged that I was actually Italian, the floodgates opened and Mrs Schmidt started reminiscing about jaunts on the Amalfi Coast and honeymoons and meals by the sea and gondolas and serenades. It was like being in a Fifties film.

Anyway, Mrs Schmidt seemed to like me a lot and by the time we had finished tea, which of course I couldn't refuse, she had reduced the price of the apartment considerably. But as she was amusing us with her stories and serving tea and walking back and forth on her stiff legs, I started to feel a touch of remorse at the fact that I didn't really have a cent to spend on an apartment on the Upper West Side, and when the woman started talking money, I wavered and tried to play it safe.

"Look, madam, I don't know, I wouldn't like to—"

"It's too much, isn't it? What do you think, Josh, is it a bit too much?"

Clearly confused by this unpredictable turn of events, Josh opened his eyes slightly and shrugged.

"Yes, it *is* too much," Mrs Schmidt went on. "Let's say a thousand five hundred."

"Madam, you're very kind, but really…"

"A thousand two hundred."

"Look, madam, I don't know what to say, I think there's been a—"

The lady looked at Josh and smiled. "These Italian professors drive a hard bargain. All right, let's say a thousand and long live science."

I looked at Josh for a moment, as if he knew about my lie and I was hoping he'd back me up.

"But I'm not sure I—"

"Including charges."

"All right, madam, what can I say? I think it's perfect."

At the door, a few minutes later, I thanked her and told her I would be in touch as soon as possible.

"In the meantime I'll take it off the market," Mrs Schmidt said, taking my hands in hers. Then she drew me to her and kissed me on both cheeks—"as you Italians do," she said, very pleased with herself—before saying goodbye and watching us go.

The frustration I felt on the train back to Princeton was in direct proportion to my satisfaction, barely five days later, in going back to Mrs Schmidt and telling her that I was taking the apartment. Seeing that I was there, and that Mrs Schmidt seemed to like me so much, I even asked her if it wasn't worth skipping the agency and doing everything between ourselves.

"I think that's an excellent idea," she said under her breath, laughing and taking me by the arm. "You Italians are so clever!"

I loved everything about New York. I loved the icy wind in winter, the plumes of steam rising from the manholes, the black-clad policemen, the red and white fire engines, the can-laden carts of the homeless, the yellow taxis, the skyscrapers and the art galleries, the people who always ran rather than walked and in the subway read the newspaper folded in order not to bother everyone else. I loved the fact that if you took thirty people at random on the street there were no more than ten of the same colour. I loved Central Park and the lakes and lawns and the guitarists who sang there when the weather was good, I loved the diners and the hamburgers and the pubs and the endless bars where even if you went back ten times in a row you never saw the same faces. I loved the boats on the Hudson and the Statue of Liberty and the fire escapes on the outsides of the buildings and the smell of burning meat in SoHo and the rectangular porphyry of its streets and the glittering doorways on the Upper East Side. I loved the hotdog stands and the Puerto Rican dishwashers and the way the Italian newspapers left your fingers black. Yes, in New York I even loved being Italian: it was as if there, that narrow strip of land floating in the Mediterranean lost all its flabbiness and weariness and became a glittering and surprising place from which it was a privilege to come, a privilege constantly celebrated by everyone. I loved my two-room apartment and my neighbour-hood and my books piled everywhere and the bar around the corner with its excellent cappuccinos and the Greek newspaper vendor and the all-night deli and even its awful Chinese owner, Ghon, who treated me like dirt and who once, after I'd already been living there a year and saw him almost every day, refused to lend me ten cents: I loved a place where dirty stinking Chinese bastards could feel free to treat me like dirt. I loved the bookcase I'd built by myself from pine planks, and the sturdy man in the hardware store who had sold me what I needed and his big yellow tape measure tied to his belt and his Canadian check shirt. I loved the fact that everything was exactly as it should be, the dignity with which the ticket collector on the train that took me back and forth from Princeton attached cards to the backs of the seats, the way he clicked his fingers and his straight back and his gruff politeness if you happened to ask for information. I loved the Public Library and its vast stale-smelling reading room and I loved Battery Park and Shakespeare & Co. and the distinct impression that everybody was on the thrilling edge of desperation.

And this love—apart from those surprising occasions when I felt proud of my origins—had been transformed over the years into a subtle and insidious sarcasm about the little village in Lower Tuscany that I came from, with all its unwritten rules and its rituals and its fruit tarts on Sunday and its festivals and all that junk I felt liberated from every day I saw the sun come up between the water tanks on the roofs of Manhattan.

Suddenly, though, a grey pall had fallen unexpectedly over those water tanks and over Mr Ghon and over all the rest, and without my realizing it I found myself crouching on the ground, my hands covered in blackish sand and an orange metal shovel at my side, planting nasturtiums in my parents' garden. By now, I had been teaching at Columbia for a couple of years, and overnight a new element had wormed its way into my life, an element whose very existence I had previously dismissed: doubt. At the time, it was nothing but the merest hint of a feeling, but thinking about it now, it was as if all at once that life that had seemed to me so solid and unmistakable had simply become one among the billions of possible lives, and all the others I had never lived were knocking insistently at my door. The rhythm of those knocks rapidly transformed itself into the metre of the old, simple, terrifying question: what's the point? At the same time, it had seeped out through the cracks in the cocoon of my studies and encroached on the outside world. Gradually, every single event of which I was aware and every one of my actions and every thing I had ever researched became refracted in a sinister way, so that for a few moments they appeared different from what they were. When one morning a chorus of voices in my head asked me what the point of a good coffee was, I realized the moment had probably arrived to run for cover.

Whenever I went back to San Filippo, the only people I was glad to see were Giorgia and Paolino. At more or less the same time I'd started my relationship with Trisha, Biagio had met Kate, and Greg was—to use his words—exploring the depths of perdition, Giorgia had been walking home alone on the evening of the annual spring festival. I never found out what had happened during the festival, but for some reason the image I've always carried with me is that of a young woman who was a bit shaken, a bit scared. As she was walking through the village, she noticed that on the opposite side of the square a light was still on. Paolino was in the doorway of his workshop, adjusting something on the engine of an old three-gear Beta.

"Hi," she said.

Paolino looked up for a moment and gave a little smile. The last time Giorgia had addressed him directly had been two years earlier, when she'd asked him for a cigarette.

"What are you doing?"

Paolino again looked up and sighed. "What do you think?"

The year before, Paolino's dad had had a stroke and was now confined to a wheelchair. Paolino suddenly had to take care of the workshop alone, and in order not to lose customers and to continue to pay his father's medical expenses, he often worked after dinner. He told me it wasn't actually that much of a burden: he liked working with his hands, and he didn't have much else to do. That evening, it was a good excuse not to take part in the festival.

"Can I stay?" Giorgia asked.

Paolino shrugged, and she sat down nearby on a Vespa without an engine. They didn't say much more to each other, and yet Giorgia stayed there all evening watching him work. There was something hypnotic about those hands moving over the engine and adjusting and fitting parts, something Giorgia could not tear herself away from. All at once—she confessed to me years later, one evening when I was having dinner at their house, while Paolino was gone for a moment—it had seemed to her that those hands could fix anything, and she had suddenly felt safe. At that precise moment she realized that she had been wrong about everything in her life, and that what up until a second earlier she'd thought was beautiful actually wasn't beautiful at all, and everything that had seemed to her important wasn't worth a cent. Suddenly it was Paolino who seemed beautiful to her—a bit dirty maybe, but they could do something about that—and the way he worked the most solid thing she'd ever set eyes on. Giorgia had chosen him, and paradoxically had to work quite hard to convince him. Paolino's incredulity was not so difficult to understand: it was strange, to say the least, to have the prettiest girl in the village hanging around him. Maybe also the most available, although certainly not, until now, for someone like him. And yet in the end she had managed to overcome his suspicions and get him to yield. Apparently, there had been some banter about it, but it hadn't lasted long. "Welcome to the club," Mauro said to him with a laugh one day, sitting on the back of a bench as Paolino was coming out of the social club after buying cigarettes. Paolino stopped, turned back and without uttering a word gave Mauro a punch so hard it sent him flying two metres backwards. An hour later Mauro was still babbling incoherently. Nobody ever ventured to say anything again, and six months later Paolino and Giorgia married. I have to admit: no other couple, among all those I've known, has ever shown itself to be so well matched. Giorgia's most unpleasant aspects, her sarcasm and coquettishness, disappeared after she got together with Paolino. And Paolino demonstrated that he had an unpredictable sense of humour, and even—in his way and in his own time—a certain love of gossip. He even started using shampoo. They laughed a lot in their house, and talked without hurry or fuss. They had three children, with barely two years between them. It seemed as if they didn't want to stop. Two girls, Giulia and Lisa, and a boy, Dario, like Paolino's dad. Before going back I always take a trip to FAO Schwarz and have fun buying toys I don't think you can find in Italy, though lately it's got harder because everything reaches Italy now. But the kids are always happy and when I arrive they run to me and ask for their gifts and call me Uncle Jacopo. Paolino and Giorgia even asked me to be Dario's godfather. I told them I wasn't very suitable, but they burst out laughing.

"Neither are we."

Sometimes, when they were smaller, to free their hands Giorgia or Paolino would put one of them around my neck. It was funny to see those little animals moving over me like larvae. As soon as they started crying or vomiting I gave them back.

2

IT WAS TRUE, Greg had done a lot for Biagio. But never in such a brazen way as six or seven years earlier. We hadn't heard from Biagio in a while, and we were quite worried. The last person I'd spoken to, an Australian friend of his I'd met on a trip to Sydney, had told me things weren't going very well for him: he lounged about between the house and the beach, and wasn't a particularly pleasant sight. One evening this friend had seen him in his dressing gown by the foreshore, as the sun was going down, with a couple of those horrible, gigantic Australian bats hovering over his head. "He looked like some kind of run-down vampire," he said.

Biagio's best year may well have been his debut in the 500cc races. It was a risk that Lucio had taken: he'd become convinced that the one way for Biagio to really make his mark was if he could tame those monsters of two hundred and something horsepower; 250cc bikes were for precise, regular, methodical riders. Once you understood them, they couldn't surprise you any more, and whoever made the fewest mistakes won. The 500cc were another matter entirely: they were crazed fillies, untameable monsters of engineering, which had defeated dozens of riders. Of course, with them, too, you had to make fewer mistakes to win, but the bikes forced everyone to make a few, and in the end all you had to do to go fast was stay on your bike and be unaware of the speed you were going at. Biagio was as unaware as you could hope for, and Lucio told himself that if he continued to mature and kept his mistakes to a minimum, his good moments would outweigh the bad. Lucio was a perceptive man: in the first championship he rode, Biagio managed to come fourth. There are still those who talk about his skirmishes with Kevin Schwantz, whom he actually managed to beat by two points in the final rankings. They even became good friends, and at the end of every race would do a high five and congratulate each other. That must have meant a lot to Biagio: he always told me that Schwantz was the greatest rider of all time, and now they were racing like little boys and laughing together like schoolmates. They were very similar, in fact: both very talented and very undisciplined. When Schwantz announced he was quitting and was asked who he thought his heir was, he declared with a laugh that he didn't know, but that he saw all his own craziness in Biagio.

The thing that spread Biagio's name and face around the world was an advertising campaign. Lucio's 500cc team was sponsored by Pall Mall, who, halfway through the season, started circulating posters and newspaper ads with a photograph of Biagio barechested in the famous open-armed pose adopted by Jim Morrison. Pall Mall was well known as the cigarette that the Doors singer had smoked. Actually, Biagio's smooth hair and thin features and blue eyes weren't very reminiscent of Morrison's, but despite that you couldn't help thinking there was something in their eyes that made them very similar. Under the photograph, a caption in scribbled handwriting said: *Genius has no rules.*

Apparently it was a very successful campaign, and sales of Pall Mall soared in several countries. Biagio, of course, made a lot of money from it. The slogan turned out to be more revealing than people might have thought: Biagio really didn't have any rules, although at first that was considered amusing, and everyone was happy. Both he and Kate became celebrities, and they never lost an opportunity to appear in clubs and at parties, often drunk and wearing large sunglasses. But that was fine; that was exactly the kind of personality everybody wanted, and as long as he went like a rocket on the track and battled it out with Kevin Schwantz, everything was perfect. The two or three times he fell or made terrible mistakes, the journalists suggested with a laugh that he might have had a bit too much to drink the night before. And yet nobody said anything: those ridiculous posters circulating around the world claimed he was just one more mad genius, and everyone wanted to believe in that fairy tale.

At the end of the second season, for reasons that have never been completely clear, Pall Mall decided to abandon Torcini's team and sponsor a satellite of Suzuki. Obviously they wanted to take with them the rider linked with their biggest and most successful campaign of the last few years. Through his agent, Biagio at first declared that without Torcini he might even quit racing. But then Pall Mall made an incredible offer, and, after a whole day shut up in an office with Lucio, Biagio issued a statement saying he would follow Pall Mall and join that Suzuki satellite. Pall Mall were hoping to plan their campaign for the coming year: Suzuki was the bike that Schwantz had ridden up until then. Going from

Team Torcini's Honda to Suzuki, they hoped to capitalize on the American's inheritance.

Things didn't go exactly as planned. It was harder than anticipated for Biagio to get used to the new bike, and on both occasions when he lost his temper and tried to go faster he fell badly, narrowly escaping serious injury. The campaign stressing that he was Schwantz's heir was shelved. In the meantime, Biagio and Kate continued their partying and clubbing and weekends on boats. He skipped press conferences and presentations with the sponsors, or else turned up with swollen eyes, speaking even more incoherently than usual. The Jim Morrison comparison had become a burden round his neck, and most importantly, Biagio was no longer battling it out on the track with a former world champion for third place in the race and the rankings. Towards the end of the season, he even talked about making a break from Pall Mall, but then everyone decided to honour the contract. Apparently it was Biagio who wanted to leave, but then had to give up the idea: Lucio told me one day that to have someone like Biagio in your stable you either had to think that he was useful or like him a lot, and nobody, except Pall Mall on one side and he on the other, was willing to take the risk. In the meantime, Lucio had his hands tied with other riders and new sponsors.

Everything blew up the following year, two days before the Italian Grand Prix, again at Mugello. On the Thursday just before the weekend of trials and races, a magazine published photographs of Biagio bathed in sweat and with an idiotic grin on his face, his arms around Kate and two transvestites. The headline was *Jim's Sunset*, and the article claimed that the photographs had been taken in a club in Torremolinos on the night before the Spanish Grand Prix two weeks earlier. In Jerez, Biagio had got everything wrong: he had committed stupid mistakes in the trials and then, having started out eleventh, had skidded badly in his attempt to catch up, bringing down two other riders and injuring his calf. By an ironic twist of fate, the Grand Prix was won by the same Alberto Puig he had been hit by five years earlier right there in Jerez.

The photographs caused a great stink. Pall Mall and the team said they were indignant and that if Biagio didn't clean up his act and demonstrate, if nothing else, a bit of professionalism, their relationship had to be considered at an end. On his side, Biagio issued a communiqué stating that the photographs were definitely not from two weeks earlier, but from the previous winter, and had not been taken in Torremolinos, but in a club in London. Not many people believed him, but as someone wrote in the *Gazzetta*, it didn't really make much difference. Biagio avoided TV cameras and reporters the whole weekend. In the trials, surprisingly, he came fifth, and the race itself was perhaps the best of his life. In four laps he managed to move up into second place, right behind Mick Doohan. Nobody could believe it, but he actually looked as if he might be able to overtake him. He threw himself into the Casanova-Savelli like a diver and climbed the Arrabbiata like a rocket, on Doohan's tail all the time. Sitting in an Italian restaurant in Baltimore where I went to watch the races and the occasional football match, I touched my heart from time to time to make sure it wasn't bursting. When I heard a couple near me laughing and wondering who this sensation was, I couldn't hold back. I turned and told them his name was Biagio, and he was my oldest friend. They nodded and said, "Great," but they didn't sound convinced. I don't think they believed me.

Five laps from the end, at the entrance to the Bucine, the downhill bend before the finishing line, Biagio got on the inside of Doohan and overtook him. On the home straight, though, Doohan's Honda seemed to have something in reserve and at the San Donato he managed to pull away first. At the same point in every lap, at the entrance to the Bucine, Biagio would gain a few metres and overtake Doohan with ever greater fluidity. It was as if he were taking the measurements of the track. At the last entrance to the Bucine he went in so fast that I let out a cry: he passed Doohan with his rear wheel off the ground, and at the exit, I don't know how he was still on his bike, he was going faster still, taking advantage of every centimetre. His front wheel glided for about forty or fifty metres, and I told myself he would end up on the grass and against the wall, but he managed to keep the bike on the track and pass the finishing line first. Even before getting to the end of the home straight, Doohan came to him and shook his hand and raised his fist and shouted to him that he was one of the greats.

Later, on the podium, once the national anthems were finished, and while Doohan and Cadalora were spraying him with champagne, Biagio picked up his magnum and started drinking it all in one go without his lips touching the bottle. There was something miraculous about seeing that big bottle being emptied into that tiny body, and everyone stopped to watch. After almost a minute Biagio angrily threw the Magnum aside, raised his head, puffed out his cheeks, raised two fingers to the sky, and sprayed out a gigantic cloud of champagne. Even today, in those bars with Ducati shields and photos of motorcycle racers on the walls, I sometimes see the image of Biagio on that podium, in the blue Pall Mall leathers, with his fingers raised and a big cloud of champagne over his head.

At the subsequent press conference, he was visibly drunk. He was greeted with a roar of applause, and after the attacks of the previous days even I, who was completely uninvolved, found it hard to hold back a shudder of irritation. Once he sat down and silence fell, he declared that this had been his last race and that he wasn't enjoying it any more and had no more desire to race and they could all go fuck themselves. There was an icy silence. Then a few journalists screamed no, it wasn't right, he couldn't just go. He looked at them, muttered that they were a bunch of clowns, again told them to fuck themselves and left the room. They all started laughing, obviously thinking he was drunk and this was just another of his acts of bravado. But they were wrong, and his career stopped right there at Mugello, where it had started.

He withdrew with Kate to the house by the sea he had bought in Sydney, near Bondi Beach. News about him started to arrive in fragments, and it wasn't good news. After a couple of years Kate disappeared too, and nobody ever discovered what became of her.

Lucio wasn't in a very good way either. The team had been through two or three difficult years and he no longer had the funds to carry on and had only managed to cope by finding collaborators and organizing driving courses. Greg heard about it and had one of his assistants call him and arrange a meeting. So Lucio found himself at the window of an elegant building overlooking the Tiber and the Palace of Justice, in the conference room of one of the biggest companies in the country. A young woman in a grey tailored suit led him in and asked him if he would like something to drink.

"No, thanks," he said.

"Signor Mariani will be with you in a moment."

About ten minutes later Greg appeared, followed by another young woman in a suit. He walked towards him and held out his hand. "Hello, Signor Torcini."

Lucio found it hard to see in this pale figure in a sweater and grey slim-fit trousers, as long and thin as an asparagus, the quiet fair-haired young man he remembered from the Rocky Road, the man Biagio had often talked about over the years. He had always found it hard to associate that memory with the weight the name Gregorio Mariani bore, now more than ever.

"I don't want to steal anyone's time," Greg said, without even sitting down. Then he turned very slightly towards his assistant and had her pass him a small sheet of paper. Greg took it with two fingers. "Do you know what this is, Signor Torcini?"

Lucio must have watched this little performance with a ironic eye, and he was unable completely to suppress his sarcasm. "A piece of paper?"

"It's a blank cheque, Signor Torcini. To set up a new team. A team I'd like you to run. I assure you, Signor Torcini, that I'm not in the habit of writing blank cheques, but when I do they really are blank."

Greg and Lucio looked each other in the eyes for a moment. When Lucio told me this story I suspected that Greg was going mad.

"This cheque is yours on one condition."

Again a moment's pause.

"And what condition is that?"

"Biagio."

"Biagio what?"

"The one condition is that one of the riders is Biagio."

Lucio looked at Greg for a moment or two without saying anything. "I don't even know where Biagio is. And, assuming I can find out, I have grave doubts that he'll be in any condition to race."

"That, Signor Torcini, is not my problem. If you bring Biagio here, and he's willing to race, you have at your disposal all the money you need to set up a new team. If not, then it's been a pleasure to see you again and I wish you all the best." Without turning, Greg handed the cheque back to his assistant, then stepped forward and held out his hand again. "Goodbye, Signor Torcini, and good luck. The young lady here will leave you all our contacts and, if you like, some small expenses to go and find Biagio. She'll also provide you with the information we have concerning him. Thanks again."

Lucio shook hands with him and watched him leave the room. He came back two months later, with a somewhat older but apparently calmer version of Biagio, surprisingly ready to race for him. But Lucio suggested dropping the Grand Prix and entering him for the Superbike Championships instead. It was a less frenetic, more human environment, he said, where it was easier to do well. And by now the Grand Prix had become as much of a horrible carnival as Formula One.

"As you wish, Signor Torcini," Greg said to him when they met again in Rome. "As I promised, you have carte blanche."

He then told him that he could discuss the details with his assistant.

"Forgive me, but I must go now." He shook hands with Lucio, then with Biagio. "And you, don't do anything stupid," he added.

When Biagio told me about this whole pantomime, I could hardly believe it. "What did you say to that?" I asked Biagio, with an amazed half-smile.

"What could I say, Jacopo? I told him to go to hell."

Fortunately, Greg had given a little laugh, then turned and left.

They set up a satellite team of Ducati and for a couple of seasons things went quite well. Biagio and Lucio, with a great laugh I imagine, called it Team Rocky Road, and even Greg seemed quite amused when he told me about it. Along with Biagio, Lucio hired a young Japanese racer who fortunately turned out to be much better than expected. They had a number of good races, and in the championships they always reached fifth and sixth place in the general rankings.

Biagio was seen by everyone as a bit of a hero, like a colleague who had been to hell and back, and they treated him with great respect. After the two races he managed to win, they were all quite moved and they embraced him and cheered him. Biagio was certainly pleased, but it also made him uncomfortable.

"They treat me like a madman," he told me one day over the phone.

At the end of the second championship he decided he didn't want to any more, and this time everyone accepted it as natural. He moved to a house on the island of Elba, near Capoliveri, and spent all his time there, mostly by himself. A young Indonesian girl lived with him for a while, but then she left too. He didn't want to have anything more to do with San Filippo, and when I asked him why he didn't find a house closer to the village, he told me that since Betta had died there wasn't anything left for him there. "Dad and Graziano are both drunks, and in Australia I got used to the noise of the sea."

Not long after arriving in San Filippo to spend a few weeks with my family, I decided to go and see him. I asked Dad to lend me his car and drove to Piombino to catch the ferry. As I stood with the wind on my face and looked out at the Tyrrhenian, I told myself it had been a great idea and that I might stay a few days longer. The next day, I was already on my way back.

The directions I had to get to the house were surprisingly quite precise, and it didn't take me long to find it. It was a small two-storey colonial-style stone house, surrounded by a forest of shrubs and swept by the wind, facing the Golfo Stella and the southern coast of Elba. If you went along a path for a few dozen metres towards the sea and leant over, you could see the quarry of Punta Calamita. The bedrooms were upstairs. On the ground floor, once past the entrance hall, there was a big living room with a beautiful stone fireplace, and at the back was a spacious kitchen with a terracotta tiled floor, as well as another room, now bare, that must once have been a dining room.

It would have been a really nice place if every corner of the house hadn't been filled with that disturbing smell of rottenness. The windows were opaque and probably hadn't been opened in months. There were big damp stains on the ceiling, and a uniform film of dust covered every object left lying around. The only sign of a recent human presence was the hollow in the worn green velvet sofa, which in the middle of all that neglect looked more than anything else like the inside of a sarcophagus. The kitchen table was covered in all kinds of junk, and the sink was filled to the brim with dirty dishes and plastic cups. I was about to open the fridge when it struck me that that might not be a good idea.

"Doesn't anyone ever come?" I asked, putting my bag down by the kitchen door and looking around, trying to temper my disgust.

"To do what?"

"I don't know... to clean."

Biagio went to the fridge and took out two beers. "A woman sometimes comes."

Luckily the front of the fridge door was towards me, preventing me from looking inside. Biagio seemed to have shrunk: he wore big wraparound dark glasses that he never took off, his hair was dirty and floppy, and although he had always been thin, he now looked flaccid and sickly. He dragged himself from the dusty interior of the house to a deckchair he'd set up in the yard next to a little table. The effort of taking a second deckchair outside and opening my beer for me was the only real sign that he acknowledged my presence. It wasn't that having me there made him uncomfortable: it was more like indifference. It was as if nothing that was happening could possibly interest Biagio, let alone disturb him. We sat there on the deckchairs for the rest of the afternoon, with me occasionally venturing a few sentences to which Biagio replied with simple gestures or brief little laughs. In the evening, when I asked if he wanted me to cook something, he told me he wasn't very hungry, but that there might be a couple of pizzas in the freezer that we could heat up. After dinner we went back inside the house to watch a film and, as he had on the deckchair, he simply sank into the hollow in the couch and stopped moving. He finally took off his dark glasses: his eyes were as blue as ever, but opaque and dull, as if there were an unbridgeable gap between them and the person behind them. True, Biagio had never been much of a talker, and it was quite normal for us to spend a lot of time together in silence, but there had always been something in his presence, a kind of vibration or magnetic field, which seemed to reorganize the world around us, if only for a few minutes. At a certain point everything had taken a different turn, but as boys it was as if despite himself he had always known how things were, and somehow you too were touched by the same awareness. Now nothing seemed to remain of that vibration, that magnetic field, or it was so distant as to be confused with all the rest. That was what he was, distant. Biagio was distant: he had gone a long way inside himself, far from the surface of his eyes and his skin, and far from anything surrounding him. In the old days, even when he was silent, he'd sucked you in like a vortex.

As soon as the film finished, in the hope of overcoming my anxiety with a bit of reading, I told him I was tired and went upstairs. Biagio simply nodded and said goodnight. I had chosen a room that was bare except for two wrought-iron beds. In a chest of drawers in the corridor I found some sheets that looked a bit cleaner than the others, and lay down on the bed half dressed. I've never been a fastidious person, but the idea of any part of my skin touching any surface in that house for a few hours filled me with unease.

In the morning I got up early and, just to do something, went downstairs and started cleaning up. I opened all the windows, found a dishcloth and tried to dust as best I could.

I discovered some big black bags into which I threw all the food left lying around and the plastic dishes from the sink and the waste paper strewn in every corner of the living room. I gave the place a good sweep: the balls of dust were as big as cats and twisted around the broom like a Rastafarian's dreadlocks.

"Leave that," Biagio said behind me, as I was sweeping. He had already put on his sunglasses and sounded quite annoyed.

"Don't worry. At least I'm doing something."

He looked at me for another moment, then went and got his first beer of the day from the fridge, walked outside and took up his place again on the deckchair.

Some time later, after sponging down the worktop in the kitchen and opening the cupboard under the sink to see if I could find anything to clean the bathrooms and the windows with, I was assaulted by a wave of stench. In the adjoining cupboard was a green plastic bucket with some rubbish in it in a black bag that had been there for God knows how long. Screwing up my face, I opened the bucket and took out the black bag. I was already closing it in a hurry when something attracted my attention. Holding my breath and making an effort not to vomit, I took a closer look. From underneath some wet leftover food, a long narrow object stuck out which for a few seconds I wished with all my heart I hadn't seen. I looked around, grabbed a roll of kitchen towel, tore off two sheets, folded them a couple of times and, holding them between my fingers, plunged my hand into the bag. I moved a few mouldy scraps to one side and, trying not to touch anything, pulled out the object. An insulin syringe. As I stared at the traces of dried plasma at the base of the needle and imagined, with nausea rising in me, everything they meant, the picture finally started to compose itself in front of my eyes. How could I not have realized? This explained all the mysteries about Biagio: his decline, his detachment, his lack of interest, his solitude, his apathy, the image of him in Sydney in his dressing gown, his silences, and for some reason, also the image of him when he was small, walking around the fields at night.

I admit it: I was overcome with an embarrassing but undeniable wave of terror. I placed my hand on the edge of the sink, and as I was trying to hold back the gush of acid rising in my throat I started to see all the tiny objects in the kitchen—and immediately afterwards in the rest of the house—as if they were set dressing for a horror movie. For a moment I gazed into a cold dark place, the depths of which made me violently dizzy. Sometimes, over the years, when things had been going badly, I had wondered like an idiot if that was what people called *the abyss*. Well, here at last was the answer: no. This was a much blacker, deeper monster, faced with which—I'm ashamed to confess—I was unable to do anything but run away. I wrapped the syringe in a thick layer of kitchen towel, went to the bedroom where I had slept, threw the wad in my bag along with the few things I had taken out the previous evening, and went out again. Biagio was still there on his deckchair, sipping a can of beer and looking at the gulf. I told him I'd called my parents and my mum was apparently feeling ill again, I was sorry but I had to go. As I expected, Biagio didn't seem very interested in the news, although he did make the effort to stand up and hug me.

"Try to keep well," I said to him, feeling vile and mean.

"You too," he replied, sitting back down and looking at the sea again.

An hour and a half later, going back on the ferry, I was struck by an intense mixture of deliverance and guilt. Half of me—not the smaller half—was goading me and calling me a coward; the other half was unable to hide its relief at having managed to get to a safe place before it was too late.

When I got home, I simply took a long shower and went to bed. The next morning, as soon as I woke up, I set about planting and watering my mother's nasturtiums and pansies with even greater passion than before, and started pulling out the few weeds from the rest of the garden. Two days later, bent over a flower bed, digging a small hole in the dark earth with a shovel, I heard and then saw Greg's helicopter hovering over the village and descending towards the villa. I went back inside the house, took off the apron that Mum had lent me to work in the garden, washed my hands as best I could in the kitchen sink, went upstairs to my room for a moment and finally went out. It was a hot, humid day, more like August than the end of June, and with every step I took I could feel sweat breaking out on my chest and making my T-shirt stick to me. I walked with big slow strides, stooping more than usual. I crossed the village, weaving between the English and German tourists, past the main square, which increasingly resembled the piazzetta on Capri, and kept going until I got to the gate of the villa. When I got a reply through the entryphone, I simply gave my first name, as I'd done when I was little. Incredibly, the gate opened without my being asked anything else. At the end of the cedar-lined drive, at the top of the stone steps in front of the main door, a butler I'd never seen was already there waiting for me.

"I'm sorry, sir, but there's nobody at home," the butler

239

said. He looked Filipino, and was wearing a big white jacket.

"I saw that thing arrive," I said pointing up at the sky. "Tell Signor Mariani that Jacopo is here and is waiting for him in the study," and I went in before he even gave me permission. The butler stood there for a moment, stunned, then followed me along the corridor and through the blue drawing room, and when I entered Greg's study he switched the lights on.

Greg had adapted as his study what had once been the real heart of the villa, a vast drawing room with a coffered ceiling and a monumental fireplace surmounted by the family arms. The time when guests had been received here and parties had been given was long gone, and Greg, to stir his megalomania, had had the idea of putting a big dark wooden table at the far end of it and making it his study. My two-room apartment on the Upper West Side could probably have fitted comfortably into a quarter of this room. After a couple of minutes a maid appeared, greeted me shyly and started opening all the windows and the frosted glass doors, gradually flooding it with natural light and gusts of hot summer wind.

On one side, under a window, stood Sandra. For a moment I was overcome with an irrepressible sense of nostalgia. I looked at the shiny egg of the engine and the fibreglass fairing that I had made with my own hands almost twenty years earlier. I placed my fingers on the twist grip of the accelerator and, as I lightly pulled the brake lever, I felt a strong impulse to shed a few tears.

"What are you doing, spying on me?"

I raised my head. Greg had gone straight to the back of

the room and put some papers down on the desk. He was wearing grey trousers and his shirt sleeves were rolled up.

I again looked at Sandra and pulled the brake lever a few more times. "Is it her?"

Greg raised his eyes a moment, then started looking through some papers. "Of course it's her."

I let go of the grip, looked at Sandra for another moment or two, then walked towards Greg's desk. "I thought you left it to Paolino."

"Paolino? What's Paolino got to do with it? It was mine and I took it back."

Before collapsing into one of the three red velvet armchairs in front of the desk, I took the wad of kitchen towel from the back pocket of my trousers. I slowly opened it and threw the syringe on the desktop. Greg glanced first at the syringe, then briefly at me.

"Thanks. Another time, maybe."

"Idiot. It's Biagio's. I went to see him on Elba."

Greg sighed, clicked his tongue rather oddly a few times, and sat down. "And?"

"He's in a bad way, Greg. He spends all day sitting in a deckchair looking at the sea and drinking beer. God knows how many of these things he does a day. The house stinks like a corpse."

"How does he get hold of it?"

"I have no idea. I didn't see anyone come to the house, but I was only there for one night. I wanted to stay longer... then I saw this and left. I don't know—I was afraid. It's tough being there, it's upsetting."

Greg was listening to me without saying anything.

"I asked him if someone at least comes to tidy up a bit, and

241

he told me a woman comes from time to time. But I don't believe that. The house seems abandoned. Maybe she's the one who brings him this."

Greg drummed on the arms of his chair for a few moments. "And what do you think we should do?"

"I don't know, Greg. Go there, take him away, put him in a home, shoot him in the head. I really don't know."

Greg looked me in the eyes for a moment, then down at my T-shirt. "You're dirty."

I looked down and with two fingers held the white cotton a few centimetres away from my chest. There were in fact stains of sand and grass on it, as well as blue streaks from some flowers. "I've been gardening."

Greg's mouth creased into a smile. "Is that the end result of all your academic efforts?"

"I know about nasturtiums."

Greg shook his head. "All right," he said, turning serious again, "let's think it over for a bit and then talk again. Now fuck off, I have work to do."

He shifted closer to the desk and gathered the papers that he had been leafing through earlier.

"And this?" I asked indicating the syringe.

"You can stick it up your arse."

"I think that's more your style."

"I wouldn't even feel a little thing like that, kid. I'm used to much bigger sizes."

I gave a little laugh, wrapped the syringe in the kitchen towel again, stuck it back in my trouser pocket and left.

I don't know what I'd give now to be able to say that I spoke to Greg again the next day and that we had found a solution and went to our friend's house and took him away and managed to stop his downward spiral. We could have gone there in Greg's helicopter and landed directly in front of the house. We could have taken Paolino with us. It would have taken us a moment to load that heap of skin and bones into the helicopter. In the state he was in, Biagio probably wouldn't even have resisted. We could have done a whole lot of things, a whole lot of damned things that will now continue to knock at our doors like the living dead. But it didn't happen, because, like the good racer he was, Biagio was quicker than us. He hadn't been lying when he'd said that a woman came to clean the house. Twelve days later, she showed up and found Biagio lying dead on the sofa in the living room. The stench was already unbearable, and the doctor who came to issue the death certificate said he must have been dead at least three days. If I think about it, I can almost see him: alone, lying in that cavity in the sofa as if in a sarcophagus, one arm hanging over the side, his mouth half open, his skin and face hollowed by death like rotten wood.

So yes: Greg had in fact already done a lot for Biagio. Once the corpse had been discovered he had even used some of his contacts to get the body transferred quickly to San Filippo. We wondered if Biagio would have preferred it like that, but in the end we told ourselves that it was definitely better than having him buried in a cemetery somewhere on the island of Elba.

Why then, when I asked Greg if he was coming to the funeral and he gave me that curt reply, did I start despite myself to slip into that pit of apathy? Greg had often made an effort for Biagio, even though it had been a while since he'd stopped wasting much time on what he couldn't understand or touch or buy. And yet, from the very moment when—through my parents' telephone—Greg's words had struck my eardrum, they started to bounce around in my head like the tolling of a gong, preventing me from seriously considering any other thought and pulling me into a relentless vortex of confusion. *Dazed*: that's the word. For some weeks now, or maybe unconsciously for a few months, my neurons hadn't exactly been models of reactivity, but from the very moment my hand put the grey receiver of my parents' phone back on its cradle, that's the word that best described me.

The next day, at the funeral, facing a crowded church—people had come from all the neighbouring villages, in the hope, I imagine, of seeing TV cameras and reporters—Don Roberto said that he had never known Biagio, but that over the years the love of his fellow villagers—those were the words he used—had conveyed the image of a gentle young man with a sunny disposition who always had a good word for everybody. I could barely hold back my laughter. He discussed the famous words "and the last shall be first" and concluded by praying to the Lord to help this sensitive soul find a little peace. That idiot Cardini, the mayor, spoke next and gave an incoherent speech about misfortune and temptation and solitude and how the State was now incapable of helping its most isolated citizens. Feigning emotion, he beat his hand on the lectern and almost cursed as he declared that this sad passing should be a spur to everyone to fight with all their might the widespread solitude that surrounded us. Then he paused theatrically for a moment.

"It is therefore with great pride," he went on, "that the municipal council has already engaged a prestigious sculptor of international fame to make a monument to our talented and unfortunate fellow villager."

The church resounded with applause and Cardini was unable to hide his satisfaction, however hard he tried. Inside me, I heard in the distance the echoes of an angry crowd shouting and whistling and cursing, but I couldn't find the strength to follow them.

On the way out some ladies in their Sunday best, with handkerchieves in their hands, answered the questions of two or three reporters spread around the square. They approached me, too, but even before they could say anything to me I muttered that if they didn't get out of my way I'd kick them from there to kingdom come. In a corner of the square, I spotted Lucio. I'd informed him two days earlier. We walked towards each other and hugged, but briefly. Then he put his hands on my shoulders.

"I'm sorry," he said.

I nodded and said nothing. We stood for a few moments watching everyone coming and going and I wondered what Biagio would have said if he had been there.

"Are you going to the cemetery?" Lucio asked.

The coffin came out of the church, carried by Graziano and some people Biagio had never even met.

"No, I think I'll go home."

Lucio nodded. We watched the coffin disappear into the long dark Mercedes and begin its slow journey to the cemetery, followed by that flock of people. When the square was empty again, I looked up and for a moment watched the branches of the pines moving slightly in the wind. This, then, I found myself thinking for some reason, is what remains, though I wasn't very sure what that meant.

"All right," I said. "I think I'm going."

Lucio nodded again. "Yes, me too."

For the first time I looked at him a little more closely: he had grown older, and he looked like the uncle I had never had. I hugged him again quickly and gave him a slight pat on the back of the neck.

"Phone me," he said.

"Yes."

"Please."

I smiled, said, "Yes," again in a low voice, then put my hands in my pockets and walked away. At home I wandered for a while in the garden, kicking at the stones around the flower beds. Everything looked very tidy. I went back inside, called the airline and had my return flight brought forward: I would leave in two days' time. When my parents came back, they told me a place had been found for Biagio right in the middle of the cemetery, not far from his parents, and that Buti had promised to make him an appropriate headstone.

Two days later, Amanda came to pick me up from the airport. It was the kind of gesture that wasn't common in our relationship, but it didn't have any effect on me. Even seeing her didn't move me all that much. Usually seeing her again gave me a strange sense of disorientation. Sometimes, after only a few hours, seeing her at the corner of a street or at the door of the apartment, I wondered for a moment if she was really smiling at me, and controlled the impulse to turn and see if there was someone behind me. I couldn't quite get used to the idea that all that beauty was at my disposal. Such an original beauty too, the kind of beauty constantly on the verge of collapse, which only made it all the more intriguing. Looking at her closely, you knew that that big nose and those round cheekbones and full lips could easily turn into something graceless and irritating. And yet it never happened: I often caught myself looking at her in the morning when she woke up, or at night, tipsy after a party, or in the evening in pyjamas in front of the TV with a big tub of ice cream in her hand, trying to discover if her face had finally lost its harmony. But the features and curves of that face seemed to resist any attack, and I had the feeling I was hearing stories about the eternal war between harmony and disorder.

Amazement. That was what I had felt from the first moment we had started seeing each other. Whenever we found ourselves talking about when exactly our relationship had begun, we immediately agreed on one Tuesday evening, just outside the main entrance of the New School. A couple of years earlier, a woman who taught comparative religion had contacted me and told me she'd attended a lecture of mine and had been struck by something I'd said: "Today, this is our religion." It was a kind of joke, but it corresponded to a quite serious and long-held belief of mine in the element of the unknowable in physics. Patricia, the teacher in question, told me she was working on a wide-ranging book on comparative religion, in which she had long been thinking of including a section on contemporary physics, rather on the same lines as Fritjof Capra's *The Tao of Physics*, but also encompassing non-Oriental religions. So we met for a coffee and became quite good friends. She was an amusing character, was Patricia, and good at organizing quite brilliant dinner parties I surprisingly didn't mind going to. The year after we met she asked me to give, within her course, a brief cycle of two or three seminars on the most crucial aspects of contemporary physics, focussing in particular on what brought scientific analysis closer to the extreme limits of the universe. I had discovered that it was amusing to find images that attempted to explain some aspects of my work that for me now had a meaning exclusively in mathematical terms, and in those few hours I suddenly had the impression that physics was a much broader and more fascinating field than I might have imagined. Perhaps what partly deceived me was the rapt looks of those listening to me.

The New School had been founded in 1919 by a group of academics from New York University, with the intention of establishing a more flexible and liberal kind of university. The nicest thing about it is that anyone, of any age and with any qualification, can pay to follow a course on the academic programme as an external student. If he wishes, he can also try his hand in the final exams, which are obviously compulsory for anyone attending the entire course of studies. In the case of Amanda, she had found herself in a somewhat idle period, work-wise, and the idea of gaining a smattering of knowledge about the main religious currents of the world for a few hours a week had appealed to her. It had also been the result—or the fault—of 9/11. Over the years, her doubts about what was so different between her and those people who had flown into the World Trade Center and the Pentagon and a field in Pennsylvania had gnawed away at her and the idea of finding out more about the subject was something that intrigued her. On the evening of the second lesson, I found myself standing on Fifth Avenue outside the school for a few moments, a bit unsure, watching the cars go by. I didn't much feel like going straight home and I wondered who I could call in the area who might invite me to dinner.

"It was really fascinating," I heard someone say on my right.

Not far away, bending forward slightly to see my face better, was Amanda, smiling at me. During those first two lessons I had already noticed her sitting among the others, and had tried to look at her as little as possible. Now here she was, looking me in the eyes and expecting an answer, and I felt very embarrassed.

"Thank you," I managed to say in a whiny voice.

Shamelessly, she asked me if I felt like going for a drink, and we went to a bar somewhere in the neighbourhood. I was by now a respected scientist, who'd long stopped being surprised by the most formidable mechanisms of the universe, and yet being there in the company of this woman with such a magnetic face filled me with dismay. My voice seemed to tremble and I kept giggling idiotically in a way I'd never done before. Amanda meanwhile looked very much as if she were trying to ensnare me: could it be possible that such a beautiful woman—and, as I've said, beautiful in such an original way—really wanted to ensnare someone as gauche and boring as me? The whole situation made me awkward and distrustful. After the second glass she asked me how come I couldn't look her in the eyes. At last I looked up and straight at her. Immediately my defences collapsed and I felt like a little boy.

"Because I'm afraid I'd never look anywhere else again."

"Hi," she said at the airport, giving me a big hug when I came out through the sliding door with the other passengers.

"Hi," I replied.

We didn't say much to each other in the taxi. She asked me how the journey had been and I said: fine. As the cab slowed down for the tollbooth, she looked at me and stroked my cheek. I gave her something that was as close to a smile as I could get it and went back to looking out of the window.

Driving back into the city did not stir any great emotion. Previously, when the skyscrapers of Manhattan had appeared in the distance, and especially when I approached the bridge and crossed it, a kind of electric charge had always surged through my arteries and I was reminded of why I had decided to live here. There is no better way to understand the attachment or revulsion we have for a place than to leave it and then come back: the degree of unease or excitement that assails us on our return is the measure of our affection. Looking again at the outline of New York had always been very similar to knocking back half a bottle of wine in one go.

The black taxi driver asked for confirmation of the address. Amanda asked me if I preferred to go to my place. I shrugged and shook my head. It really didn't matter.

That was how it was: it didn't matter. I felt nothing: nothing as I got out of the taxi with my case, nothing as I climbed the stairs to Amanda's apartment, nothing when we later went for a bite to eat at Vito's, our favourite restaurant. Nothing as we strolled through Alphabet City, nothing when we got home and washed and went to bed and she huddled beside me and we fell asleep and nothing the next morning when we woke up in the same bed. Nothing. Nothing when two days later I went back to my own apartment, nothing when I opened the windows and saw my papers and my notes and my calculations on the whiteboard. Nothing when I went to the university and said hello to a few of my colleagues and talked to a few students who wanted information about my courses or how to be part of one of my research groups. Nothing when Amanda suggested we take a trip round the United States and nothing when I accepted. Nothing when we flew to Chicago and I got to the home of Fred, perhaps the only really amusing fellow student I had ever known, in fact the only one I'd really stayed friends with. Nothing when Fred took me around the faculty and one of his colleagues, after we were introduced, opened his eyes wide and asked, "*The* Jacopo Ferri?" and nothing after Fred told him yes and nothing after his colleague told me he was a fan of mine and that he'd found an article of mine in *Physics Review D* two years earlier quite illuminating. Nothing when Amanda and I hired a Toyota and nothing when she drove for hours between fields of corn—I told her I wasn't in the mood to drive—and when, just like in the movies, we made love in a seedy motel in the Midwest and nothing when I put my hand on a gigantic sequoia and thought it was the most imposing creation I had ever touched. Nothing even when we got back to New York and Amanda went back to work and I started going to the university again and nothing even on the day the classes restarted and I launched into my usual introduction to the complex question of dark energy.

Nothing until that night. I was sleeping at Amanda's. The previous evening we had been to dinner at the apartment of James and Clara, two friends of hers, and as I came back from the bathroom I'd heard Clara ask Amanda how things were going and she answered that it was getting to be a strain, that I didn't react to any stimulus and she didn't know what to do any more. For a moment I wondered if things hadn't worn themselves out and we wouldn't eventually separate, which was what always seemed to happen to me. Incidentally, even at that moment I felt nothing. This was the way things had ended up with Trisha too: we had simply stopped understanding each other and overnight the softness of her skin had stopped being crucial to me. I had told myself—unlike her—that maybe the world outside the two of us wasn't so bad after all, and one day she had simply gone back to sleeping at her place and started hating me as much as she hated most of humanity.

In bed, Amanda tried to rub herself up against me, but it didn't have much effect. Later, in the middle of the night, the echo of a sinister laugh jolted me from my sleep. I sat up in bed, trying to calm down and slow my heartbeat. I wiped my forehead with the back of my hand and took a deep breath. I went to the kitchen to get a glass of water, then to the bathroom. I splashed water on my face and looked at myself for a long time in the mirror. My heart was still beating like a bass drum and my stomach was churning. That damned laugh continued to boom in my head. I knew perfectly well who it belonged to. I thought of going back to bed and trying to sleep, but I knew I couldn't. So I went back to the bedroom and slowly, trying to make as little noise as possible, started dressing. I was already lacing my shoes when Amanda turned to me with a frown.

"What are you doing?"

"I can't sleep," I whispered. "I'm going to my place. Go back to sleep."

"To your place? What time is it?"

"I don't know," I whispered again. "About three. Go back to sleep."

Instead, she sat up and turned to me fully. "Three? What are you going to do at your place at three in the morning?"

I shrugged. "I can't sleep anyway. An idea came to me. I want to see if it works."

Actually, in the three years we'd been together, I'd demonstrated to Amanda that I wasn't prone to that kind of impulse. We had talked about it once: good ideas, I told her, come when you're working, and you learn with experience that the ones that come to you when you're doing your shopping are often false. So are those that hit you when you're sleeping, so you might as well sleep. But in the past few months, obviously, all the moulds had been broken, and now Amanda, fortunately, preferred not to ask any more questions. She gave me a kiss and lay down again and asked me if we would see each other the next day.

"Of course," I said.

We didn't see each other the next day. Or the day after or the one after that or the one after that. I kept telling Amanda that I'd finally found the solution to a problem I'd been struggling with in my work for months and that I absolutely had to see it through to the end. On the third day, addressing my answering machine for the umpteenth time, she asked me what she was supposed to do.

At the university I said I was sick. I spent three whole days at the computer, cruising the internet for hours on end, looking for answers to the questions which had suddenly started eating away at me, but which in reality—even though I hadn't realized it—had been eating away at me for weeks now, preventing me from feeling anything. Using every search engine I could find, I looked for addresses and phone numbers, and called whoever I thought could help me, at any hour of the day or night. I forgot to eat and slept in fits and starts.

When, at seven in the evening on the third day, I typed out one last brief e-mail message and pressed *send*, a sense of heat and torpor fell over me like a tree trunk. It was the reply to a mail from Greg four days earlier, in which he asked me if I was in town and if I felt like meeting. I struggled out of my chair at the desk, dragged myself into the bedroom, took off my trousers and, before my head even touched the pillow, fell, until the next day, into the deepest sleep I had ever known.

3

THE HUGE TAXI DRIVER with the turban dropped me in front of the glass entrance of the building. Watery green reflections filtered out from inside and spilt onto the sidewalk. The blacked-out glass doors slid open as I approached, and I stepped into an area of intense white light. To the left of the entrance, behind a highly polished black lacquer desk, a square man with a shaved head and wearing a black suit gave me the memory of a smile and said good evening. I took out my ID card, put it on the desk, and said I was there to see Mr Mariani. A tiny trace of my fingerprint remained imprinted on the black lacquer of the desk and as the square doorman typed my data into the computer, I couldn't help pulling my cuff out with my fingertips and trying to wipe it away.

"Very good," the doorman said, giving me back the card and pointing with the other hand to my right. "Elevator number two, code 136. Welcome back, Mr Ferri."

The elevators went directly up to the suites, and once the data had been put in the computer every visitor was given a personal code. That meant that, in the unlikely event of the doorman being absent, nobody was able to just go to the elevators and straight up to the desired floor. It particularly meant that every single entrance and exit by a visitor was individually recorded. This was another of the delightful little characteristics of the Gold Club, the highly exclusive international society which—for an annual fee that most ordinary people could not amass even in a lifetime—provided, in all the most important cities in the world, suites, chauffeur-driven cars, a considerable number of hours on private aircraft, a dedicated butler twenty-four hours a day, and a personal telephone assistant who followed all your movements and knew all your schedules, tastes, preferences, vices and obsessions. All of this, obviously, in the most total secrecy. Greg didn't have any real obsessions, but one evening at dinner he told me with obvious amusement how a Lithuanian friend of his named Sergej found, every time he got in one of the cars provided by the Gold Club, an espresso ristretto and a lit Tuscan cigar, in tribute to the happy time he'd spent in Rome at the age of twenty, soon after escaping from the Soviet Union. Apparently for Sergej, the mixture of his Roman memories and the luxurious lifestyle he had somehow managed to achieve in the meantime created a short circuit that always led him into a wonderfully overblown nostalgic state.

I asked Greg one day why the Club maintained such secrecy.

"Let's just say that some of the members often risk the anger of their competitors, and also of some governments."

"Ah," I said, then asked him why the hell he bothered with all that pantomime.

He looked at me reprovingly. "I have a ton of money and no relatives. Let me satisfy my little whims."

I had no idea what floor the elevator was going to, but to judge from how long it took, it certainly wasn't the second.

The doors opened to reveal a vast, glass-lined room. Straight ahead towered the monolith of the AT&T building, and beyond it, the skyscrapers of the Financial District glittered in the night like ships at anchor. On the left of the room, a uniform sheet of yellow and blue fire emerged from the base of what seemed like a huge aluminium frame.

"Hello, Skinny."

I turned to my right. Greg was sitting at a black table at the corner of the window, his blond hair barely illuminated by the one light on the table. He finished tapping something on the keyboard of a computer, then sat back in his chair and looked at me. I slowly crossed the room and approached the window. If I'd suffered from vertigo I would certainly have felt uncomfortable. From a hi-fi I could not see came a piano piece by Haydn.

"Would you like a drink?"

I shrugged and for a moment kept looking out of the window. Greg lifted the receiver of the telephone on the table.

"Two vodka martinis, please," he said, then hung up and stretched again on the chair. After a few moments he stood up, slowly walked across a good part of the room and went and sat down behind me on one of the two black leather couches that faced each other at right angles to the fireplace.

"If you've come to look at the view you could have stayed in your pigsty of an apartment. You only had to tell me and I'd have sent you a postcard."

I waited a few seconds, then turned. I didn't really know what to do or where to begin. Greg was sitting there with that usual half-smile of his which had always amused me, but was now getting on my nerves like a guitar being tuned.

I went straight to the couch until I was very close to Greg. He raised his eyebrows and looked me up and down from behind the black frames of his glasses. The next instant, I threw myself on him and aimed my right fist directly at his face. But Greg was faster than I'd anticipated, and by springing to the left managed to avoid the blow almost completely. I lost my balance and fell forward. My fist ended up stuck between the cushion and the arm of the couch, with my wrist twisted in an unnatural fashion.

"Aaah!" I screamed like a little boy.

"What the fuck are you doing?" Greg yelled above me.

Then I felt an anvil descend on my right side and the air abandoning every corner of my lungs and a dull pain in my ribs. For a brief instant, as I fell to one side and tried to cry out, I felt as though I were going to die of suffocation. I was on the floor next to the couch now, bent double, not sure whether to hold my wrist or my chest. After what seemed an eternity, I managed to get my breath back enough to produce a groan, and got up into a kneeling position. The pain in my ribs was easing off, becoming diffused, but my wrist was still throbbing, crying vengeance like a crazed animal.

"Have you gone mad?"

Greg was standing behind the couch with an expression on his face I'd never seen: a mixture of anger and surprise and fear I wouldn't in all honesty have thought him capable of. He passed a hand over his cheek and looked at it.

"You hit me! What the fuck's got into you?"

I wanted to say something, anything to wipe out that clumsy attempt to strike my oldest friend.

"For Christ's sake! Why the fuck did you hit me?"

With no small effort, I moved back as far as the edge of

the couch opposite. I bent double again. My wrist was still screaming with pain, and I wondered if I'd broken it.

"You know why," I finally managed to murmur, then coughed twice and screwed up my face with the pain.

"Shit!" Greg cried. "I know? I KNOW? No, God dammit, no, I don't know! Jesus, I ought to call the doorman and have you kicked out of here!"

I glanced at him, then lowered my head again and tried slowly to move my wrist. It was still hurting like hell but, although it creaked in a rather sinister way, it seemed to be moving all right.

"Forget it. You're a mess, but you're not exactly dangerous."

He was agitated, more agitated than I had ever seen him, which struck me as a fairly acceptable result.

"Shit!" Greg said again, but more softly, jerking his head to one side. He touched his cheek again and looked at his hand.

"I didn't even hit you."

"Actually you did, damn you. A glancing blow, but you did hit me. If you'd hit me properly you'd have taken my head off. But what the fuck's the matter with you?"

For a few seconds I kept moving my wrist a bit and throwing him a couple of quick glances.

"I know everything, Greg," I said softly after a while.

"Everything about what?"

"I managed to track down the former president of the Cirri Foundation. I talked to him and Lucio and several others. I spent three days in front of the computer and on the phone, sleeping three hours a night. I've reconstructed everything."

I finally raised my head and looked Greg straight in the eyes. He stared back at me, but didn't say anything. After a few moments a little bell rang in the room. Greg let a couple of seconds pass, still staring at me.

"Fuck off," he snorted, before going towards a narrow counter that emerged like a breakfast bar from the wall opposite the windows. He walked around it, opened a kind of dumbwaiter in the wall and took out a tray with two cone-shaped glasses on it. As he came back towards the couch, I stood up and went back to the window. I tried to move my chest and ribs: they hurt quite a bit, but nothing was broken.

"I should smash this on your head," Greg said, slamming the tray on the glass surface of the table. Then he sat down, picked up one of the glasses and took a sip, giving me a final furious glance. But after a few moments he gave a deep sigh followed by a little laugh. "Did you have to hit me?"

I turned. "I don't know, you tell me: did I have to hit you?"

Greg drank again. "What do you want me to say, Skinny?"

"Why you did it, that's all."

"Honestly, I don't understand why you're so pissed off."

"Oh, really? You don't understand?"

"No, I don't understand. I gave you everything you have. You should thank me, you should drink a toast to me, not come here and try to hit me and stand there like an idiot."

At last. This was what had obsessed me and worn away at me slowly since that damned phone call, the day before Biagio's funeral, this was what, from the moment I'd hung up my parents' grey telephone, had been burrowing away inside me like a termite.

I've already done as much for Biagio as I could. Now it's up to you.

Here was that sentence again: and yet, without my realizing it, until that sinister laugh a few nights earlier, it hadn't been the sentence that had taken away my breath and my ideas for weeks. It was, though, a sentence so simple as to seem exactly the same. The mere replacement of one word by three others: "I've already done as much for all of you as I could." That wasn't what Greg had said, but it was what had bounced around my head until it made me feel nauseous, preventing me from feeling anything else. As if half of me already knew and wanted to inform the other half, without success. Until that night, in Amanda's apartment, when Greg's laugh had thrown it in my face more strongly than usual. I had woken with a start, with my heart pounding like mad and sweat on my neck and forehead. For *all of you*? What did that mean: for all of you? What had Greg done for us? What had Greg done for *me*?

Obsessed by that shadow, and with the terrifying sensation of losing control and going mad, I had left Amanda's apartment and gone back to mine. I had gone on the internet and investigated every useful lead and called whoever I could think of at all hours of the day and night, hoping that all my doubts would be swept away and vanish like a passing madness and I could at last go back to my lessons and my books and my relationship with Amanda and everything that up until that summer I had called "my life". But none of the people I contacted had removed my doubts. In fact, they had confirmed them, and all at once what I'd lived through until a few months earlier seemed hardly to belong to me at all.

It was Greg who'd had the Rocky Road tarred, Greg who had made sure that Lucio had come to see Biagio ride, Greg who'd somehow put that damned card in my book and had me entered in the selection process for the scholarship, through the foundation of which his father had been one of the biggest sponsors. And it was Greg who had allowed Paolino to be granted the finance to open his dealership and expand. Suddenly, through those simple interventions, the chilling, slender shadow of Greg hovered over every single part of our lives, with his hands in his pockets and that sinister smile on his lips.

"And who told you I wanted it? Who told you any of us wanted it?"

Greg gave an affected laugh. "You can't be serious."

"Of course I'm serious. Very serious."

"Why, did you want to stay in San Filippo?" he asked, passing a hand over his mouth.

"Maybe, yes. What do you know about it? You should have asked us."

"Asked you what?"

"You should have asked Biagio, for instance, if he wanted Torcini to be contacted. Or you should have asked me if I wanted you to help me get a scholarship."

"What difference would it have made? Would you all have said, 'No, thanks'?"

"How do you know? Maybe, yes. It's too late now."

"What the fuck are you talking about, Skinny? Would you all have turned down the most important opportunities of your lives?"

"That's exactly the point: it wasn't the opportunity of our lives, it was an opportunity for *you*."

True, none of us had ever admitted it, but as I've already said, I'm sure that more or less consciously, from the moment our eyes fell on the black surface of the Rocky Road, our lives had secretly been opened up to a vaster world. Suddenly, strange and surprising things had started to happen, about which we preferred not to ask too many questions, but which filled us with a new, thrilling enthusiasm. We found motorcycles forgotten in sheds and roads mysteriously covered in asphalt, we rode fast bikes and people offered to race us and postcards appearing in our books transported us to great universities abroad. Who would have taken the trouble to say no to all this? Something greater than us was dragging us—perhaps despite ourselves—outside the village where we had grown up and where, until that moment, we had been happy, and who were we to oppose it?

If, though, all these mysterious forces were nothing but thin, invisible threads in the hands of a man as limited and shortsighted as the rest of us, that changed things. If Greg had asked us, if Greg had come to me one day and said, "Listen, Jacopo, our family is a partner in a foundation that among its other activities selects candidates for major scholarships. Do you mind if I put your name forward?" how would I have reacted? Would I have applied anyway, or would the honest, pure part of me have said, "Thanks, but I don't need help from anybody else"? And if that had happened, what would have become of me? What would have become of all of us? What about Biagio? Would he have gone to those motorcycle trials knowing that one of the sponsors was his best friend? I remembered it well, that sense of inadequacy, the day we went to Mugello, that question buzzing in both our heads, and especially his: "What are we doing here?" Imagine if, on top of that, we had suspected we were only there out of friendship.

"All right, Jacopo, do me a favour. This conversation makes no sense: take a sleeping pill and go to bed, then maybe we can talk about it again calmly and remember the good old days. Right now I'm tired and you punched me and you're really starting to piss me off."

"I don't need a sleeping pill."

"The drink is getting you all worked up."

"I don't give a damn about the drink."

"A pity, it's a good drink. They aren't easy to make."

"Who told you we wanted to go?"

"Come on, Skinny, stop it. Did you really want to stay in that hole all your life?"

"How do I know? And above all, how did you know?"

"For God's sake, what's happening to you? Where is that lucid, disenchanted person I always loved talking to on the phone? Can you call him, please? Because I can't talk to you. What is it? Would you have preferred to study mathematics in Rome and be a scientist in a country as broke and chaotic as ours? Or maybe you'd have preferred to teach at the wonderful Fermi high school in Posta!"

"What do you know about it? Maybe, yes."

"Fuck off, Skinny. You get excited about Ozawa's concerts at the Boston Opera House, you investigate the behaviour of dark energy, and you develop credible ideas about the destiny of the universe."

"Theories, Greg, mathematical models. I realize you're not too familiar with certain expressions, but that's all they are."

"Don't get on your high horse: I'm already trying to resist the temptation to call the Polish doorman and have you kicked out. I wouldn't stretch the point if I were you."

"I'm not developing any credible idea, just making mathematical gambles. And for a while now everyone's been amusing themselves throwing them back in my face."

Physics Review D, after a bit of sparring back and forth, had refused to publish either of the last two articles I had submitted, which had never happened before and which certainly did not help to lift me out of what now appeared increasingly like the beginning of my premature decline. My only published article challenged the theory of the expanding universe, maintaining that the Big Bang was not where time and space had formed, but simply *one* of the times and spaces. In collaboration with Yuko Atori, a Japanese friend and colleague of mine, through the analysis of seven years' data from the WMAP space probe, I had managed to establish that in background cosmic radiation, the oldest perceptible signal in our universe, appreciable uniform variations in temperature could be found similar to those of spherical waves, the origin of which we claimed could be attributed to gravitational wrinkles caused by the collision of black holes preceding the Big Bang. This was compatible with the picture of a universe which one day would start shrinking again, increasing in density until it reached a new point of infinite density and set off a new Big Bang.

The article had been greeted with a certain suspicion and many of my colleagues had raised a number of objections about the reliability of the theory, the most common being that the temperature fluctuations of background cosmic radiation were too marginal. Oscar Liebowitz had gone one step further: he had written a decidedly astringent article in *Science* in which he knocked down both me and my theory. He claimed to be upset that a serious scientist like Yuko Atori should waste time on such nonsense, especially with someone who seemed for some time now to have wandered into Wonderland. To demolish my theory Liebowitz had claimed, ironically, that with a bit of intelligence and imagination—characteristics I obviously did not lack—you could see whatever you wanted in cosmic background radiation. The article was illustrated by an image of cosmic background radiation—a kind of planisphere dotted with blue and green thermal streaks, with just a few sporadic hints of yellow and red—and above it, surrounded by dark blue shadows, the words *God Exists*. Two days after the publication of his piece, going down into one of the bleak little classrooms in Pupin Hall in Columbia for one of my classes, I had found another map of cosmic background radiation attached to the blackboard, with the words *We still love you, prof* above it.

"Very witty," I admitted reluctantly, giving a little laugh.

Two years earlier, Oscar Liebowitz had been offered the post of director of the Astrophysics Department of the new Kavli Institute in Dallas after I had already turned it down. One evening, over a beer, I'd heard from a mutual acquaintance that Liebowitz was embarrassed by the fact that he had been offered the job only after it had already been offered to a scientist ten years his junior, but obviously, on the few occasions we met, he behaved with the formality for which he was well known. One day however, after a lecture of mine at the University of Dallas which he had decided to attend, we found ourselves alone together in the elevator.

"A bit lightweight, that talk of yours, Dr Ferri," he said as soon as the elevator doors had closed, continuing, as if everything were normal, to stare at the numbers on the button panel as we descended to the ground floor. Usually, we used each other's first names in public in a show of friendship.

I turned and looked at him. He seemed smaller than usual, his skin cracked by some psychosomatic disorder. There was an almost imperceptible hint of a smile on his lips. So as not to go all the way down with him, I pressed the button for the second floor. When the doors opened I stepped out, then stopped the door with my hand, looked him straight in the eyes, and gave him an icy smile.

"Professor Liebowitz," I said, "having to chew the food someone else has spat out every day must have left a bitter taste." Then I said, "Have a nice day," and left with a big smile on my face. As I wasted a few minutes wandering through the second floor of the University of Dallas, I convinced myself that few things in the world were as satisfying as a well-placed barb. As a friend of mine would write one day in one of his books: "Never underestimate the terrible resentment of dwarves."

So I wasn't too surprised by the smug sarcasm with which Liebowitz had slammed the article by me and Yuko. Unfortunately, half of me couldn't help feeling dejected and sniffing the acid smell of failure everywhere. The other half just smiled and kept repeating, "I told you so." Yes, in reality I had known that sooner or later this obsession of mine would bring me to a halt. I had known it ever since that spectre had insinuated itself into my thoughts. After a certain point, I had become obsessed by the idea of being able to find concrete and credible theories that would predict the fate of the universe. In reality, what little fame and authority I had rested on my lengthy study of the very subject of cosmic background radiation, more specifically its anisotropies, its irregularities. But what my obsession was actually about was the limits of the universe. I didn't really want to accept it, but that was the way it was. However, because of the principle of indeterminacy, going all the way back to the real origin obviously wasn't possible. So my interest had shifted to the future. All my studies, though, seemed to confirm the idea of what was commonly called the Big Chill, a kind of general cosmic death. The universe did not seem to have any intention, as I had hoped at first that I could demonstrate, of slowing down or actually stopping its own expansion—let alone starting to contract—and, however lacking in harmony it might seem to me, everything in fact appeared destined to move apart until it disintegrated and disappeared. The problem, though, lay precisely in the word harmony: I couldn't accept that the extraordinary elegance I had grown accustomed to see in the universe was destined for something as cold and bleak as a general collapse. Emotion had, so to speak, penetrated the hitherto solid borders of my research. My subsequent study of cyclic cosmic waves was a way of gathering everything I had constructed and studied into a credible theory that could finally save the elegant idea of a cyclical universe in constant expansion and contraction, like the wrappers of an infinite and very tasty series of sweets. Moreover, it could quite easily be only one of the possible universes. In short, there could be as many sweets as you wanted, and the universe, that even larger one, the father of all universes, could go back to being a gentle, colourful place. That was why half of me, in writing the article with Yuko, had been convinced for months that I had finally found the project of my life, the one for which we would be remembered, a turning point in the history of modern astronomy. The other half of me—unfortunately the more serious and rigorous half—knew it was only a clumsy attempt to bend mathematics and physics and the WMAP data into a naïve sensation devoid of concrete and serious evidence. That was why my more lucid colleagues had taken it for what it in fact was: an interesting but basically weak theory.

"So what?" Greg said, sitting there on his black leather couch with the glass in his hand. "Nobody knows more about the world than you people. It was you who told me that once, overcome by one of your ridiculous scientific ecstasies: 'There's no branch of science or philosophy that has ever investigated the universe so profoundly.' That's what you told me."

"And what do you think the point of it is?"

"I don't know," he said, finishing his drink and putting down the glass. "You tell me."

"There *is* no point, no point at all."

"Stop it, you're talking nonsense. Go home and look at yourself."

"No point to any of it. And do you want to know why?"

"Enlighten me."

"Because advancing in the study of science only means advancing towards an awareness of our limitations."

Greg raised his eyebrows and continued to stare at me.

"Precisely," I continued. "At first it all seems beautiful: the laws of gravity, the curvature of space and time, neutrinos, gluons... it all seems to be there to give colour to a universe that never ceases to amaze you. Then, while you're stooped over a desk solving equations with your eye fixed on that kaleidoscope, you realize the years are passing and the only thing you've really learnt is that a human being will never understand a fucking thing about what surrounds him, and above all that the whole human race and this whole planet that everyone worries so much about will vanish in what for the universe is no more than the infinitesimal fraction of a yawn. Everything becomes insignificant, Greg. Nothing matters any more. And the beauty of it is, you don't even notice it. It's a slow, unconscious process of erosion: moment by moment, every new revelation about the universe darkens another fragment of your days, until you're not surprised by anything any more. What can still surprise us when we already have intergalactic collisions, black holes, fossil radiation and supernovas? Everything surrounding us becomes simply an accumulation of vibrating particles which will dissolve in the clicking of a finger or contract into the void it came from."

Greg was still sitting there motionless, staring at me and smiling. I stared back at him, biting the inside of my lip slightly. For a moment the music faded, and I almost thought I could hear both of us breathing.

"Amanda wants children."

Greg said nothing.

"Do you think she's wrong? We've been going out for three years and I've never even suggested living together, let alone having kids."

"Why?"

"What do you mean 'why'? How can I bring children into the world, make them work as hard as everyone has to work, most probably suffer, and then as soon as they've developed enough brains to ask me a few questions tell them, 'You know, I was joking. There's no point to any of this. Everything you construct, everything you strive for will be swept away like the contents of an ashtray in the wind'?"

Greg continued looking at me for a few seconds. "And so your great new insight is that if you'd stayed in San Filippo everything might have been better?"

"I don't know. Maybe, yes. At least I didn't know."

"Is that what you really wanted? A nice little wife to fuck in the missionary position, mass on Sunday, gathering blackberries in summer with your kids?"

"What's wrong with that?"

"Did you want a life like your parents?"

"My parents are satisfied with their lot."

"Sorry to tell you this, Skinny, but your parents are the dullest people I've ever met. Whenever I went to your house, even if it was only for ten minutes, it took me the next two days to shake off the boredom."

A smile escaped me. Then after a moment I became serious again and bowed my head. "I doubt everything, Greg."

"What do you mean?"

"What I said. For a while now there hasn't been anything I haven't doubted. Everything appears blurred and indistinct."

"Well, congratulations."

"On what?"

"You doubt, you're alive, you're a man at last."

"What are you talking about? It's all blurred and grey. Is that life?"

"In your opinion, Skinny, why are we here?"

"Oh, my God, how should I know why we're here? I don't even know if I still like coffee or not."

"Here in this city, I mean."

"In this city?"

"Yes."

I stared at Greg for a few moments, feeling myself slipping into a terrifying and absurd whirlpool of incoherent arguments.

"Original sin, Skinny."

"Original sin? What's original sin got to do with it?"

"Why do you think they call this city the Big Apple?"

"I don't know."

"Neither do I, but it's always amused me to think that it's the greatest monument to the forbidden fruit, to man's irrepressible tendency to rise above himself."

Again I couldn't hold back a smile. "Are you preparing for another conversion?"

"Stop it," Greg said irritably. "And put it any way you like, but at a certain point in the history of this strange evolution of the ape something happened. And who cares about his discoveries? They all derive, every one of them, from the biological joke of opposable thumbs. We agreed on that once: nature couldn't have found a more effective tool for training our brains than this damned crooked finger. But that's not the real, the inexplicable miracle: it's that after a while this animal started to ask himself questions. He removed himself from the world around him and found the freedom to doubt. That's what we are: doubt."

I looked at him for a few moments. "Well, because of how we are, it might have been better not to ask ourselves all these questions."

Greg gave a forced laugh. "Oh, come on. Someone like you spends every day asking the most ambitious questions a human being has ever asked himself. Why do you think you get that thrill every time you come out of that damned 59th Street station?"

I looked at him without saying anything.

"Because you feel at home, Skinny. Because it's music to your ears."

I lowered my eyes and gave a deep sigh. "I don't know."

Greg looked hard at me for a few seconds. "What is it you want? Thanks to me you've seen the world, you've known the abyss of desire. You've learnt to suffer."

*

Oh yes, the gods knew I'd learnt what desire was. Knives in the chest and organs that turned in on themselves. Red hot pincers had squeezed my soul and genitals until they bled, and all because of the unlikeliest of women.

It all started on an ordinary late April evening. I was at dinner with Fausto, an acquaintance of mine, the New York correspondent for an Italian TV channel. The first word that comes to mind when I try to define him is: clichéd. His Italian shoes with their eye-catching stitching were clichéd, as were his mirror-filled Midtown apartment, his off-colour jokes and especially his passion for young girls. The way he'd laugh on the street and rub his hairy hands and point out a girl of barely twelve and say, "The things I'd do to her…" didn't necessarily make him as odious as he perhaps hoped. More than anything else it made him not very original. For some reason, though, Fausto had taken a shine to me. I don't know if it was the brilliant answers he told me I'd given during the interview that first brought us together, or the day he asked me to replace a friend of his in a soccer game in Central Park and discovered I was a decent midfielder. Whatever the reason, he'd convinced himself that I was a person worth spending time with. His insistence sometimes made it difficult for me to refuse, and as it was a time when I was reluctant to stay indoors anyway and Fausto was always full of plans, always had interesting places to suggest going, I always seemed to end up letting him drag me along.

It was at the end of one of these strange evenings that I found myself in the back seat of a taxi, clinging to the body of a Latino girl. She said her name was Tara, and we had met only a few hours before at Novecento, the restaurant on West Broadway where she worked as a waitress. Fausto, with a lot of cunning and a number of lies—that despite my age I was in the running for a Nobel Prize, that he was interviewing me about it, that they were throwing a party in my honour in TriBeCa that evening, and then that the supposed party had been cancelled at the last moment because of an accident—had managed to lure Tara and another girl who worked with her to an ultra-exclusive club hidden in the basement of the Mercer Hotel, right there in SoHo. An endless supply of bottles of vodka and the girls' excitement at spotting a couple of movie stars had done the rest.

Some time later, standing on the sidewalk, Fausto suggested we all go to his place.

I tried to regain a modicum of clearheadedness. I imagined us in Fausto's living room, which looked like a pimp's hangout, probably getting through another bottle of something, and the dawn coming all too soon.

"I don't know," I said, "I think I'll skip it." Then I looked at Tara and asked her if she'd come with me.

She burst out laughing. "Yes, sir, of course I'll come with you."

By the time we were in the taxi we were finding it hard to keep our hands off each other and we started some serious groping. I felt as if I were going to explode. When we got to my building, I threw too much money on the plexiglass plate, told the driver to keep the change, and we jumped out of the cab. Tara stumbled and fell to her knees on the ground. Laughing, I picked her up and helped her up the few steps that separated us from the front door.

"This is where my landlady lives," I whispered once we were inside, putting a finger to my lips.

"Oh yes?" Tara said. As I turned away to lock the front door behind us, she climbed a few steps of the staircase that led to the upper floor. She turned her head slightly, threw me a glazed smile, grabbed the hem of her skirt, pulled it up above her hips, pushed out her arse and wiggled it. The black thread of a G-string vanished between two buttocks as round and firm as nectarines.

"Jesus," I said. I approached her slowly, and as if my legs were giving way, collapsed on one of the steps and buried my face in her arse. She wiggled again, as if to let my face get further in. I put my hands on her buttocks and parted them and put my nose and tongue half in. Then I pulled back and, feeling all the oxygen abandon my lungs, lifted the G-string with my index finger and moved it aside. I again sank my mouth and tongue into the fold between the buttocks and between the moist lips, before I rose— with something appalling and unknown unleashed inside me—unbuttoned my trousers, climbed two steps and sank into her. Tara placed her hands on another step, emitted a little cry, and started panting. I grabbed the G-string with both hands and tore it. As I took her, I opened her buttocks as far as they would go and, clenching my teeth until they hurt, stared at that dark little star that seemed to be there, winking at me, inviting me. I started massaging it with my thumb, ever stronger, until I let a whole phalanx disappear inside. I felt something rising inside me that I'd never felt, something animal, fighting me inside and swelling my throat in the hint of a snarl. I spat between her buttocks and sank my thumb even further inside.

"*No atrás,*" she said suddenly in Spanish, though still panting and moving.

I didn't listen to her and slipped the other thumb inside her too.

"No," she sighed again, still moaning.

I felt that fierce animal continuing to swell my throat. It had nothing of the yearning I'd felt in the days of Trisha for her soft cunt and her skin, let alone the sublimated eroticism I thought I'd felt for Anna, the doctorate colleague in Baltimore I'd decided to become infatuated with and soon got bored with. It was something different, something shattering. Something *older*: older than me and older than man. It was as if I found myself torn in two: half of me had gone back to its most primitive urges, the other was in the most refined vanguard of evolution. And they were both struggling and snarling, trying to bring what they had started to a conclusion: I lifted myself from inside her, jumped up another step, again spat at her behind, took out my thumbs, opened her buttocks wide, and entered.

"No," she howled again, not very convincingly. I started to slip in and out of her, first slowly, then more violently, that constant muted snarl still vibrating in my throat. She was moaning ever more loudly, and the stairs were starting to creak. I felt the muscles of my legs and back hurting and when she was about to cry out, I tried to cover her mouth with one hand and she bit it, and when I was about to come and took away my hand and grabbed her hair and gave her a big slap on the arse, she turned her head aside and shrieked, "*Ahi, corazón, qué rico!*"

So it was that graceless, ridiculous expression of pleasure that started my brief, shambling relationship with Tara.

Everything went well until about a month later. We had seen each other a few times, always alone. We'd go out for a bite to eat, maybe catch a film, then drop into a bar somewhere, fill ourselves up with vodka like the first evening and go back to my place. Once we actually took the vodka to bed with us, and ended up falling asleep in liquor-soaked sheets.

Tara often talked to me about her half-Venezuelan origins and her new-age parents who had moved before she was born to a hippie commune in California. When she talked about those years, her eyes gleamed like a little girl's and she said they had been the happiest in her life. I asked her once what had made her leave, but she muttered something about an accident and changed the subject. She also often talked about her name, Tara, and told me it belonged to an Indian goddess, the mother of all the goddesses and a source of light for the buddhas. Thinking back on it now, I can't help realizing that whenever she talked about those years in the commune and about her name, there was always something slightly excessive, slightly forced in it, but at the time I dismissed it without further thought.

All that mattered was that she seemed quite stuck on me and called me her "little genius". She found it a bit hard to distinguish between astrology and astronomy, and often asked me to explain some sign of the zodiac. I would smile: part of me wondered what the hell I was doing with someone like her, but I would tell myself that that arse and that mouth were a more than valid answer to any question. I think what confused her was the word *predictions*: to simplify things, I had told her I studied the behaviour of the stars and made predictions about the future of the universe. So from time to time, leafing through a magazine, she would read out a horoscope and ask me, quite seriously, if I agreed. The fact that I was a distinguished scholar had reawakened in her a deep interest in horoscopes.

So that was how it went on: my conceited awareness of my intellectual superiority helped me quench any doubts I might have had as to why she kept going out with me and waving that arse in front of my eyes, and I had the unconscious illusion that this whole relationship might have been weird but was somehow solid. Up until that evening.

We had arranged as usual to have a bite to eat somewhere and then decide what to do. It was her day off and she had told me to call her on her cellphone about seven to make arrangements. At seven she hadn't answered, or at 7:10 or 7:17 or 7:32 or 7:50 or 8:02. After four rings, the answering machine came on and at the third attempt I left a message, saying hello and that it was after seven and I was waiting to hear from her and I was at home and she should call me. I'd never had any great desire to get a cellphone, and to keep in contact with people I used a white AT&T answering machine, which when it was empty displayed a single—and until that moment anonymous—luminous red zero. When there were messages, the number flashed. After an umpteenth attempt, at 8:23, which made me feel weak and nauseous, as if a rat were starting to gnaw at my stomach, I decided it was better to go out, if for no other reason than to eat something. When I got back, I ran up the stairs, convinced I would find a message from Tara on the answering machine and would finally hear her apology and we would meet and I would overcome that sudden terrifying sense of disorientation. But that damned zero was still there, as calm as could be. I lifted the receiver to make sure it was working. I redialled Tara's number, but again there was no answer. Feeling stupid and ridiculous, and overcome with an undeniable sense of panic, I left her another message, telling her obstinately that I was still at home, waiting for her, and that she should get in touch.

About ten I called Fausto.

"Listen," I said after our hellos, "any idea what's happened to Tara?"

"Who?"

"Tara."

"Who's Tara?"

"Come on, Fausto, the girl from Novecento we went to that club with."

"Oh, yes… She was hot. Are you still seeing her?"

"Yes, we were supposed to meet tonight."

"She stood you up, eh?"

"Something must have happened. Maybe you've spoken to her friend…"

"No way, I never saw her after that night. I don't even have her number."

"All right, thanks anyway."

"You sound down. Come out with me. We'll find a couple of whores."

"No, thanks, Fausto, maybe another time. I have to get up early tomorrow."

With images of Tara going round New York with some of her girlfriends and a few men starting to invade my thoughts, I tried to calm down by watching an old film with Marilyn Monroe and Cary Grant, but it didn't help much. So I threw myself on the bed and tried to read. I slept in fits and starts, one hour at a time, but couldn't stop myself going into the living room to check that damned red zero in the dark, hoping every time that she had called while I was asleep to say something had come up and she was sorry and would call me tomorrow. Obviously there was never anything, just that damned little luminous circle staring at me like the eye of the devil. I saw Tara in clubs, her arms round a huge tattooed guy with a cock as big as a pole throbbing inside his leather trousers. I saw his hands on that round arse and those thighs and that skin as smooth and dark as leather. I had to masturbate twice, and both times I thought I was also doing it with the tattooed guy, which left me feeling even more nauseous than before.

The next day, pale and dead beat and with two green chasms under my eyes, I went to the university and told everyone I was coming down with something and might even have a fever. After lunch, when I got back home, I saw at last a little bar flashing on the answering machine.

"Hi, it's me," the voice said. "Sorry about yesterday but something bad happened to a friend of mine and I rushed out and left my cellphone at home. Talk to you later. Bye."

The tone was, understandably, somewhat cool. I immediately felt stupid and ridiculous, and went into the bathroom to wash my face and look in the mirror and see if there was something in my eyes of the man I thought I knew.

Two evenings later we saw each other again. We had agreed to meet in Washington Square and then grab a bite to eat on Bleeker. Everything felt different. I tried to seem casual, but wasn't very successful. I had lost my desire to laugh and I had no idea how to get it back, and if we didn't laugh and talk crap to each other, we didn't know what to talk about. She told me that two evenings earlier the junkie ex-boyfriend of a friend of hers—the father of this friend's child—had died. She had gone running to her friend to take her out and in her hurry had, as she had told me, left her cellphone at home.

"But where did you think I was?" she asked, smiling.

I shrugged. For the first time I started to suspect that a relationship with a woman is very similar to a long and complex trench war, and that every small tactical error is very difficult to make up for. After dinner we didn't stop for a drink anywhere: I was tired and I had a difficult class to give the following morning, so I told her I preferred to go straight home. In the bedroom, we didn't tear the clothes off each other as we usually did, because I wanted to take things more calmly and gently, but I was sober and frustrated and I came even before she could give a moan.

"Is that all?" she said, laughing, as I got up to go and wash.

From that moment, and for some weeks, my relationship with Tara—if you could call it that—was nothing but a rollercoaster of disappointments and torments. From time to time she'd be impossible to get hold of, which only made me all the more desperate to reach her. Every time, like a primal trauma, I would be overcome with the same nausea and vertigo that had carried me away that first evening by the answering machine. I even started drinking a fair amount. I would buy bottles of Belvedere, the vodka from that first night, and get through them sprawled on the couch watching old films, with a cushion behind my neck. I often masturbated sniffing the couch and the little table, searching for traces of her smell. I even found myself licking the edge of the chest of drawers in the bedroom where, one of the first times, I had laid her and forced her legs open and licked her. As I ran my tongue along the cold edge, I was thinking that Tara's arse had been in this spot, maybe her cunt too had touched it, and the most throbbing erection of my life swelled in my hand. A few moments later, after coming on the floor, I sat down broken against the chest, put a hand over my face and started sobbing.

I was still seeing a lot of Fausto. Maybe it was because he was, paradoxically, my only link with Tara, or maybe it was just that he was the only person who could get me out of the house and keep me out until oblivion overtook me. It was a different time from any other I've known: we went from parties in which all I did was drink and babble incoherently to clubs I would never have believed existed.

One evening, as we were leaving a bar in the Meatpacking District, Fausto laughed and told me to follow him. We crossed the street, opened a little door hidden in the wall, and went down two flights of stairs. Immediately to the left of the entrance, bars ran from the ceiling to the floor, separating a dark corner from the rest of the room. Behind the bars, a hairy, overweight man was tied to the wall completely naked and was being whipped by a woman dressed in latex.

It was one of the few times Fausto and I had a conversation that was slightly more serious and personal: we talked about Italy and the reasons he hadn't gone back and how, if things had worked out, we would both have preferred to live there and not in a country which, however welcoming, was still a foreign country.

As we talked, sipping our drinks, we moved to a room where there were hammocks and two or three wooden pallets. On one of the pallets, a woman was being masturbated in an almost surgical manner by three men, and emitting loud cries. Walking around the club, well-dressed customers alternated with completely naked people and wild-eyed men with huge erections in their hands. The surprising thing, though, was my absolute imperviousness. The fact that we were chatting as we moved though a club where people were being touched and penetrated in front of everybody, surrounded by half-naked maniacs with eyes popping out of their heads, didn't seem to matter. Over the years I went back to the Hellfire a few more times, and every time it was like entering a parallel world governed by its own rules, where what you saw lost any feeling of strangeness.

Fausto grew bored with my attempts to extract from him an opinion or any words of comfort about my relationship with Tara.

He sighed and cut me short. "Forget about her," he said, raising his eyes to heaven. "It's not worth making a fool of yourself over a girl like that."

I think it was those simple words that made me suddenly choose Fausto, the apparently least appropriate person, as my mentor. And yet it was only a marginal symptom of the general paradox in which I'd become hopelessly entangled: what was I doing with Tara? Was it for this that I'd spent the best years of my life? Once, in a few pleasant moments of solitude, happening to look up at the star-filled sky, I let myself wallow in mathematical models for describing gravitational waves. What was I doing with this simple-minded creature who found it really hard to understand the difference between a star and a planet, and was convinced that the moon shone with its own light?

"What are you talking about?" she'd replied with a laugh when I tried to explain to her that the light of the moon was actually the reflected light of the sun. "It's a different colour!"

And yet my attempts to draw Tara into a steady and definite relationship were increasingly energetic, and also increasingly clumsy. She responded by standing me up more often. One evening when she told me she had to work, I took up position on the other side of West Broadway and waited for her to come out of Novecento. I had put on an improbable Mets cap and even a jacket, although it was quite hot, and I raised the collar to hide my face. I was convinced she had lied to me and that she wasn't in the restaurant. But then I saw her come out and say goodbye to the other waiters and waitresses. I thought for a moment of catching up with her, then simply started following her. She walked north as far as Prince Street and turned right. On the corner of Broadway she went down into the subway, inserted and withdrew her Metrocard from the respective slits in the turnstile and took the stairs that led towards the northbound platform. I started waiting, half turned away, about twenty metres from her. Once on the train, I sat down quite far from her, but in a seat that allowed me to keep my eye on her. She simply sat there with phones in her ears and a book in her hand. I couldn't see the title, but from the colours and squiggles on the cover I guessed it was a romantic novel. She looked like anyone else, an ordinary defenceless human being in the immensity of a big city, sheltering behind the silence of her music and her book. The fact that I was aware of what she really was, what kind of creature was concealed within those clothes, and the fact that she couldn't see me, made me feel as if I were a government spy, or an alien from another planet.

She stayed on the subway to 57th Street, and then past that, on the elevated, as far as Queens. On one of our evenings out she had told me she lived in a little row house in

Astoria, and it was clear now that she was going home and that I was an idiot and that things might have gone well for a while, but the time had come to get out of this madness once and for all. As I was wondering if I would also get off when we got to the end of the line and say something to her, Tara stood up, put her book back in her bag, and walked to the carriage door. It was the 30th Avenue stop, which, as far as I knew, wasn't the stop near where she lived. Doing everything I could to hide behind someone, I got to the door and, still keeping a few dozen metres behind her, followed Tara off the train and down the iron staircase of the elevated and outside, and found myself surrounded by the square apartment blocks of Queens. It was like a scene from *The Warriors*. Tara walked east for three blocks, then turned right and across a half-empty parking lot. At the far end of the parking lot she headed for the back of a brick building and knocked at an iron door. After a few moments, it was opened for her and she disappeared inside. On the front of the building, above a glass door and the big man standing in front of it, there was a red neon sign saying *Boom Bar*, with the illuminated drawing of a buxom, knowing girl in a bikini. I stood there for at least ten minutes, in a daze, at the other side of the little square, wondering what to do, then slowly, as if in a trance, dragged myself to the entrance. The man at the door was wearing a sweatshirt and wide black trousers and a shiny silver chain around his neck.

"I.D., please."

I took my identity card from my pocket and showed it to him. As always happens in New York, he checked it carefully with a torch and gave it back to me, stared at me for a moment, then said, "Go ahead."

Beyond the door was a little room separated from the club by a dark blue velvet curtain. A girl at a table asked me for twenty dollars. It was a perfectly ordinary strip club, with its armchairs and its sofas and its bar and its coloured lights and its half-naked girls swaying their hips and opening their legs in time to the music on stages or around shiny steel poles. The same kind of strip club where I'd once gone with a fun-loving teacher of mine from Princeton to discuss my research. I ordered a neat vodka from a dark-skinned barman on steroids and sat down at a corner table.

About twenty minutes later, she appeared from behind the curtain of the main stage, along with two other girls who were paler and taller than her. She was wearing a skimpy fuchsia bikini and two shiny boots with platforms nearly two inches high and heels of at least six. She had more make-up on than usual and her hair was pulled back in a tight ponytail that made her look more adult and ruthless. She went straight to a pole to the right of the stage. From the back of the room I watched her rub herself against the pole and shake and bend, smiling at a few customers who approached and slipped some dollars into her G-string, and I didn't recognize a single thing I was feeling. About ten minutes later she moved from the main stage to a smaller one, surrounded by a series of tables and armchairs. After a few moments I got up and sat down like an automaton on one of the armchairs close to this smaller stage. Two other men also approached her. One of them slipped a five-dollar bill in her G-string and stood there for more than a minute watching Tara opening her legs in front of him and putting her hand behind his head.

"You're gorgeous," the man said when she started dancing

again round the pole. She smiled and winked at him, then continued dancing for herself. After a while she winked at the other man, then turned towards me, gave a little smile, and as she was already turning her head gave me another, sharper look. Dreary pop music was bouncing off the walls, and my heart seemed to be beating like a bass drum in time to it. Tara moved around the pole and glared at me again. Then she continued dancing for five minutes without looking at me, smiling a couple of times at the other man and finally accepting one of his dollars in her G-string. She then came down off the stage, danced her way to my armchair, rubbed herself against me for a moment and coldly whispered in my ear to take out twenty dollars and put it in her G-string. I took my wallet, dug out two ten-dollar bills and stuck them under the side of the G-string. She then sat down on my lap, facing me, unhooked her top and took it off. I had the feeling that everything around me was vanishing and for a moment I had the illusion that I could kiss her and lick her and take her right there on that chair. I passed a hand over her side and went closer to kiss her, but she pushed me back in my chair with one hand.

"You can't touch me," she said, as coldly as before.

She then finished off what must have been the simple ballet she performed for all her customers, made me lift the bikini top over her head and pulled me towards her breasts.

"Now get out of here and wait for me outside, and don't let anybody see you," she whispered in my ear, then got up and put the bikini top back on and went back to the main stage. So as not to be too conspicuous, I stayed there for another ten minutes and finished my vodka, then stood up, nodded goodbye to the girl at the cash desk and the guy at the door as I went out and headed for the far end of the parking lot. I settled down to wait round the corner, leaning on the boot of a car. By the time Tara appeared, two hours later, I was already thinking of leaving.

"Hi," I said, somewhat embarrassed, when she emerged from the parking lot.

"Move," she said looking behind her and continuing to walk quickly. "If they see me leaving with a customer they'll fire me."

I walked quickly behind her as far as the subway station and up onto the elevated. As we waited, I smiled at her and tried to kiss her on the cheek. She threw me a glance, then again stared along the platform to where the train was due to arrive.

"How did you get here?" she asked.

"I followed you."

She looked at me gravely for a moment or two. We heard the noise of the train and waited for it to arrive, then sat down side by side on one of the blue plastic benches. We didn't say anything else to each other. When we reached the end of the line, two stops later, we got off and I followed her down Ditmars Boulevard and along one of the streets on the left. She went through a small iron gate and opened the door of a small two-storey brick building, identical to all the buildings in the street. She climbed to the upper floor, opened another door and let me into a small untidy two-room apartment, full of clothes and magazines left lying around. There was a smell of incense and dust and even before taking off her jacket, Tara hastened to light two scented candles.

"Sit down, I'll be right back," she said, throwing her jacket on the sofa and disappearing into what must have been the bathroom. I moved a few garments, sat down on the couch and leafed through a fashion magazine. For a few minutes I heard the shower running. Then I heard something fall, maybe a jar. When she reappeared, Tara had a long blue towel tied round her breasts and on her head the kind of turban women use to dry their hair. She walked straight to a small old stereo and put a disc in, then approached, moved aside the little table in front of the couch with her foot and sat down astride my legs. Through the folds in the towel, I could see a few short hairs of her shaved pubis. She unrolled the turban, opened the towel and, as I started running my fingertips over her skin, gave me a long kiss. Then she stood up, held out her hand and led me towards the bed. She undressed me very calmly, laid me down on two pillows and finally mounted me. We made love for a long time, silently, and although I was fairly sure she didn't come, it struck me this might be the first time we had really made love. Afterwards, she got up and went back to the bathroom. After a few moments I heard the water running, then the sound of a hair dryer.

As I lay there, still buried in a mire of mixed emotions I couldn't identify, my eyes fell on some sheets of paper on one of the little shelves next to the bed. I took them and leafed through them. They were in Spanish and looked important. Attached to one of the sheets was a faded little yellow plastic card with a photograph of Tara. She looked very young and innocent, and I wondered what the girl in the photo had to do with the woman I had seen stripping a few hours earlier at the Boom Bar. Or, to tell the truth, with the woman who had just stripped me and laid me on the bed. Under the photograph was the name *Rosalita Hernández*, with some other numbers and a date that made her three or four years older and next to it what must have been her place of birth: *México, Distrito Federal*.

Tara reappeared completely naked, went to a chest of drawers without even looking at me, opened one of the drawers, took out a pair of shorts and a T-shirt and put them on. Then she looked at herself in the mirror for a moment.

"Well, Rosalita?" I said, smiling. There was no particular reason why I said it, nor, to be honest, was I even thinking about what those papers and that card meant. Tara looked at me in the mirror, then turned, looked at the papers I was holding in my hand and again at me.

"What the fuck are you doing?"

She seemed very serious and very angry and I felt an icy wave flood through my veins. "Nothing, I just happened to notice these—"

"WHAT THE FUCK ARE YOU DOING?" she suddenly screamed.

"Nothing, I was only—"

She leapt at me, tore the papers from my hand, threw them on the chest of drawers and turned with her face suddenly hard, staring at some indeterminate point on the floor. "Get out," she said.

"Tara, I don't give a damn about these—"

"GET OUT!" she screamed hysterically.

I suddenly felt as though my head were in a vice. I sat down on the edge of the bed and started getting dressed. She stood there motionless, staring at the same point on the floor, nervously biting her lip. I finished dressing, then looked at her.

"Tara, I don't—"

"You have to go."

"I don't want to go. I'm not interested in those papers. I only want—"

"YOU HAVE TO GO!" she screamed again in that hysterical voice.

I tried to reach out my hand and touch her arm. "Tara…"

She knocked my hand away, pushed me aside and strode across the living room. I couldn't really believe it, but I actually saw her slap her face a few times. She opened the door to the apartment, went across the landing and started beating on the door opposite.

"COSTA!" she screamed.

Tara had told me, with a laugh, about a neighbour of hers, a Greek named Costa, who sometimes gave her a hand to mend a pipe, carry a piece of furniture or put up a shelf. She always said she didn't know what she would have done without him, and that once he had even saved her from an attempted assault near the building. I had always assumed Costa was a muscular guy with tattoos all over him, but kind and affectionate in his way. But the man who came to the door in an undershirt a few moments later was middle-aged with a paunch and a long lock of hair brushed over a bald patch.

"What's going on, Tara?" he said, sleepily. "It's five in the morning."

"This asshole hit me," she said, gesturing behind her without even looking at me.

"What?"

Costa looked at her, then at me inside the apartment, trying to connect the two.

"This son of a bitch slapped me twice and now he won't go."

"But it isn't true!" I cried, my voice sounding ridiculously boyish.

"Oh, no? Look," said Tara, or Rosalita or whoever she was, turning her face from side to side in front of Costa.

Costa opened the door fully, tied a towel round his waist and came slowly towards me. In a flash of lucidity I told myself, with a certain interest, that this was perhaps the first time I had experienced real terror. The voice that emerged from my mouth was like the squeak of a mouse.

"Look, Mr Costa, there's been a misunderstanding."

Costa approached and stopped in front of me. For a moment I fooled myself that I could reason with him, then all at once I felt my cheek explode. I was flung to the floor on the other side of the room. He kicked me twice and I screamed, begging him to stop. I couldn't say anything except, "Stop, I can explain, please stop."

"Did he have anything else?" Costa asked, turning towards Tara.

"That jacket."

Costa picked up my jacket from a chair, approached me again, gave me another few—fortunately inaccurate—kicks, and grabbed me by the hair. I managed somehow to get up and follow him, bent double, my head attached to his hand.

"Tara," I said as I passed, reaching out a hand towards her. She brushed it away and went back inside. Costa dragged me down the stairs, still bent in that ridiculous position. Once outside the little gate, he threw my jacket into the middle of the street, then changed the hand with which he was holding my hair, lifted my head, and as I let out another scream landed a second punch on my cheek. I was thrown to the ground and for a few moments all I saw was darkness and a thousand coloured flashes. When I opened my eyes again, I was flat on my face on the sidewalk.

"And if you try to come anywhere near Tara again I swear I'll put a bullet in your head."

I heard him spit, presumably at me, then out of the corner of my eye saw him go back up the few steps that led inside the building and slam the door behind him.

As I got up, I noticed someone peering at me from behind the curtain of a little house on the other side of the street. As soon as our eyes met, the figure disappeared behind the curtain. I dragged myself to the middle of the street and picked up my jacket. I tried to pull myself together and figure out where I was. Half my face throbbing like the open heart of an animal, I walked slowly towards the subway. The train was there at the end of the line, waiting to set off again. A couple of shady individuals who got on with me sniggered and pointed out my obviously swollen face to each other. I told myself I would phone Tara the next day, or else I'd go to the restaurant and we'd talk and everything would pass. For a moment, I even persuaded myself that I'd be able to help her and maybe for the first time I realized that I really loved her and I didn't care if she wasn't Venezuelan and had never lived in a commune in California and was probably an illegal immigrant who had grown up in a shantytown in Mexico City. I didn't care about anything: we'd talk about it and I would understand her and I would marry her and protect her and cure her of whatever it was that was troubling her.

Fortunately it didn't happen. Once I had recovered, something grey and slimy continued to float inside me, but it was simply too much: she was too much, her body was too much, and her tongue, and obviously her past, and—however clever I tried to be—the distance between us was too great. I didn't see her again, I didn't hear from her, and whenever I happened to be in the area of Novecento a feeling of nausea always made me gave it a wide berth.

"So, do you think all that desire, all that suffering is any use in looking at the world or giving Amanda a home and child? What do you think I should do?"

"I don't know, Skinny, play *briscola*. What do you want from me?"

I looked at Greg for a few seconds. I wondered if he was really so sure of himself or if he was just a very good actor. "I think a lot about Paolino," I said.

"Paolino?"

"Yes, Paolino."

"What's Paolino got to do with anything?"

"He certainly doesn't go to mass on Sunday or gather blackberries. And I guarantee that with Giorgia he does more than fuck missionary style."

"So?"

"That means they're happy, Greg. I go back to the village and I go to see them and they're laughing or arguing or watching TV, but they're fine. They're healthy. Sure, they don't know. But so what? What do I do with all this knowledge? Am I so much better off?"

"Paolino is a dear boy, Skinny, and Giorgia and the kids have certainly been good for him, but I never heard him say a sensible sentence before he was fifteen. Can you tell me what Paolino has to do with you? Above all, can you tell me what he has to do with me? What do you think, that I really orchestrated all your lives? I put a few opportunities your way. Who knew you would all run with it better than anyone would have imagined? Yes, you all surprised me. Do you think I did anything more than make it possible for you to go in for that scholarship? Well, you're wrong. Do you want to know what I did? I designed and printed that card, I put it in the book for you and waited for it to arrive at the foundation. Then I simply had you chosen as our candidate. That's all. You were the person who won that scholarship and the subsequent ones, you were the one who went off at a tangent with all this madness about the universe and relativity and cosmic radiation. I left a quiet, boring wanker who only knew how to solve equations and a few months later I find a sombre, inspired guy wandering the streets of Glasgow like a character in a novel and talking about space and time as if they were his socks. You gave me a lot of satisfaction."

"What about the equation?"

"What equation?"

"The one on the postcard."

"What about it?"

"Did I solve it?"

"How do I know if you solved it?" Greg said, with a hint of irritation. "I found it in a newspaper. I never saw that card again."

"I always thought I solved it."

Greg sighed and again passed his hand over his cheekbone. "And Biagio: do you think I rode the bike? Do you think I knew that arsehole really had all that talent? I said it to Rastello almost as a joke. Once, when we'd been talking, it transpired that one of our companies was sponsoring a motorcycle team. It was a time when motorcycle racing was becoming popular and Rastello thought it was a good investment. I hadn't given it any more thought in the meantime, not even when we fixed Sandra. But then in the middle of a conversation, I said to Rastello, 'Look, there's a friend of mine on the Rocky Road who rides fast. Maybe the head of our team would be interested in him.' How was I supposed to know Rastello would call Torcini, or that Torcini would really go to the Rocky Road and ask Biagio to go to Mugello, or that that arsehole really would go that fast?"

By now I didn't believe much in all these *as a joke*s and *how did I know*s, but decided to let him go on. "And what about the Rocky Road?"

"What about it?"

"It's the only missing piece: how did you manage to get it tarred?"

Greg looked at me and shook his head, as if he were talking to a little boy. "Do you have any idea how San Filippo would have been if it weren't for my family? Do you think it took a lot to send for a roadlaying company and get the authorities to turn a blind eye?" Then he paused for another second and gave an affected smile. "And do you still think the Marshal always let us do what we wanted because he couldn't catch us? Have you forgotten we'd fixed up his barracks five years earlier? Even at the time I thought it was impossible that nobody had put two and two together, but now…"

Feeling somewhat ridiculous, I thought for a moment about those days there on the Rocky Road, about the spur, about the Marshal arriving and bawling us out and then going away. I suddenly wondered if on the way back he had laughed or shaken his head in frustration.

"There's that image of Biagio that haunts me," I said.

"What image?"

"Biagio at night, alone, when he was a boy."

"What of it?"

"Since he died I haven't been able to separate it from the image of his corpse on Elba. It's as if I'd actually seen it. Something broke inside Biagio, and it started to break as soon as he left the village. And however much you try and twist the argument, the last and perhaps only moment when I remember Biagio happy was right there in San Filippo."

For a moment Greg seemed to take his mask off and looked at me with the same eyes he'd had when he was a little boy. "Jacopo, I know, but it's been a while now since I stopped feeling guilty about Biagio."

"Guilty?"

"Yes."

"Because of the bike?"

"To hell with the bike! No, not because of the bike, because of everything else."

"What else?"

"Are you an idiot? All the rest. All the mess he made and the drugs and so on. The rest."

"But what has that got to do with you?"

"I'm sorry, but what do you think was in those cigarettes that Biagio and I had been smoking since we were kids?"

"It wasn't cannabis, was it?"

"It was grass, Jacopo. I grew it in the summer in one of the old greenhouses and discovered that method of tying the leaves with sewing thread and leaving them to dry on slices of fruit. I don't remember where I learnt it. But it worked. Then, when I started going round the world with Rastello, I'd often run into Biagio in different places. He was often in Japan or Spain or America for the Grand Prix or the trials. Sometimes, if I was in London or Paris, he'd join me directly from Italy. We'd go clubbing, take a few pills, do a few lines of coke. He swore to me that when he wasn't with me he didn't do anything, all he thought about was the bike. But it was different for him. You could see it. Since those first joints from me, his whole expression would change. How come you didn't see it? To me it was always a bit of fun, a carnival, a holiday. Even now, every once in a while, maybe every couple of years, I smoke a bit of opium. I forget everything for a day and get a few massages and the next day everything starts again. Not him. He went into it head first, his eyes got all hollow, he'd give that half-smile of his and for a few hours it was as if he wanted to take in the whole world and disappear inside it. He'd become another person. Then the next day he'd get up with those silences of his and his hair over his eyes, and each time he'd tell me that maybe, when you came down to it, it was a kind of holiday for him too."

Greg looked at me for a moment or two. An insidious lump of anxiety and nausea was doing everything it could to rise from my stomach.

"But it wasn't."

"No, not after that Australian bitch showed up. I swear to you, Skinny, I never thought the human body could contain all that shit and still laugh and chat. When she went out, she always wore big mirrored glasses. The last evening we spent together was right here, in New York. I had some business to finalize and he had a meeting with a sponsor about the photographs for an advertising campaign. We'd been to a party first, then to the private room of a club until eight in the morning and in the end we'd gone back to my hotel. The girl had managed to get some dope from somebody, and although my eyes had already started to close, she was still spreading powder and burning foil and passing the stuff to Biagio as if there were no tomorrow. She walked around the suite in ripped jeans and a bikini top and a Mexican straw hat she'd taken off someone at the party and those mirrored glasses on her nose. She was laughing and hopping around the room as if everything were fine, as if she'd only just woken up and was ready to go to the beach. She was sitting on the couch. I went to her and as a joke reached out my hand and pulled her glasses down onto the tip of her nose and asked her what she was doing. I'll never forget those eyes. She pushed my hand away and put her glasses back up, then went to the bar as if nothing had happened and poured herself half a glass of vodka. That was what she did. It was as if all the devastation that usually affects every muscle and nerve of a normal human being, in her was concentrated in and around the eyes. They were purple and unnaturally hollow, the bright blue had been transformed into a weak ash-grey corona. The pupils seemed mushy, one was larger than the other, and they were empty, completely empty, and moving in different directions. "I'm telling you the truth. It may have been partly the tiredness and the hangover, but it terrified me. I went into the bathroom and threw up and closed the windows and took a couple of sleeping pills. Before I fell asleep I was convinced I might even die. The next day, when I woke up, Biagio and that thing had disappeared. A few days later we talked on the phone and I told Biagio to be careful. Obviously he didn't take much notice. From that night onwards, I always made myself scarce when they were together. That was our last night together. I don't know if I've ever understood why."

I stood there for a few seconds, motionless, looking at Greg and trying to fit everything into a few new pigeonholes, for which I would then have to find names. I wasn't sure if I was more upset by the content of the story or that subtle feeling of jealousy over a part of our lives from which I'd been excluded and about which I'd been kept in the dark. I went to the low table, finally picked up my cocktail, warm by now, and collapsed onto the couch facing Greg's.

"My God," I said.

"Yes, that's our dear Biagio for you."

"It wasn't your fault."

"I know it wasn't my fault. I told you, I got rid of my sense of guilt about Biagio some time ago. And yet it was hard to see a friend disintegrating. I'd just like to find that bitch again. I even thought of hiring an international investigator. But what would I have done then? Let her go to hell and have done with it."

For a moment I played with two drops of condensation on the side of the cone-shaped glass. "Hasn't it ever occurred to you that he would have been happier?"

"Where?"

"In the village."

Greg opened his eyes wide and threw his head back. "Oh God... how do I know, Jacopo? Maybe yes. Maybe no. Maybe he'd have ended up dead of an overdose even earlier, like Nannini's son. He was the brightest and the darkest of us, but it isn't written anywhere that light has to last for ever. Yes, he saw the abyss, but he did what he knew how to do best, and in his way he did it in style. Who's to say his life was wasted?"

"I don't know, Greg. Even you have somehow found yourself someone who makes you feel at home, someone you're attached to. That's what we all want when you come down to it: roots, a place we can call home. What does all the rest matter?"

That someone I was referring to had emerged over time in things Greg had said to me, appearing first as a mere hint, a person he had to see or he'd been to dinner with, and had gradually become a constant presence. I'd met him one evening, in London, while I was there for a conference. His name was Richard, and he worked in a merchant bank in the City. For some reason, I had imagined an elegant but clearly eccentric person, probably somewhat elderly. Not a bit of it: he was a young-looking thirty-something like all of us, polite and well dressed, clean-shaven, with glossy dark hair and a neat side parting. I arrived at the restaurant a few minutes early, and when they both came to the table Richard gave my hand a firm shake and said that he was very pleased to meet me, and that Greg often spoke about me in glowing terms. I looked at Greg and smiled.

"Don't get a big head, Skinny. He's exaggerating to make himself look good."

The attraction of that evening, apart—I have to admit— from Richard's brilliant conversation, was Greg's obvious discomfort. All his life he had struggled to turn himself into a shadow, the closest thing he could find to the speakerphone in *Charlie's Angels*, and now here he was, sitting at a table at Simpson's in the Strand, sinking his knife into a slice of roast beef as soft as butter and chatting away like any other human being with his partner and his oldest friend.

So this was the depravity of which Greg was so proud: this kindly London broker who seemed to have a great passion for Italian shoes and romantic comedies. He asked me if I'd like to go with him the following evening to see a new show with Emma Thompson. He'd gone so far as to buy two tickets, but obviously Greg's slow emotional evolution didn't yet include comedies with Emma Thompson.

Greg's discomfort and his constant muttering as we talked were quite amusing, but he seemed to get over it quite well in the end, and from subsequent phone calls I got the impression that our relationship had warmed slightly. Eventually, Greg and Richard bought a house in Primrose Hill, and Greg now spent most of the free time he allowed himself there.

"Skinny, the relationship between Richard and me is so far beyond anything your petty little mind could conceive, there's no point your even talking about it."

I smiled and watched the drops of condensation slowly descending the stem of the glass. "Were you really in that monastery?"

Greg looked at me. "Yes, I really was," he said, with a bored sigh.

"And how was it?"

"Why, are you planning to become a monk?"

I didn't say anything.

"What can I tell you, Jacopo? It was a monastery in the middle of the mountains. Monks and prayers and all the rest. It was very cold and the food was disgusting."

I continued looking at him without saying anything.

"Do you want to know if they've found the solution? Yes, they've found the solution. Many haven't, but some have understood: they know and they're happy all the same. And so what? What should we do? Should we leave all this and disappear into the mountains? That would be nice, Skinny, but the reality is that they know how the universe is, but they don't know how things are down here, and don't have much to leave behind: a few sheep and a patch of frozen ground. They're better off in a monastery than going around in their tents. I don't know about you, but I'm better off here. Rubber mattresses are amazing. Have you suddenly realized that this is our great mandala? Congratulations. Enjoy it! What do you care?"

I sighed, then turned my neck from side to side and heard it crack. I squeezed my right wrist. It still hurt a lot, but I could move it.

Greg was looking at me with his arms stretched along the back of the seat. He was smiling.

"You punched me."

"You deserved it."

4

WHEN I FOUND myself back on the street half an hour later, I decided to go for a walk. A cool wind was blowing, which forced me to raise the collar of my jacket and stoop slightly. The city seemed calmer and more silent than usual. I thought I could smell roast meat in the air. I walked toward Canal, and then further north, along West Broadway. For the first time in at least five years I passed Novecento. I stopped and approached the window, putting my hands around my face to look inside. I saw my ghost and the ghosts of Tara and her friend and Fausto sitting there at the table and walking around the place with plates and orders in their hands. Rosalita Hernández. Who would ever have thought that we had really been so close? I moved away from the window and for a moment it seemed to me that I saw behind me, in the shimmer of West Broadway, the figures of my friends and me and Tara standing in the middle of the road looking at an imaginary horizon. The morning the towers had collapsed I had been in that area, at the apartment of a weird Canadian girl I'd been trying vaguely to have an affair with for some weeks. The first tower collapsed as I was crossing Washington Square. I heard people shouting and running, looking south, covering their faces and mouths. It took me a while to realize what I was watching: the outline of a single tower immersed in smoke. The world as I knew it had come to an end, and every frozen corner of my body told me so. Within a few minutes, Fifth Avenue was deserted. There were men and women in tears talking on the telephone, others huddled in groups around the news coming from car radios or from the TV sets that some people had put in the windows. Scattered here and there were people standing looking north. They were staring at the Empire State Building, waiting for one of the two planes still in the air to hit it. There we all were, all at once, me and Greg and Biagio and Tara or Rosalita or whatever she was called, and maybe the rest of the world: all standing, disoriented, with our backs to a past that had been bombed out of existence, looking at what remained while waiting for another collapse.

I went up West Broadway as far as Prince Street and turned left, then turned right and continued uptown, on Thompson. Beyond Houston, I passed the Italian bar where a few years earlier I'd gone to watch Biagio's last appearances in the Superbike Championships, then the two chess forums where I had been soundly beaten by a twitchy little boy and an elegant old man in a double-breasted suit.

The fountain in Washington Square was full. I decided to stop for a while and sit down on the edge. The building on the corner of Fifth was reflected in the motionless surface of the water and every now and again a slight gust of wind made the reflection shimmer. Just to be on that side of the fountain and continue looking north I took my shoes off, rolled up the hems of my trousers and dipped my feet in. The water was quite cold, but I soon got used to it. A young black guy approached me and asked me for a cigarette. I told him I was sorry, but I didn't smoke. He nodded and told me I was right.

"It's a nice night," he said looking around and up in the sky. He sat down on the edge of the fountain and kept looking around without saying anything. He had a funny round face and I wondered what he was doing around there at that hour. After a couple of minutes he wished me a good day, took a long, deep breath, and went on his way.

The taxi driver I approached muttered that it was his last run and I lived too far away, but in the end he took me and even thanked me for the two dollars extra I gave him as a tip. I decided to take another sick day and not set the alarm. My little apartment still bore the signs of all those hours I'd spent looking for confirmation of Greg's machinations: sheets of paper scattered on the table even more untidily than usual, Post-its stuck everywhere, half-filled glasses. The smell of obsession still hovered. I opened the windows that looked out on the street and let a little air in. I also took a big black bag and threw in it all the papers and notes and scraps that reminded me of that pandemonium. I thought of taking a shower, but in the end decided to leave it till the next day and settled for washing my face. And finally, having drawn all the curtains and made it as dark as possible, I collapsed on the bed, exhausted.

Two days later I told Amanda that I'd passed a real estate agency by chance and that they had a couple of interesting apartments on offer: we might be able to go and take a look. Her hands were smeared with paint and she had an orange-coloured band around her head. As soon as she opened the door, she said she had to finish something and ran back to her studio. When I told her about the apartment she stopped and looked at me. She held her hands up like a surgeon before an operation and frowned.

"What did you say?"

She looked like a little girl, with that band on her head and those hands full of paint, and once again I wondered what a woman like her was doing with someone like me.

"I said I saw photos in an agency of an apartment that seems perfect for us."

She looked at me for another moment or two. "Are you sure?"

"I think so."

I started to find my classes enjoyable again from time to time. I even asked Jerry, the head of the department, if I could do more popular classes, maybe intersecting with other degree courses. I missed those short seminars at the New School, the effort of looking for ways to explain the laws that govern the universe to those who didn't know much about it, that gleam in their eyes when they seemed at last to grasp a concept that had previously been impenetrable. I missed the labour of finding the right images and words. Perhaps I missed the words and that was it. And even though words could not explain much of what I was studying, it was still true that they could change the perspective of these young people for ever, even if only by a few hundredths of a degree.

I looked through some notes from more than a year before, which I'd put aside to give vent to my sudden mad obsession with omniscience. They were still in a rough state, but there were a few aspects worth developing. I got back in touch with some ex-pupils and tried to set up a research group. We did some good work on the correlation between the emissions of neutrinos and the gravitational waves of supernovas, and it was even published. To celebrate, I treated everyone to a steak dinner at Peter Luger.

In the end we didn't move to the apartment I'd seen in the photograph at the agency. Eventually, we ended up in an apartment belonging to Columbia University, on 118th Street. We got it thanks to the university, and it was the only way to have a place big enough for both her studio and my study. It even has a little terrace, where we sunbathe a bit before it gets too hot and sometimes even have dinner al fresco. Amanda wasn't too keen on it—she didn't like leaving Alphabet City and her Puerto Rican friends, but she was surprisingly happy to live with me. I told myself that maybe that's what it's all about: to make someone else happy.

I think Mrs Schmidt's children were very relieved too: for quite a while now she's been in a retirement home in New Jersey, but she made it a matter of honour that I should stay in the apartment for as long as I wanted, and at the rent agreed at the start. I was the one who took her to hospital the night she collapsed. From time to time I pay her a visit, and always find her all dressed up, with her hair nicely combed. The first few times she took me by the arm and showed me off to everyone as her young Italian boyfriend. Now she doesn't walk so well any more, so we spend most of the time in her room, chatting over a cup of tea. I always take a little bottle of whisky with me and pour some in her cup, without the nurses seeing. I've even taught her how to play *briscola*.

Mathías was here recently too. A film by a young Brazilian director that he produced was in competition in a festival in New York. We went to an Allman Brothers concert at the Beacon Theater. They played a version of "Mountain Jam" that lasted at least half an hour and brought tears to our eyes. After the concert we went for a walk along Columbus and dropped into a little bar. He was wearing a white shirt, and his big, already greying mop of hair fell partly over his eyes. Since I'd last seen him he'd married and had a son, then fallen in love with another woman and left his wife, who made him buy her a house and plagues him constantly about his responsibilities.

"You're a parody of yourself," I said to him.

He laughed and ran his hands through his hair, then looked at me and said that I seemed different. I'd never thought I would, but I told him the whole story. He listened to me gravely, without saying anything and without taking his eyes off me. When I'd finished he sat looking at me for a while, still without saying anything, then took a sip of his beer and put the tankard back on the table.

"A funny thing, luck," he said, continuing to stare at the tankard and removing a residue of froth from the edge with the tip of his thumb.

Most of the time, I don't think about our story. But I do often think about Greg's final words. I was already in the elevator, and just before the doors closed, I put my hand out to stop them and again looked Greg straight in the eyes.

"Why?" I asked.

I wasn't completely sure what that why meant, but I couldn't hold it back. Greg stared at me for a few moments and sighed. I thought he would tell me to go to hell and close the elevator door without adding anything else.

Instead of which, he said, "Pleasure, Jacopo. Pure pleasure. What else do you think matters? Do you really believe there's anything else worth living for? Congratulations, you've got there at last: sooner or later our species and our beloved planet will be swept away like a grain of sand. To tell the truth, I had hoped that with all the money that three universities invested in you, you'd have got there a bit earlier, but better late than never.

"And yet there's one thing that nobody will ever be able to take away from us, because it fades the moment we achieve it, before we can even lay our hands on it. Pleasure. That's what I felt when we were fixing the bike and when we stood on the Rocky Road and when I was drawing and printing that postcard and when I heard about you growing up on the streets of Glasgow and New York and when I watched Biagio come round those bends like a bullet. And that's what I feel when I have myself oiled and massaged and when I spend time with Richard. Pleasure, my boy. That's all."

I was almost there. Yes, I told myself in the following days and weeks: what else do we need in fact? We get on with our lives, we look the other way, and when the monster gets too close, when we feel its hot breath on our necks and its shadow falling over us, we go and have a nice massage, we make love with our woman, we go and hear a good concert. Pleasure. Beauty. We couldn't have better rafts at our disposal to stay afloat.

But that's too easy, my dear Greg. You're too intelligent and too disturbed to really believe that a couple of massages and a concert can save us from the abyss over which we float. It's true, as we'd said: it isn't the brilliance of our ideas that makes us apparently so unlike the animals that surround us. The difference lies in the fact that we doubt. But why do we doubt, Greg? You know why as well as I do: because if the answer to all questions was really pleasure, or beauty, we'd have stopped asking ourselves questions long ago. We continue to plague ourselves with questions because we are and always will be unable to answer the only one that matters. Here it is, the monster an ape spotted one day in the recesses of the world. Here is the puppet master who plays with our days. We study the odyssey of that swarm of ants we call the human race, we admire its works and its discoveries, and all we see is the constant, niggling dance of moves and countermoves with that beast of whose existence we are aware but who we never manage to track down.

The terror and wonder of nothingness: it would have been nice to tell another story, but I think that's how this one is going to end.

APOLOGIES AND ACKNOWLEDGEMENTS

The day when, already having signed the contract for this book, I was faced with the inescapable duty to start the first draft, it suddenly seemed to me an impossible enterprise, like climbing an inaccessible peak: at any rate an enterprise considerably beyond my abilities. I would never have got even halfway if it had not been for the invaluable help I received on the journey.

However, before thanking those who gave me a hand, I have to make a few apologies: in my dreams of glory for my character, I misappropriated other people's successes. I must therefore apologize to Alberto Puig for the skirmishes at Jerez in 1992, and to Bradl and Shimizu for stealing their places on the podium. I have partly compensated Puig with a victory five years later, again at Jerez. I also apologize to Kevin Schwantz for having him actually beaten by two points in the 1994 rankings, and to the great Mick Doohan for having him beaten at Mugello in 1997. What can I say? We all need our little satisfactions, and can only hope they are harmless.

I must also apologize to Roger Penrose for borrowing and partly twisting his model of Conformal Cyclic Cosmology for the trivial purposes of the story.

But coming to those who supported me in the undertaking,

my first thought goes to the adorable Anna Zoccarato and Vito and my friends in Glasgow for their kindness, their willingness to help, and all their stories.

Thanks, too, to Alberto Nicolis: even before we had a chance to talk, the mere fact that he was only thirty-five and already teaching at Columbia had already dispelled half my doubts.

My warmest embrace goes, however, to Professor Nicolao Fornengo: if my character has any credibility, it is thanks to the time that Nicolao devoted to me, and his anecdotes and his e-mails and the books he recommended I read. Among other things, exchanging ideas with such a sharp mind was an infinitely satisfying experience. Thanks, too, to Paolo, who introduced us.

Another flood of hugs, and something more, goes to Matteo and Derick, who have been supporting me for ever, and to Nicole and Olivia, who have consequently had to give me accommodation.

Thank you, finally, to Nico. He knows why.

PUSHKIN PRESS

Pushkin Press was founded in 1997. Having first rediscovered European classics of the twentieth century, Pushkin now publishes novels, essays, memoirs, children's books, and everything from timeless classics to the urgent and contemporary.

Pushkin Paper books, like this one, represent exciting, high-quality writing from around the world. Pushkin publishes widely acclaimed, brilliant authors such as Stefan Zweig, Marcel Aymé, Antal Szerb, Paul Morand and Hermann Hesse, as well as some of the most exciting contemporary and often prize-winning writers, including Andrés Neuman, Ellen Ullman, Eduardo Halfon and Ryu Murakami.

Pushkin Press publishes the world's best stories, to be read and read again.

*